T0190971

## Also by Catherine Bruns

ITALIAN CHEF MYSTERIES
*Penne Dreadful*
*It Cannoli Be Murder*
*The Enemy You Gnocchi*

COOKIES & CHANCE
MYSTERIES
*Tastes Like Murder*
*Baked to Death*
*Burned to a Crisp*
*Frosted with Revenge*
*Silenced by Sugar*
*Sprinkled in Malice*
*Ginger Snapped to Death*
*Icing on the Cakes*
*Knee Deep in Dough*
*Dessert Is the Bomb*
*Seasoned with Murder*
*Bake, Batter, and Roll*
*Crimes and Confections*

CINDY YORK MYSTERIES
*Killer Transaction*
*Priced to Kill*
*For Sale by Killer*
*Killer View*
*With Option to Kill*
*Killer Under Contract*

ALOHA LAGOON MYSTERIES
*Death of the Big Kahuna*
*Death of the Kona Man*

MAPLE SYRUP MYSTERIES
*A Doomful of Sugar*
*Syrup to No Good*

# IN THE BLINK OF A PIE

### A Maple Syrup Mystery

## CATHERINE BRUNS

Poisoned Pen
PRESS

Published by Poisoned Pen Press, an imprint of Sourcebooks
P.O. Box 4410, Naperville, Illinois 60567-4410
(630) 961-3900
sourcebooks.com

Printed and bound in the United States of America.
KP 10 9 8 7 6 5 4 3 2 1

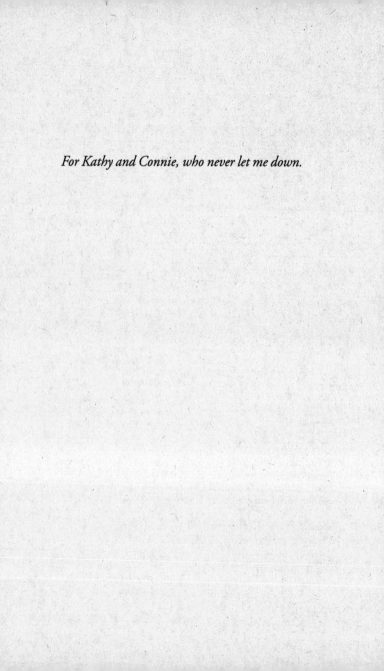

*For Kathy and Connie, who never let me down.*

# CHAPTER ONE

**"CAN YOU BELIEVE THIS WEATHER** that we're having?" My best friend, Heather Murray, asked as she spread a checkered red cloth over a picnic table. "I can't remember Vermont ever going through Indian summer this late in November before."

"Well, I guess there's a first time for everything." I laid the freshly baked pies down on the cloth and then gently inserted red flags with numbers printed on them into the top crust. "This works so much better. It would have been so cramped if we'd had to hold the contest inside the sugar house, or even the café for that matter."

Heather's blue eyes sparkled. "This was such a terrific idea, Leila. A pie-baking contest right before Thanksgiving! How many entries do you have so far?"

"I'm not sure," I confessed. "I guess I should have been a little more specific about where and when to drop the pies off." Some people were leaving them with Heather and me at the sugar house while others brought theirs to the café inside the main building of Sappy Endings.

Sappy Endings was a maple syrup farm located in Sugar Ridge, Vermont, that had been started by my father twenty-six years earlier. The town was rural and small with less than two thousand people, most of them hardworking folks like my family. Last fall, I returned home from Florida after teaching there for five years, but it hadn't been for a happy reason. My father, Victor Khoury, had been murdered. Even though his killer had been found and brought to justice, my life would never be the same again.

"Noah just texted that he and my mother are bringing more pies down from the café."

Uttering Noah Rivers's name caused a pleasant tingle to run through me. The man had given me fits when I'd first returned home. In my defense, I wasn't in a good frame of mind then due to my father's murder. When Noah had learned that my father had left me Sappy Endings in his will, he'd been nearly as surprised as I. It hadn't exactly been love at first sight for either one of us.

"I think it was a mistake to let people register up to the day of the event," I admitted. "I should have cut off entries yesterday. All these last-minute pies are making it difficult for me to keep track of everything. Next year, I'll create a Google form ahead of time and post in on the website."

"That's a good idea," Heather said approvingly. "By the way, did I mention how wonderful it is that the farm is donating a share of each entry fee to the Sugar Ridge Food

Bank? You have no idea how many turkeys this will help us provide to families in need for Thanksgiving."

In addition to Heather's full-time job as an at-home hair stylist, she was very involved with the local food pantry. Heather recruited donations year-round and assisted her church with handing out food every week. During the holiday season, she stepped things up. She was already in the middle of organizing a giving tree for Christmas as well.

"I wish it could be a larger donation," I said. "But we need to keep money aside for prizes and the clown I hired to entertain the kids. Plus, with the cost of supplies rising—"

"Say no more. It's extremely generous of you," Heather said. "I know it's not easy. Especially now."

We both fell silent as Heather stacked paper plates, cutlery, and napkins at one end of the table. I checked my list of entries again, counting them for the tenth time this hour. One of the loveliest things about having a best friend is that we often knew what the other one was thinking. Heather understood what I could not bring myself to say. Although my first year as manager of Sappy Endings had started out well, we'd seen a significant drop in sales over the summer. If my father were watching from Heaven, he would be shaking his head in sorrow. I was definitely no Victor Khoury.

My first anniversary at Sappy Endings had come and gone last week. In his will, my father had stipulated that I run the farm for one year after his death. At that time, I could do as I pleased, which included selling it. No one would blame me if I did. As it turns out, my father had known me better than I knew myself. He'd realized long before I did that the family maple syrup farm would become a part of my heart and soul, like his, and that I would never walk away.

"We will weather the storm together, *habibi*." *Habibi* meant "my love" in my father's native Arabic. He had told me this several times while I was growing up when it looked like the farm might not survive for another year. I thought the recent drop in business might have been due to the increase in syrup prices, but Noah assured me that wasn't the issue.

"All of the farms are suffering this year," he said. "Everyone's tightening their belts with the soaring cost of inflation. Things will be better next year."

Like my father, Noah was an integral part of Sappy Endings. He had been born and raised in South Carolina but spent many years on a maple syrup farm in Upstate New York after leaving the Marines. My farming experience paled next to his. After all, I was still learning.

"Leila, look!" a bubbly voice sang out.

I cleared my mind of worry and bestowed a smile upon the blond little girl running in my direction. She gleefully waved a hand full of blue-colored papers at me. Six-year-old Emma Rivers threw her arms out as she reached me, but her pink sneaker hit a rock in the dirt and she went flying across the grass, as did the entry forms. When I rushed over to see if she was okay, Emma looked up at me with tears in her eyes.

"Are you all right, sweetheart?" Her jeans had a hole in the knee, but that might have been there before.

She put her arms around my neck and sniffled, causing my heart to dissolve into a giant puddle.

"I'm sorry." Emma dried her eyes on my denim shirt. "I was only trying to help."

I kissed the top of her curly head as Noah came toward us with three freshly baked pies in his hands. He laid them on the table and then lifted his daughter's chin with his index finger. "Guess it's a good thing I didn't let you carry the s'mores pie, huh?"

Emma glanced from me to her father and grinned. I'd seen pictures of Noah's late wife, Ashley, around his house, and Emma was the spitting image of her mother, except for the eyes. They were Noah's eyes—the same striking ice-blue color with long dark lashes surrounding them.

"Do I still get to be your special helper when you judge the pies?" Emma asked excitedly.

When I looked into her sweet little face, the word "no" didn't exist. Even if Emma had been my own daughter, I couldn't possibly love her any more. I would never try to take the place of her own mother, and Emma seemed to accept my relationship with her father without question.

I laughed and hugged the little girl tightly against me as I looked over her head at Noah. His eyes softened when our gazes met. I knew Noah was happy Emma and I got along so well, but it had been no effort on my part. Emma was easy to adore.

"Of course, you can still be my assistant," I said. "Now, let's pick up all the entry forms and sort them by pie."

"Yay!" Emma clapped her hands in delight, then wiggled out of my arms and began to help Heather pick up the papers. When there was a neat stack on the table, my mother appeared, bearing two more pies between her delicate hands.

In the past year since my mother and I had been living under one roof, the strain in our relationship had finally lessened, and we'd become closer. I'd learned a lot from our time together, but our current living arrangement would be coming to an end soon. Noah wanted me to move in with him and Emma after the holidays, and I suspected my mother wasn't pleased about it.

"Leila, dear, here's some more entries." My mother set the pies down on the table. One had a golden-brown lattice crust that revealed pieces of apples underneath and smelled strongly of maple and cinnamon. The other pie had its crust shaped into small leaves around the edge of the plate. The one requirement we insisted upon was that every pie needed to have Sappy Endings organic maple syrup or maple sugar as one of their ingredients. Although the pies were also judged on appearance, it wasn't required to shape the crust into maple leaves or decorate the top with them. Of course, a little extra promotion never hurt, especially when the product smelled so delicious.

I double-checked my numbers again. "This currently puts us at twenty-eight entries. And I just received an email from a woman bringing a sweet potato pie. My guess is that we'll easily go over thirty."

My mother clucked her tongue in dismay. "You should have let me handle this, dear. After all, culinary events are my specialty."

My mother was a wonderful cook and baker, and if she

wanted to boast about her skills, she certainly had every right. Besides keeping the house in immaculate order, she cooked and baked every day. This was in addition to working full-time in the café. While sales of syrup had dropped, the café's business had remained steady and helped us stay financially afloat. My mother's maple lattes were a huge hit among our customers, as were her baklava and maple doughnuts. Like the contest entries, every item in our café contained some degree of maple syrup.

Mom pushed her short, dark hair away from her face. "There's quite a crowd of people at the gate. Is it okay to let them in?"

Noah picked up Emma and swung her onto his shoulders. "I'll go take care of it. I've set up some extra lawn chairs in case people forgot to bring one with them. Afterwards, Em and I will carry the coffee urn down from the café."

My mother beamed at him and Emma. "Wonderful. Thank you, Noah."

"Yes, I think we're as ready as we'll ever be." I wished that I had put more thought into the contest but had only come up with the idea a few weeks ago, when Heather mentioned that donations were low at the food pantry.

My mother was right—I should have let her handle the event. She was so efficient with everything she did. At the same time, she was buried in the café, especially since her newest assistant had quit last week, after only one month on the job.

My mother studied the pies on display with a critical eye. This was going to be an interesting competition with her as a judge. My perfectionist mother always managed to find fault with everyone else's cooking.

As if she'd guessed my thoughts, Heather leaned over and whispered in my ear. "I didn't know that your mom was going to judge the pies. What if she doesn't like *any* of them?"

In spite of myself, I laughed out loud. "That's why Noah and I are also judging. This way we can decide on a winner even if she doesn't care for any of them."

"Noah's judging too?" Heather looked surprised. "The Maple Messenger said that you were the only judge."

"I know, but Simon's assistant got it wrong." My brother was head reporter for our local newspaper, and usually had his facts straight, but this time, someone had gotten the details wrong. "Mom and Noah will be sampling the pies as well. After we've taste-tested and announced the winner, the crowd will be invited to try them too."

Heather wrinkled her nose. "I know that you're charging a fee for each entry, but maybe you should charge for the pie eating as well. How else can the farm make any money?"

"There's a small fee to sample the pies," I said. "We're providing the ice cream for free, though. And we have latte samples for people to try. There will be enough of a profit, even after the donation to the food pantry, so don't worry."

"I'm glad that Noah's helping with the contest." Heather winked. "You two are so in sync these days. Honestly, you're just the cutest couple. But your mother looks so tired lately."

There was no doubt about that. "She *is* tired. That's why I didn't want her to make anything for the event. Mom didn't even need to be a judge, but she insisted."

"Have you guys had any luck hiring someone else for the café?"

"None." I sighed. "The ad's been online for a week now, but we've only had one applicant so far—a woman named Janice who showed up here on Monday. Mom insisted on handling the interview by herself."

Heather's eyes grew round. "You're kidding."

"Don't I wish." The damage had already been done before I even realized that Janice was there. I had only talked to the woman for a few minutes, and she couldn't wait to leave. My mother meant well, but she expected everyone to be an expert in the kitchen like herself. Two days later, I had called and left a message for Janice, but she never responded.

"Your mom can be intimidating," Heather agreed. "Don't worry, you'll find someone. Look, here they come!"

Our table was quickly surrounded by spectators who oohed and aahed over the display of pies. Two more people chose to drop off their pies and entry forms while I entered them on my clipboard. Heather took charge of the numbered red flags and stuck them into pies. Noah brought the coffee urn over while my mother hurried back to the main building for the espresso machine. I was bombarded with questions from the crowd. They ranged from how many pies a person could sample to if there would be media coverage.

"Absolutely. My brother Simon will be doing a feature story on the contest for tomorrow's paper." I didn't bother to tell the woman who'd inquired that Simon was following another news story out of town and might not make it back in time for the actual contest. One way or another, he had promised me a nice write-up for the farm and, if possible, on the front page.

Emma came hurrying towards me, balancing a pie between her hands. She looked like she was headed straight for disaster. I stepped forward and made the stop signal with my hands.

"Whoa!" I laughed and quickly removed the pie from her hands, thankful it hadn't landed face down on the grass. "I hope this is the last of them."

Emma nodded solemnly. "Yep. It was sitting on a table in the café when I went up there to get napkins, like Selma asked me to. I told her that I'd bring the pie down to you."

"You're such a good helper."

"I know." Emma smacked her lips together. "Yum. It sure smells good."

I glanced down at the pie. It was pumpkin, my favorite, and perfect for this time of year. An intricate maple leaf had been designed in the top crust. If this pie tasted as good as it looked, we might have the winning entry on our hands.

"Thank you, sweetheart," I told Emma. "Was the registration form with the pie? Or did you see the person who left it?"

"Oh! Here it is." Emma produced the crumpled form from her pocket and handed it to me along with the fee clipped to the top. I assigned the pie a flag with the number 31 printed on it and quickly wrote down the name of the contestant—Sandy Sweets. *How ironic.* There was no cell number included, but the man or woman had included an email address. The pie was pumpkin maple, and a half a cup of our syrup was included as one of the ingredients. I didn't bother to look through the rest of the form.

"Everything seems okay here," I said out loud.

My mother appeared with the espresso machine, which she quickly set up at another table. "Mom, did you see who dropped off this pie?" I asked.

She leaned over to look at the pie and shook her head. "No, I was on the phone."

I watched as she quickly mixed the ingredients necessary for her famous maple lattes—coffee, nutmeg, maple syrup, and whipped cream. When it came to cooking, my mother always made everything look so easy and effortless. Heather went over to help her fill the sample cups as people crowded around them. The cups disappeared as soon as Heather set them down.

"Thank you, dear," my mother said. "Would you mind going up to the café and grabbing a few extra spatulas? I don't think we have enough."

"Of course not," Heather said. "I'll be right back." She glanced over at me. "Did you need anything?"

I shook my head. "No, thanks. Once you bring those back, my assistant and I can start eating."

"Wow." Emma stared at the pies in fascination. "Can I taste *every* pie?"

"If you do, I think you'll have one heck of a stomach-ache." I chuckled.

She looked disappointed. "But *you* get to taste all of them."

"Not all of them." I corrected her. "Your daddy, my

mother, and I are each going to taste ten pies." Now that we had 31 entries, I'd actually be tasting eleven. A spoonful of each one. I'd only had a piece of manoush bread earlier this morning, so my stomach was growling with hunger.

Emma looked confused. "Then what happens?"

"Then, each one of us picks out our two favorite pies, and the other judges sample them. We'll narrow all the pies down to two entries—the winner and runner up. After the winner is selected, everyone gets to sample them along with some vanilla ice cream. But you can be in on the final decision, okay?"

"Yay!" Emma clapped her hands. "I love pie. Chocolate and apple and pumpkin…"

Heather returned with the spatulas and laid them on the table. She placed a hand on my arm. "There's a woman up in the café who said she's here to apply for the job. I told her to wait, but do you want me to go back and tell her to come down here?"

I glanced over at my mother. She was laughing and talking with Margaret Middleton, the woman who had lived across the street from our home for many years. "No, thanks. I'll go talk to her myself." I was worried my mother might scare off another one.

Noah stood in front of the assorted lawn chairs, speaking into a bull horn to get everyone's attention. "Good afternoon, everyone. I'm Noah Rivers. Thank you all for attending Sappy Ending's inaugural pie contest! We are not accepting any more entries at this time. The pies will be judged by our manager, Leila Khoury, the culinary genius of Sappy Hour Café, Selma Khoury, and yours truly."

"Never hurts to suck up to a future mother-in-law," Heather teased.

My cheeks warmed, and I gave her a playful nudge. I wished that Noah hadn't already made the announcement; I wanted to talk to the woman in the café. In Noah's defense, we were running behind schedule and had to get on with the festivities.

"What's the prize for the winning pie?" a woman called out.

"The winner will receive a year's supply of our maple syrup, a trophy, and the opportunity to have their pie featured in our Sappy Hour Café during Thanksgiving week," Noah announced. "While we're tasting all of your delicious masterpieces and trying to decide on a winner, please help yourselves to free samples of our organic syrup and Selma's delicious lattes. There are some games set up in the sugar house for the kids that our friend Heather will assist with, and we might even have a clown friend dropping by any minute!"

Everyone cheered and clapped while I moved swiftly over to my mother, who was still chatting with Margaret. "Mom, why don't you and Noah go ahead with the tasting. I need to run up to the main building for a few minutes."

My mother narrowed her eyes. "Leila, we don't want to keep everyone waiting. What's so important that you can't put it off until later?"

I debated about what to tell her. "Um, I have to talk to a vendor about a syrup delivery. It can't wait. I'll only be a few minutes."

Margaret gave an exaggerated cough. "Perhaps you should have hired a professional judge for the competition, Leila, dear."

I turned and gave her a long look. Margaret was in her mid-sixties and a few years older than my mother, with short gray hair that had once been a vibrant auburn. Her green eyes gleamed like a cat's whenever she learned a juicy tidbit of gossip. She was of medium build, with transparent skin that looked like she never saw the sun. Margaret wore a wide-brimmed straw hat with red and blue flowers that reminded me of Minnie Pearl. The only thing missing was the price tag.

Margaret had settled in Sugar Ridge about fifteen years ago with her husband, who had died a year later from a brain aneurysm. My mother had developed an instant friendship when she first brought over a plate of baklava to welcome Margaret to the neighborhood. I knew she felt sorry for the woman since she was all alone, but I found her smart aleck remarks tough to take at times.

"We don't need a professional judge, Mrs. Middleton," I said in a polite tone. "This is just a tiny competition. It's not like it's going to be on national television."

"It's really to help the food pantry," my mother put in hastily. She held a cup out to Margaret. "Wouldn't you like to try one of these?"

Margaret pushed the cup away, and a few drops of the latte spilled onto the tablecloth. "Selma, you know that I don't like anything with coffee."

A petite redhead with porcelain skin quickly rose from

her lawn chair and came to Margaret's side. I struggled to keep my mouth shut as my mother wiped up the mess in record time. For such a strong-willed woman, mom always let Margaret have her way. I didn't like the way she took advantage of my mother.

"Ma." The redhead spoke in a soft, subdued tone as she touched Margaret on the shoulder. "Why don't you come over here and sit with me? The contest will be starting soon."

Abigail Middleton lived in New Hampshire, where she worked as a nurse in the emergency room. She was here this weekend to visit her mother and had accompanied her to the farm.

"Food pantry," Margaret grunted, as she shook off Abigail's hand. "Those people probably don't even need the help. They just go in there with some sob story so that they can get free groceries."

Her rude remark shocked me. My mother's face turned a crimson shade, but she said nothing. When I turned my head away, I thought I spotted the face of a former student of mine in the crowd. I blinked, and the image of a muscular young man with short, dirty blond hair disappeared. How silly. There was no way that Cameron Wilton would be here today. I must have imagined it. The last time I had seen him, Cameron had been a skinny teenager with a long, scraggly ponytail who sat slouched in the back row of my classroom, quiet as a mouse.

"No one wants to work these days," Margaret continued on.

Her statement jolted me out of my thoughts. Margaret's

remarks were highly insensitive, and I was grateful that Heather hadn't overheard. She devoted much of her free time to the food pantry and was passionate about helping the less fortunate. Margaret's comment would have deeply hurt her feelings.

I fought to control my temper. "Mrs. Middleton, there's many people who depend on that food pantry—"

She waved me off impatiently. "Oh, Leila, you have so much to learn about the world. You're too young and silly. Since I haven't submitted a pie, I would be more than happy to help judge the contest in your absence."

"That won't be necessary. We have it covered." I did my best to ignore her and addressed my mother. "Mom, feel free to divide the pies up however you wish for Noah and me. He doesn't have any allergies. Oh, and the only pie that contains nuts is number ten, the apple walnut. I put a sign next to it, just to be safe."

I walked swiftly up the path to the main building while Margaret clucked her tongue in disgust. "My goodness. That daughter of yours has quite the attitude, Selma."

*Thank you, Margaret.* Her words made me smile. If this incident had occurred a year ago, I wouldn't have hesitated to get in a jab at Margaret's expense. Patience had never come easily to me, but since my father's death and taking over the farm, I'd finally started to develop some.

On the other hand, Margaret, who was more than twice my age, never had anything nice to say about anyone. As my father used to tell me, "Some people will never change, *habibi*, and you must learn to accept that."

I glanced up at the picturesque sky and smiled as his face came to mind. "If more people were like you, Dad, this world would be a better place to live."

# CHAPTER TWO

**AN ASSORTMENT OF COLORED LEAVES** littered the grassy path that led from the sugar house to the main building of Sappy Endings. This was where the café, gift shop, and my office were located. As I walked along, I made a mental note to call the groundskeeper about leaf removal next week. It was going to get worse before it got any better. The unusually warm weather would not last much longer, and I suspected that the trees in our sugar bush—a community of maple trees tapped to yield sap which were then processed into syrup—would be bare by Thanksgiving. All too soon the grass would be replaced by several inches of the cold white stuff, but I didn't mind. One of the things I had always loved about Vermont was the change in seasons.

When I'd left my hometown over five years ago for hot and humid Florida, the absence of seasons had been one of the things that I had never gotten used to. Summer, fall, winter, and spring all felt the same down there. Variety had been missing from my life in so many ways.

My parents had fallen in love with the town of Sugar Ridge at first sight. They had settled here shortly after their marriage. Simon and I were both born here. Even though it wasn't as small as some Vermont towns, Sugar Ridge was dominated by friendly and hardworking people who took the time to get to know one another. My father always said that the healthy air quality had something to do with everyone's pleasant demeanor. I took a moment to inhale it deep into my lungs and was sure that he'd been right.

It was funny the way that life worked sometimes. When I'd left Florida with a broken heart and was barely speaking to my mother, I'd been certain that I would never return to stay again. My father's death had brought everything into perspective, and today, I couldn't imagine living anywhere else.

A young woman sat alone at one of the tables in the empty café. Her shoulder-length, black hair was the same shade as mine but devoid of any curl. She stared across the walkway at the gift shop, which we'd closed and locked while the contest was going on. After the winning pie was announced, we would throw open the doors and welcome a barrage of customers to stock up on maple syrup, candy, and homemade candles for the upcoming holiday season.

One could only hope.

"Hi, can I help you with something?" I wished I had thought to ask Heather for the woman's name.

The woman jumped slightly in her seat at the sound of my voice and turned around to face me. Her complexion was much lighter than my almond-colored skin, and her gray eyes reminded me of the sky on a stormy day. "Sorry," she said. "I didn't hear you come in. Are you Leila?"

"That's right." Something about the woman struck a familiar chord with me. "Wait a second. Don't you work at Bagel Palace?"

The woman smiled and held out her hand. "That's right. I've waited on you a couple of times. My name's Jenna Fleming." She stared at me with an anxious expression. "I hope this isn't a bad time. It looks like you've got some kind of event going on outside."

"This is fine." I pulled out a chair and sat across from her. "How long have you lived in Sugar Ridge? I don't think I've ever seen you in here before."

"It's been about seven years," Jenna said. "My parents moved here while I was in high school, but my mother homeschooled me. I graduated college last year and have been working at Bagel Palace ever since." She grinned. "Noah still works here, right?"

"Yes, and I'm guessing he must be one of your best customers. He's quite the bagel connoisseur." Noah was a huge fan of bagels and cream cheese. I liked them well enough, but my breakfast preference was for my mother's homemade manoush, a flat bread flavored with herbs that went well with everything.

Jenna laughed. "He sure is. Jeez, he must come in three or four times a week. Sometimes he brings his daughter in too, if he's dropping her off at school. Anyway, the last time Noah was in, I mentioned that I wanted another job, and he said that his girlfriend had an opening at Sappy Endings. How long have you two been dating?"

"About a year." After my father's killer had been brought to justice, Noah and I started seeing each other outside of work. He was a wonderful man, and unlike any I'd ever known before. Even with our busy schedules, we tried to get together two or three times a week. A year later, we had finally said those magical three words to each other and were both ready for a permanent relationship.

I studied the resume that Jenna had brought with her. "So, you've been working at Bagel Palace for about a year and a half. Can I ask why you're interested in working here?"

Jenna shifted in her seat. "Bagel Palace is okay, but I'd really like to do more baking. I graduated with a business degree and would love to run my own café someday. I figured this would be a great way to get started."

My heart gave a little jolt of excitement. Jenna sounded like she would be a perfect match for Sappy Endings. Hopefully mom would like her. I loved my mother, but she could be a bit picky at times. She'd had two assistants in the past six months. The first woman had been close to my mother's own age and seemed to resent being given orders by her, but that was part of the job. Mom had been running the café single-handedly since my father died, and we'd learned how to stay out of each other's way.

Alicia, who'd quit two weeks ago, was closer to my own age. After a rough start, she finally seemed to be catching on. My mother could be tough to please, but she thought Alicia had promise. Then, in a matter of a week, Alicia's boyfriend had proposed, and they'd eloped and moved south, where he'd accepted a new employment offer. Alicia ended up only giving us a couple of days' notice, which did not go over well with my mother.

"What do you do at Bagel Palace? Wait on customers?"

Jenna smiled and nodded. "A little of everything. I also cash customers out, make coffee, hot chocolate, and macchiatos. I don't have any real baking experience, except for—well, you know, baking with my mom and stuff like that when I was a kid. I'd really like to learn more. Noah told me your mom runs the café, and she's an awesome baker."

"It's true. She's also a great cook." A surge of pride ran through me. In addition to helping my father run the farm for years, she'd managed to make sumptuous meals for the entire family every night. My parents had left Lebanon shortly after they were married and settled in Vermont with hopes to start their own business. Mom still prepared Middle Eastern delicacies almost every evening, and Simon and I never complained.

"Is there someone I could contact for a reference?" Jenna hadn't listed any names on the short resume.

"Oh sure. Max Delray is the owner." She recited his number for me, and I jotted it down. "You'll see on my resume that I held a job on campus at SUNY Fredonia in their cafeteria. This was prior to Bagel Palace. If you need another name, I can check to see if anyone I worked with is still there."

"No, that's okay. I know Max from the times he's been in here. His reference will be more than enough, thanks. Would you have a problem working Monday through Friday, and every other Saturday? During the summer, we close at two o'clock on Saturdays, but right now, we're gearing up for our busiest season."

Jenna's leaned forward eagerly across the table. "The hours are fine with me. When's your slow season? Summer?"

I laughed. "There's always something to do around here. After the sap is gathered and the syrup is made, spring is already underway and it's time to start giving tours. Plus, I've been working on setting up more events for the summer and fall seasons, like our pie-baking contest that's happening today."

"Oh!" Jenna's eyes widened. "That explains why the woman I talked to earlier left here with like ten spatulas. For the record, I know a little about tapping trees. That usually happens in February, right?"

Most Vermonters knew when sap collecting season was, so this didn't come as a surprise to me. "Yes, usually February, but it really depends on the weather. If it's warmer than usual, we might start in February, but sometimes it doesn't happen until the beginning of March. Like life, it can be a crapshoot sometimes."

Jenna nodded in understanding. "I've read about tapping trees and the process of making syrup from the sap. I went on a tour here once. The man who told us about the farm was really nice. He was a sweet older guy—maybe he doesn't work here anymore? I remember that he gave me a piece of maple candy to try, and it tasted so good."

Her words tugged at my heart. The man had undoubtedly

been my father. He had loved nothing more than to explain to people how syrup was made. His maple candy had been the best around and was my personal favorite. Sweet and creamy. I still devoured a piece whenever I made it in the sugar house. During the process, I always felt a little closer to him.

"That was my father." My eyes grew moist, but I quickly blinked the tears away. "He passed away a year ago. A year ago this month, in fact."

"I'm so sorry. I didn't know." A stricken look appeared in the young woman's eyes.

"It's okay. And thank you."

An awkward silence fell between us until Jenna spoke up. "Um, are there, like, any benefits with the job? Max doesn't provide health insurance for his workers."

"We can work something out." Medical coverage was expensive, and neither Max nor I were required to provide it since we had less than twenty employees. My father had generously included family coverage for Noah, and I felt certain I could arrange something similar for Jenna.

Even though sales for syrup had been down recently, we still needed to hire someone. The café was doing well, and its business always increased around the holidays. I knew that my mother preferred to be at home crocheting, baking, or spending time with Toast, our orange-haired fluffball of a cat.

I glanced at my watch. "Sorry to cut this short, but I need to get over to the sugar house. Let me give Max a call, and then I'll get back in touch with you if I need more information."

"Sure, no problem." Jenna pushed back her chair and rose. She was shorter than me, about five foot two inches, with a slender build. "Thank you for meeting with me, Leila. I appreciate it and hope to hear from you soon."

"Thanks for coming out. I promise to get back to you within a couple of days, one way or another." I had a good feeling about this young woman. If she was a fast learner, she might even be able to take over the café by Christmas.

I walked Jenna to the front door of the building, which led to our parking lot.

"Would you like to come down to the sugar house with me and watch the pie-baking contest? We have every kind of pie you can imagine, plus homemade vanilla ice cream. Noah made the ice cream himself." I'd helped pack the ice in the machine last night, but Noah had done the rest. He made a gallon of vanilla with maple sugar, heavy cream, vanilla extract, and salt, and then another gallon this morning.

Jenna hesitated for a moment, then shook her head. "I'd like to, but I'm supposed to meet my boyfriend in a little while. It sounds like fun, though."

"No problem. Have a great day, and I'll talk to you soon." I opened the door for her, and then watched as she walked slowly towards a maroon-colored Chevy sedan with large rust patches on the side. She turned and waved at me.

I locked the front door then quickly went down the walkway and out the back entrance to the sugar house. The musical notes from *Sugar pie, honey bunch* met my ears. I smiled, thinking of how clever it was of Noah to suggest the pie-themed music, which we had streamed through

Pandora in the sugar house. Some of the other tunes we'd picked out included "American Pie" and "High Hopes" by Frank Sinatra, which Emma had learned the words to in kindergarten.

The clown had arrived and was in the sugar house, entertaining several children with his magic tricks. Heather stood in the doorway watching the show but left her post when she caught sight of me. "How did it go?"

"Good, I think. Her name is Jenna Fleming, and she works at Bagel Palace. Noah told her we were looking for help. I'm going to call her boss on Monday for a reference."

Heather wrinkled her brow. "Fleming. I don't think I know her. How old is she?"

"She graduated from college last year so twenty-two or twenty-three, I guess?" I was about to go on, but a slight commotion from the pie table managed to distract me. "Oh shoot. I don't know what's wrong with me—I need to start tasting the pies. We're way behind."

Heather grabbed hold of my arm. "Hang on a second. There's something I should tell you first. Or maybe prepare you is the right word."

"What's wrong?"

She swallowed hard. "There's someone here that you're not going to want to see."

A vision of Cameron flashed through my mind. "You saw him too? I thought he was a figment of my imagination."

Heather gave me a blank look. "He? Who are you talking about?"

I quickly realized that she must have been referring to

someone else. "Never mind. I forgot for a second that you never met him. Cameron was a former student. He was in my history class during my first year of teaching. I thought I saw him in the crowd." I did a rapid calculation in my head. "Let's see. He'd be a freshman in college by now."

Heather shook her head impatiently. "No. I'm talking about Taylor."

"You're kidding." I froze in my tracks. "What is *she* doing here?"

Taylor Hudson had been my roommate during our freshman year of college. We'd hit it off immediately, but our friendship had quickly disintegrated the night I came back early from the library and found her going through my purse. My money had gone missing on a few occasions, but I'd never actually caught Taylor in the act. Taylor promised never to do it again and begged me not to tell anyone. Foolishly, I had believed her.

Heather threw up her hands. "Who knows. Didn't she end up going to culinary school? Maybe she's entered a pie. Look, there she is, taking pictures of them with her phone."

After my confrontation with Taylor that night, things had gotten worse instead of better. Mysterious charges started showing up on my credit card, which had conveniently gone missing. By then, I'd had enough and went to the Dean's office. When confronted, Taylor tearfully admitted to the crime and returned my credit card. She was expelled from school, which led to her parents discovering that she had a serious drug problem.

Taylor called me one night a few weeks after being expelled

and accused me of ruining her life. She could have applied to return to school the following year, but never came back. I later discovered that she had attended a rehab program, taken some time off, and then enrolled in culinary school.

At that moment, Taylor looked up from her phone, and our eyes met. Dread settled like lead in the bottom of my stomach. She began to stroll casually towards me. I wanted to walk away, but that would have been the cowardly thing to do. My father used to say that we all needed to face our fears instead of running away from them. Of course, he was right, but going for a jog sounded pretty good right about now.

"Here goes nothing," I said to Heather.

Taylor had always been a beauty, and she'd only improved with age. Tall and slim, her golden hair cascaded down her back in perfect waves. Her wide-set, amber-colored eyes bore into mine, cold and angry.

Before things soured between us, we'd shared some fun times, specifically cramming for exams all night with cookies and ice cream to give us the sufficient fuel we needed. Taylor and I shared our hopes and fears for the future. It was the first time since my friendship with Heather that I'd felt close to anyone else.

"Hello, Leila."

Her cordial tone surprised me. The last time Taylor had been at the farm, she'd acted rude and condescending—at least to me. Back in June, Noah had been in the process of ringing up her maple syrup purchase in the gift shop when I came into the shop. Taylor had been flirting shamelessly with him until he casually introduced me as his girlfriend.

Taylor's jaw had nearly hit the floor, and she quickly left the store without another word.

"Hello, Taylor. What brings you here? Did you enter a pie?" I didn't remember seeing her name on any of the entry forms, but I'd only given them a quick glance.

"Oh please." She snickered. "I can't be bothered with these insignificant competitions. I'm planning to enter the Pillsbury Bake-Off next year. No, I'm here with a couple of friends who wanted to tour the sugar house." Her lips thinned into an icy expression. "To be honest, I think they want to drool over the hunky guy who works here."

"That would be Noah." Heat crept up my neck.

"Noah and Leila are practically engaged," Heather added.

"Oh, are you still seeing him?" Taylor tried to sound casual, but I spotted a vein bulge in her forehead. "That's too bad. With his looks, I figured he would have found someone better by now. Excuse me." She lifted her nose in the air and walked away.

Heather cursed under her breath as she watched Taylor make her way towards the sugar house. "She's horrible! You should have told her to get lost."

"It's not worth it." I sighed. "Taylor's never going to forgive me for what happened."

"Taylor should be thanking you instead," Heather remarked. "If she hadn't been expelled, her parents may not have found out about her drug problem until it was too late."

"Let's not talk about it anymore." The memory gave me no pleasure. Several of my peers who discovered what happened had turned their backs on me, claiming that I was a snitch. They weren't aware of Taylor's drug problem, and for my part, I never told anyone about it.

Heather pointed at the pie table. "It looks like someone might be trying to take over for you."

I followed her gaze. Margaret was sitting in my seat, eagerly cutting a slice out of the pumpkin pie that Emma had brought down from the café. She placed the piece on a paper plate and licked her fingers. I rushed forward before she had a chance to stick her fingers in another pie. My mother was talking to Noah about something and didn't notice. She would have died if she had seen Margaret handling the pies in such an unsanitary manner.

"Ah, Mrs. Middleton?" I gave her my most gracious smile. "Thanks for keeping the seat warm, but I'll take over now."

She squinted at me from behind her bifocals and lifted a plastic fork to her mouth. "Leila, I'm perfectly capable of judging this contest without any help. I've judged several pie and cake contests over the years for the Methodist Church."

I hoped the irritation didn't show on my face. "I'm sure you have, but this contest is being judged by the employees only. After we announce the winner, there will be plenty of pie for you to sample."

Margaret shot me a hateful look as if I'd insulted her. She shoved the fork into her mouth purposefully and licked her lips. "Oh, my. Delicious. Pumpkin is my favorite. Well, don't eat too much, Leila, or you'll lose that slim figure of yours."

She rose from the chair and walked away with her plate.

I turned to my mother. "I don't know why she has to be so difficult."

My mother sighed. "She's always been that way. I suppose she craves the attention." She pointed at the maple cream and apple walnut pies in front of her. "This has been very difficult, but I picked these two as my favorites. How about you, Noah?"

Noah was in the middle of finishing a piece of strawberry rhubarb pie and didn't hear her. I leaned over to tap him on the arm, and he looked up at me with a huge grin.

"Sorry, ladies." Noah pointed at his empty plate. "This one was fantastic. No maple syrup, but the card says they used maple sugar instead." He gestured at another pie in front of him. "My other favorite would have to be the chocolate silk pie."

I cut a small wedge of the pumpkin and placed it on a paper plate. As I reached for a fork, someone called my name. "Leila, guess what I've got!"

Emma came running towards me from the sugar house with an animal-shaped balloon in her hands. "I asked the clown if he could make a cat, and he did! And I asked for an orange one because Toast is orange."

I stooped down to examine the balloon and laughed. "This has to be the cutest thing I've ever seen." The clown had drawn whiskers on the balloon and made ears, and it did indeed resemble my farm cat, Toast.

"Isn't my kitty pretty?" Emma proudly swung the balloon around in a circle. It connected with the pumpkin pie, which was close to the edge of the table. I lunged for the pie, but didn't reach it in time. The pie teetered for a brief second, then toppled off the table and fell into the grass below, crust side down.

A few women seated in lawn chairs nearby saw the incident and gasped out loud. My mother looked shocked, but had the good sense not to say anything in front of Emma. Noah stepped around us to pick up the pie. It had broken into four separate pieces, all of which were now covered with grass and dirt.

Noah glanced over at Emma and me. "Well, it looks like we're going to have to depend on Mrs. Middleton's opinion for this one."

Emma's lower lip started to tremble. "I'm sorry, Daddy. I didn't mean it."

Noah tossed the pie pieces into a nearby trash can and picked Emma up in his arms. "That's okay, sweetheart. It's not the end of the world." He glanced over the top of her head at me, but I gave him a reassuring smile. Accidents happened and I wasn't worried. It was only a pie, after all. I'd happily refund the contestant their entry fee.

"Don't worry, Em." I touched her curly locks. "It's no big deal. Now, we have to select a winner so why don't you ask Heather to get you a glass of lemonade in the sugar house and then get ready to eat some pie with me, okay?"

Emma rubbed her eyes and wiggled out of her father's arms. "Okay." She gave us both a fleeting smile and raced into the sugar house as if nothing had happened. I glanced around at the crowd, waiting for someone to say something negative, but thankfully no one did. Margaret must not have seen the incident, or she would have been at my side like a bolt of lightning.

"Are you searching for an angry pie baker?" Noah whispered in my ear.

I barked out a laugh. "Kind of. I was afraid someone would make a big stink and get her all upset. The person who baked this pie must be a good sport. Do you want to grab Em to come back out here? I won't be held responsible for devouring the entire pie by myself."

"She'd never get over it." Noah smiled deeply into my eyes and headed for the sugar house.

With a chuckle, I picked up the paper plate and sniffed at the pie. I noticed how my mother did this before she sampled each piece. She would then examine the crust and contents with a critical eye. All I knew was that the pie looked great and smelled wonderful. My mouth had already started to water, and I had a sudden urge to satisfy my craving.

As I lifted my fork to my mouth, a blood curdling scream pierced the air, and I froze in place. Everyone turned to see what the commotion was about. A woman wearing a light blue Sappy Endings T-shirt with a maple leaf in the center came running towards our table.

"Call 9-1-1!" she screamed and pointed at the pathway that led to the main building. "A woman over there is having some kind of attack!"

I pulled out my phone and punched in the three numbers as Noah ran towards the area indicated. The woman in the maple leaf shirt and several others followed him in a panic.

By the time I'd reached them, there was a tight crowd around the woman.

"People, back up, please! Give her room!" Noah yelled.

"9-1-1, what is your emergency?" the operator asked.

I breathed heavily into the phone. "My name is Leila Khoury. I'm calling from Sappy Endings Farm. We have someone in need of medical attention right away—" I broke off as the crowd stepped back and I could see the woman lying on the ground, with Noah beside her. It was Margaret Middleton. Her entire body was racked with convulsions.

I watched with horror as Margaret's eyes rolled back in her head. Even at this distance, I could hear the woman gasping for air. Bubbles began to stream from between her lips. "Oh God. She's foaming at the mouth."

"Are you sure it's foam and not something else?" the operator asked. "Maybe something she ate?"

I wasn't sure of anything anymore. "It looks like foam."

"Can you tell me what's wrong with the lady?" the operator asked. "Is she clutching at her chest?"

My mouth had gone dry, and I struggled to speak. "No. She—she's having some kind of attack. And trouble breathing. Please hurry!"

"Help is on the way, ma'am. Is someone assisting her?" the operator asked. "Is she conscious?"

I watched as Noah bent over Margaret. My mother was a few feet away, holding back Abigail, who was sobbing hysterically. Noah tried to help Margaret sit up, but she shook him off. Margaret clutched at her throat and tried to say something.

"Is there a doctor here?" Noah shouted into the crowd. "A nurse? Anyone with medical training?"

"She's conscious." Dear God. It was truly a horrible sight to behold, and all I could do was stand there helpless as Noah tried to assist her. Margaret let out one loud, audible gurgle and went still. Noah felt her wrist for a pulse, then sucked in a deep breath.

The noise and commotion instantly stopped, and a quiet lull fell over the crowd. Noah laid Margaret's hand on her stomach and slowly rose to his feet. The crowd separated to allow him to walk towards me. His troubled eyes met mine, and in an instant, I realized what had happened.

Margaret Middleton was dead.

# CHAPTER THREE

**THE NEXT HOUR PASSED IN** a horrible blur. Paramedics arrived within five minutes and tried to revive Margaret, but to no avail. Noah had quickly composed himself and steered the crowd towards the parking lot so they were out of the way. Fortunately, the coroner had been available to come out to the farm right away and confirmed Margaret's death. My body was numb as I watched hers being loaded onto a gurney and taken away in his white-paneled van.

As soon as Margaret started having convulsions, Heather had gathered up all the children in the sugar house and brought them up to the main building for maple candy. I was grateful for her quick thinking and didn't believe the kids had been fully aware of what had happened.

My mother gently laid ice-cold fingers on my arm. I stared into her face, pinched tight with worry. "Abigail's on her way to the hospital," she murmured. "She's already called her brother. Eric will be here on the next plane from New York City."

Eric Middleton, Margaret's only son, was an attorney in New York City and didn't visit often. Abigail had divorced a couple of years ago and briefly moved back in with her mother before accepting the nursing job in New Hampshire. With her daughter no longer around, Margaret had taken to calling on my mother constantly, asking for help with grocery shopping, or she'd drop unsubtle hints about cravings for my mother's delicious grape leaves. Although they were close in age, my mother was much more active and had such refined manners that she would never refuse Margaret anything. Mom believed in being a good neighbor while Mrs. Middleton had only believed in taking advantage of people's kindness.

My mind was racing in ten different directions, but I knew that she wanted me to say something. "That's good, Mom."

Her lower lip trembled, and the sight devastated me. I put an arm around my mother's frail shoulders. Even though Margaret was disagreeable, I knew that my mother had considered the woman a friend. "Are you okay?"

Mom blinked back a tear and nodded. "I don't understand. She was fine earlier. What on earth could have happened to her?"

"Excuse me, Leila."

The voice was familiar, and I glanced up at the sound. A tall man in a blue blazer with dark hair graying at the temples stood a few feet away. Officer Ryan Barnes had investigated a murder last spring at the country club where Heather's bridal shower was held.

Great. The man must think I was some type of death magnet. I sucked in a deep breath. "Hello, Detective Barnes."

He moved closer and addressed my mother. "Good afternoon, Mrs. Khoury. Ladies, do you have a few minutes?"

I glanced in the direction of the parking lot. There were several people still milling around, and more than a few were staring over at us with interest. We needed to be out of their line of vision. "Sure, detective. Why don't we talk in the sugar house?"

Detective Barnes led the way into the building. Only an hour earlier, the room had been filled with the sound of children's laughter as they played games and drank lemonade. A discarded balloon animal in the shape of a giraffe had been flattened and lay on the floor in a sad state. Oh, the terrible irony. This was supposed to have been a day filled with good food, laughter, and fun for all. No one could have predicted such a horrible turn of events.

"I understand that you were having a pie-baking contest," Detective Barnes said.

"That's right."

His dark eyes searched mine. "Tell me what happened to Mrs. Middleton."

I shrugged. "We don't know exactly. She was fine earlier. I came down from the café and she was sitting in my chair, sampling a piece of pie."

The detective made a note on his iPad. "Was she a judge too?"

My mother shook her head. "She didn't wait for an invitation. Margaret has always been like that. Since Leila was delayed at the cafe, she offered to help judge the contest. Margaret claimed that it wasn't fair to keep people waiting. I told her that Leila would take care of everything when she got back, but she refused to listen. When Leila returned, she told Margaret that her help wasn't needed."

"What did Mrs. Middleton do then?" Detective Barnes asked.

Mom reached down and picked up the giraffe balloon. "Margaret seemed to take it personally. She picked up her plate and walked off into the crowd."

"That was the last we saw of her, until—" I couldn't finish the sentence.

The detective's trained eyes wandered around the sugar house, taking in the half-empty cups of lemonade and maple leaf coloring books that decorated Noah's desk. "Can you tell me what she ate or drank?"

"When I came back to the table, Margaret had already cut herself a slice of pumpkin pie. But I don't know what else she might have had. Do you, Mom?"

My mother pursed her lips together. "I know that she drank a glass of lemonade and ate a few pieces of maple candy."

"Did she sample any other pies?"

"Oh!" Mom's dark eyes widened. "I completely forgot. When I narrowed down my choices to the maple crème and apple walnut pies, she came over and asked if she could try the apple. I got an extra fork and gave her a mouthful."

Detective Barnes drummed his fingers against his iPad. "But you tasted it as well, correct?"

"I did," Mom admitted. "I had two or three bites because it was so delicious."

"Why would you give her some of the pie if she wasn't a judge?" Detective Barnes asked. "Weren't you afraid that other people who came to watch the contest would wonder why she got preferential treatment?"

My mother lowered her eyes to the floor and said nothing.

I decided to speak up. "I hate to speak ill of the dead, but Margaret could be difficult at times. I think my mother was afraid she would start complaining and distract everyone else from the contest."

Mom shot me a grateful look.

Detective Barnes stroked his chin in a pensive manner. "I see. And did you ladies pick a winning pie?"

I thought this was a strange thing for him to ask. "We never got a chance. The entries had been narrowed down to six when Margaret collapsed. We weren't able to finish the judging, but don't worry. Everyone's entrance fees will be returned to them."

"That's not what I was worried about." Detective Barnes strolled out of the sugar house as if he had all the time in the world. We had no choice but to follow him. He went over to the table which was still covered with pies that had barely been touched. We watched as he examined each one.

"Detective, what is it?" My mother brought a hand to her mouth. "Do you think Margaret could have gotten sick from eating something at the farm?"

Detective Barnes picked up the maple crème pie and sniffed it. "Ladies, I can't be positive, but there's a good chance Mrs. Middleton might have died from cyanide poisoning."

My mother looked like she might faint. She began to sway back and forth, and I put an arm around her shoulders to steady her.

"Is she all right?" The concern was evident in the detective's voice.

"Detective Barnes, why would you think it was cyanide? This doesn't make any sense," I said.

He lifted the apple walnut pie to his nose. "Well, for starters, there were several witnesses who said Mrs. Middleton was foaming at the mouth. That's a clear indication right there it may have been cyanide poisoning. Someone else who spoke to Mrs. Middleton before she collapsed said she told them that she felt dizzy, which is another sign. Cyanide is the fastest acting poison out there. Once ingested, a person can die within three to five minutes."

"No. It can't be." My mother's face turned as white as powdered sugar. "Why would someone do such a thing?"

Detective Barnes shrugged. "Maybe Mrs. Middleton had someone who didn't like her. You said that she could be difficult at times." He turned the chocolate silk pie tin around. "Or maybe the person who put poison in the pie didn't care who ended up eating it. There are a lot of evil people in this world, Mrs. Khoury."

He wasn't kidding. In the past year, I'd encountered more incidents of death and murder than I'd seen in my entire lifetime.

"Leila, you mentioned that Mrs. Middleton ate a piece

of pumpkin pie." Detective Barnes's eyes continued to roam over the table. "I don't see it here."

"We had a little accident with that one," I explained. "Noah's daughter Emma ran into the table, and the pie fell on the ground."

"Where is it now?" Detective Barnes asked.

"Noah threw it in the trash can." I couldn't help wondering if he would start rooting through the garbage to locate it.

As I'd suspected, Detective Barnes was headed for the nearby trash can when I stopped him. "Wait a second. I cut myself a piece but never tasted it." A chill ran through me. "Do you think there could be cyanide in it?"

"I think there's a very good chance," he said.

The untouched piece of pumpkin pie still lay on the table. I handed it to the detective. This felt like a nightmare coming true. Margaret may have died from a piece of pie at our farm, and I had come close as well. "Maybe something else she ate earlier in the day was tainted."

"Perhaps." The detective scratched his head. "We did search her car and found a discarded Hershey candy bar wrapper on the front seat. We'll see if the lab tests show anything. If not, then we'll have to wait for results of the autopsy, which may take a while."

"There couldn't be anything wrong with the pie," my mother insisted. "Wouldn't we have noticed something off with the color or a bad smell?"

Detective Barnes held the plate of pie while I wrapped a piece of plastic around it. "Cyanide is odorless and colorless, so no, you wouldn't have noticed anything wrong. It will need to be analyzed."

A young police officer, the first to arrive on the scene, strode towards us from the direction of the parking lot. He nodded politely at me. "All set, Detective. We're letting the spectators go home now. We have all their names and phone numbers. A few people may have skipped out when Mrs. Middleton collapsed, but we can't be sure."

"Thanks, Matteo." Detective Barnes turned to me. "Are there any surveillance cameras around outside?"

I shook my head. "Not by the sugar house. There's one outside the main building, but it doesn't have much of a range."

"We'll need to see all the contest entries as well," Detective Barnes said.

Matteo grinned. "Already thought of that, Detective. I made copies in Miss Khoury's office. We'll take the originals back to the station."

Detective Barnes spread his arms over the pie table. "Good. Get Officer Banks to come down here, please. I want all of these pies brought to the lab. Every one of them will need to be tested."

My mother and I exchanged horrified glances. Detective Barnes had to be wrong. If Margaret had died from something she ate at Sappy Endings, our livelihood could be in serious trouble.

---

Heather came home with us after Detective Barnes and the rest of the police department had left the farm. My mother busied herself heating up some kibbi, a family favorite, and brought out the tabbouleh she'd made the night before. Heather loved tabbouleh, a Levantine salad made from finely chopped parsley, tomatoes, mint, and onion. Mom seasoned it with olive oil, lemon juice, salt, and sweet pepper.

Although my mother's cooking was top notch, no one had much of an appetite tonight. We sat there pushing the food around on our plates while not saying much.

"The children—please tell me they didn't know what happened," Mom said worriedly.

"No, I don't think so," Heather reassured her. "I simply told them the lady didn't feel well. They shouldn't have any idea that she died unless their parents told them."

My mother seemed satisfied with her response and fell silent. I kept hoping Detective Barnes would be wrong, and that Margaret's death wasn't related to our farm in any way. "Mom, if the pie did cause Margaret's death, we need to think about what we're going to say to the media."

She shot me a disbelieving look. "That's not going to happen. Like the detective said, maybe she ate something before she left her house."

Denial was my mother's best friend. "Okay, but we need to be prepared, just in case."

"Simon will keep it out of the newspaper. He promised," Mom insisted.

Heather raised an eyebrow at me, but didn't say anything. Mom's faith in my little brother was admirable, but not realistic. "Okay, maybe Simon can keep it out of the newspaper, but he can't keep it off social media or TV. Channel Eight is sure to run something about it tonight. This could end up affecting the business."

My mother rose from the table and set her plate in the sink. "Leila, people have been coming to Sappy Endings for over twenty-five years. They would never turn their backs on us."

"You don't know that for sure," I said. "Death—or murder—has a funny way of changing people's minds."

"I *do* know!" Mom's voice rose an octave.

Heather and I both stared at her in amazement. My mother never lost her temper and was always cool and collected. "It must be something else."

I got up from my chair and went to put an arm around her. "I hope so, but like I said, we need to be prepared—"

My mother edged away from me and towards the doorway. "Sorry, girls, but this day has worn me out and I have a splitting headache. I'm going to turn in early. Leila, would you please stack the rest of the dishes in the dishwasher for me?"

"Mom, please." This was so unlike her. My mother believed in being practical and no-nonsense. She refused to face the fact that our farm could be in danger. I suspected it was more of an allegiance to my father than the business. Sappy Endings had always been his passion, and she didn't want to see his dream die.

My mother paused in the doorway for a second, her back to us. I watched her shoulders sag as if an unsurmountable weight had settled on them. After a moment, she finally spoke, her voice tight with tears.

"Good night, girls. Sleep well."

As soon as she left the room, Toast jumped off the chair he was lying on and dutifully followed her upstairs. I made no attempt to stop him. Toast was my loyal companion and slept at the foot of my bed every night. Somehow, he sensed that tonight my mother needed him more than I did.

# CHAPTER FOUR

**TO MY RELIEF, THE NEXT** day was Sunday and Sappy Endings was closed. I slept badly and didn't come downstairs until nine o'clock, which was unheard of for me on a Sunday. My mother was in the kitchen, humming quietly to herself as she made breakfast. She turned and glanced at me in surprise.

"You're not dressed yet? Hurry, everyone will be here soon."

I stared down at my pink bathrobe. "Who's everybody, and why are they coming here?"

"Heather, Tyler, and your brother. They're coming for breakfast."

I went over to the stove and poured myself a cup of *Ahweh,* the strong Turkish coffee that my mother made every morning. "Heather and Simon have seen me in my pajamas before. Tyler probably hasn't, but I doubt he'll mind." At this rate, I didn't care if the president showed up with them. There were more important things to worry about.

Mom gave me a sharp look, but didn't argue. She turned back to the stove, spatula in hand, and continued preparing lamb spiked eggs. "What about Noah and Emma? Would you like to invite them as well?"

I stirred some cream into my coffee. "They've gone to New York for the day to see his mother. I'm guessing they won't be back until Emma's bedtime. Now, what exactly is going on?"

"There's nothing going on." Mom put knafeh, a traditional Lebanese dessert, on the table. Like baklava, it was made with phyllo dough but shredded and stuffed with cheese, then topped with chopped pistachios and drizzled with sugary syrup. My mother substituted our maple syrup instead. Technically, it was a dessert, but in my opinion, went well at any time of the day.

Mom shrugged. "I couldn't sleep last night, so I got up early to do some baking. I thought it would be nice to have everyone over for breakfast."

Now I understood what she could not bring herself to say. Like me, my mother was nervous about the farm being in the news and painted in such a negative light. Unlike me, she didn't lie in bed waiting for sleep to come. Mom could never stay idle for long and had thrown herself into cooking up a storm. It was how she calmed herself.

I watched as she whipped up her special buttermilk pancake batter, one of my favorite breakfasts. Should I learn how to cook, even though I had no desire to? When Noah and I got married, I couldn't expect my mother to run over to the house and make breakfast for us every day. She would be ecstatic if I suddenly developed a culinary passion. The truth of the matter was that my only interest in food was consuming it.

Noah never asked me to cook him anything. He had made dinner for me several times at his house, and breakfast on the rare occasion that I stayed over. He'd learned how to fend for himself and Emma after his wife died and said he enjoyed cooking when there was time. Perhaps I would change my mind someday, but I doubted it.

I laid a hand on my mother's arm, and she jumped about five feet in the air. The spatula fell to the floor with a clatter. She didn't usually startle so easily. I bent down to pick up the spatula and washed it in the sink. "Mom, don't worry. Everything's going to be all right."

She exhaled sharply. "I hope you're right, but I have a bad feeling about this. I tried to call Abigail again last night, but she didn't pick up."

"She may not want to talk to anyone," I remarked.

Mom ignored my comment. "I left a message and asked if she needed anything. I saw her car across the street this morning. Maybe I'll bring a maple Bundt cake by later."

"Did Eric get into town?"

"There's an older model Nissan in the driveway next to Abigail's car, so I'm guessing yes," Mom said. "Would you like to come over with me after breakfast?"

"No thanks." She must have forgotten that I wouldn't want to see Eric. "Maybe Margaret's kids need some time to grieve by themselves."

My mother started to say something but was interrupted by a knock on the front door. Toast, who had been sitting on a chair in the kitchen, waiting for his share of breakfast, jumped down and trotted into the living room. He waited patiently by the front door as I opened it for Heather and her husband Tyler.

"Hey." Heather, smelling faintly of lilac shampoo and the brisk Vermont air, gave me a warm hug. "It's cold out there this morning. Guess the warm spell is over for good."

"Glad you guys could make it."

Tyler Murray stepped forward and kissed me on the cheek. He was a wonderful man, and the perfect match for my best friend. A pediatrician, Tyler was attractive with curly dark hair and shoulders that belonged on a linebacker. "Hey. Lei. I'm really sorry about what happened yesterday."

"Thanks. Come on in."

Heather reached down to pet Toast, who nudged her hand. "There's my favorite guy. Did you save me some breakfast?"

Toast let out a plaintive meow, turned, and went back to the kitchen, with us following.

"Hello, you two," my mother called out as she set a platter of pancakes on the table. "Sit down and help yourself. Everything's ready."

I wasted no time in loading my plate with eggs, pancakes, and *knapef*. There were also sausages and manoush. My appetite had returned in full force today, and I tried to take it as a good sign.

"Everything is delicious, as usual, Selma," Tyler remarked as he reached for a bottle of our amber maple syrup.

Heather slathered butter all over her stack of pancakes. "But didn't you say on the phone that Simon was coming too? Maybe we should have waited for him."

Mom cut up two sausage patties for Toast and placed the paper plate on the floor. The cat bolted out of the chair as if he was on fire. "Simon sent me a text a little while ago. He said he had to stop by the paper first and told us not to wait for him. Now, eat, before everything gets cold."

My mother believed that good food nurtured the soul and gave people comfort, even at times when the world seemed a dark place. As my stomach filled and my hunger lessened, I grew brave enough to tackle the proverbial elephant in the room. "Did they mention it on the news last night? I couldn't bring myself to turn on the TV."

Heather looked surprised that I had brought up the subject. She calmly wiped her mouth with a napkin. "To be honest, I didn't watch. Dad stayed up for the eleven o'clock broadcast but told me he didn't see anything about the farm."

Color poured back into my mother's pale face. "Thank goodness. Simon said that he would take care of everything." There was an unmistakable note of pride came in her voice. "I knew he wouldn't disappoint us."

I poured myself another cup of *Ahweh* and smiled to myself. Even though my relationship with my mother had improved significantly since I'd moved back home, Simon would forever be her favorite child. I'd gotten over the petty jealousy years ago but worried that mom thought Simon could wave a magic wand and make all of our problems disappear.

"Speaking of the paper, did you grab it this morning?" I asked.

Mom shook her head. "I went out earlier, but it hadn't been delivered yet. Will you go see if it's arrived, dear?"

I pushed my chair back and padded through the living room in my slippers. The sun was shining brightly outside and the frost on the grass had disappeared, but there was still a raw edge to the day. Thanksgiving would be here next week, and Christmas was not far behind. I grabbed the paper from the box and thought about Christmas shopping—which was not one of my favorite things to do. At least it would be fun picking out presents for Emma.

With paper in hand, I hurried back up the driveway, wishing I'd thought to put on a coat. I closed and locked the front door behind me and started towards the kitchen. I quickly scanned the front page and froze.

The front page contained two photos of Sappy Endings. One was of the pies, taken before any of them had been sliced into. The other shot was of the wooden sign hanging in front of our main building, depicting a jug of maple syrup and plate of pancakes with the words, *Sappy Endings, Est. 1998* inscribed underneath. The headline covered the top of the page in huge, bold black letters and read:

**LOCAL SYRUP FARM IN A STICKY SITUATION.**

A guttural sound escaped from my throat.

> Sappy Endings, a maple syrup farm located in Sugar Ridge, hosted a pie-baking contest on Saturday that resulted in the death of one local woman.
>
> Margaret Middleton, age 65, went into convulsions and died shortly after sampling a piece of pie during the contest. Police confirmed that the pie contained cyanide, a colorless and odor-free poison that can kill within three to five minutes.
>
> Proprietor Leila Khoury, who took over the farm after her father's death last fall, would not comment. It is unknown if the farm will be shutting its doors to deal with the issue.

The article went on to talk about how my father had established the farm back in 1998 and how he and the business had long been a pillar of respect in the community. As I continued to read, my heart began to thump with anxiety. The news had gotten out, and it was far worse than I'd anticipated.

Simon had been covering the story. How on earth did he let this happen?

"Leila, what are you doing out there?" my mother wanted to know.

I had no choice but to show her the article. Heather gasped out loud as she and Tyler read it over my mother's shoulders. Mom turned to page 11, where the article continued, and shut her eyes tightly, as if trying to block it out.

"Your father," she whispered. "He's up in Heaven, watching all of this with a broken heart."

Any mention of my father still reduced me to tears. We had always understood each other. The sun had risen and set on him. Some days, I was convinced that I'd never get over his death.

"I'm so sorry this had to happen to your family." Tyler shook his head sorrowfully.

Heather asked the million-dollar question of the day. "How did this article ever get published?"

As if on cue, the front door slammed, and my brother Simon appeared in the doorway of the kitchen. He was two years younger than me and bore a distinct resemblance to my father with his tall frame and short dark hair. That was where any similarities ended. While my father had a sunny and welcoming disposition, there was a brooding and self-assured quality about Simon that many women seemed to find fascinating.

At the moment, Simon looked anything but confident. His dark eyes, which closely resembled mine, circled the room. When they locked on my mother, the expression in his became one of shame and regret.

"Mom." He put his arms around her. "I don't know how this happened, I swear!"

She gulped back a sob. "How could you not know?

You're the head reporter. How could you let them do this to us?"

Simon seemed taken aback by her remark. In the past, Mom's criticism had always been reserved for me, and not him. As a child, I would have been delighted by this turn of events, but at the moment, all I could feel was profound sadness.

He exhaled sharply. "Someone emailed us the article and photos. The Features editor was monitoring the mailbox last night, and when he saw the story come in, he didn't even bother to consult me. Instead, he went right ahead and published the article. I didn't even know about it until one of my coworkers called me this morning." Simon picked up the paper from the table and crumpled it into a ball. "Do you know how this makes me feel? Like I betrayed my own family."

My mother wiped at her eyes with a napkin. "It's all right, dear. But I don't understand how one of your coworkers could do such a thing."

The lines around Simon's mouth tightened. "Hank, the editor, told me that he had to use the article. It was big news for our town and came first over my hurt feelings." His face turned crimson. "Mom, I'd gladly cut off my arm to have that story removed from the paper."

"Were you able to trace the email?" I asked.

Simon slumped into the empty chair next to my mother. "Not yet. There's a good chance it's encrypted."

Heather's eyes went round with alarm. "Someone deliberately wanted this printed so they could hurt all of you even more."

A lightbulb clicked on in my head. "What if the person who sent it is the same one who killed Margaret?"

My mother looked confused. "Are you saying that the person who killed Margaret did it so our farm would suffer?"

Simon shrugged. "Anything's possible."

I grabbed the paper from the floor and smoothed it out. My finger tapped the picture of the pies. "Whoever sent these was at the contest yesterday."

"That occurred to me too." Simon grabbed a cup and poured himself some *Ahweh*. "It's creepy when you think about it. Whoever tainted that pie was probably standing around, waiting for someone to drop dead."

Something about this didn't sit well with me. We were missing an important piece of the puzzle, but at this point, I couldn't tell what or who it might be. Simon and my mother went on to discuss the murder as Heather and Tyler listened intently. I thumbed my way to page eleven to finish reading the article. It ended with a paragraph about how I had taken over the farm and continued my father's legacy.

To my surprise, there was another photo at the end of the article—one that I hadn't noticed earlier. This photo was of me. I was standing behind the pie entry table talking with Emma and holding a paper plate. I sucked in a deep breath. The plate I was holding contained a piece of the pumpkin pie Margaret had tasted. An ice-cold chill ran down my spine as I wondered how close in proximity I'd been to the killer. Or how close I had come to being their victim.

# CHAPTER FIVE

**AS I DROVE TO SAPPY** Endings the next morning, I half expected to see a crowd standing outside that rivaled the one on Saturday. Fortunately, there were no news station vans or reporters shoving microphones in my face. The only vehicle in the lot was a truck that belonged to Noah, as he often arrived earlier than me.

My mother had a doctor's appointment that morning, so I needed to get things started in the café until she arrived. The first thing I did was brew the coffee. That much I could handle on my own. The most difficult part of running the café for me—of course—was having to do any actual baking or cooking. Mom had left some maple batter in the fridge, so I lined a muffin pan with paper cups and filled them. As much as I wanted customers, I prayed that they would be satisfied with plain coffee or muffins. The maple breakfast sandwiches and other goodies that my mother created so effortlessly would have to wait until she arrived.

Noah came into the café as I was pouring myself a cup of coffee. Although I loved everything about the man, it was that brilliant blue gaze of his that always managed to make my heart beat faster. He placed his arms around my waist and smiled, but I detected genuine concern in his tone.

"How are you feeling this morning?"

"I've been better." I put the cup down and buried my face in his chest. His muscular arms went around me, and I basked in the strength that they provided. The warmth exuding from his body mixed with the woodsy scent of his cologne—a perfect combination for someone who spent so much time outdoors. Noah lifted my chin and kissed me. Desire stirred through my body and for a moment, all of my worries floated away.

"Then again, I could be a lot worse," I murmured in between kisses.

After we broke apart, Noah gently ran a finger down the side of my cheek. "I'm sorry I didn't call last night. We got home from my mom's later than I thought. Em had a bath and we both conked out while I was reading to her."

"I figured it was something like that." It was no surprise that he had fallen asleep while reading to his daughter. Noah worked hard, and between the job at Sappy Endings and taking care of Emma, he didn't have much time to spare. My only regret was that I hadn't been with them. I loved Noah and his daughter dearly and didn't know how I'd ever managed to exist so long without them in my life.

One recent evening while visiting Noah's, I'd gone into the kitchen to make us both some tea. When I'd returned to Emma's room, I'd found both father and daughter sitting propped up on pillows with their heads bent close together and eyes closed. For a long time, I'd stood there, watching them, and said a little heartfelt prayer of thanks for the blessings in my life.

"Did you see the paper yesterday?" I asked.

He shook his head. "No, I never got a chance to read it. Please don't tell me that Simon decided to run an article about what happened."

"No, he would never do that. Family comes first with Simon. But someone else sent in an article with pictures. The Features editor went ahead and included it without bothering to consult Simon or anyone else first." I went on to relay what the article said. "It's going to ruin business for the farm, isn't it? Maybe we should lock the doors now and go home."

"Let's not jump to conclusions," Noah said wisely. "The Maple Messenger doesn't have a huge readership. More people turn to social media for their news these days instead of the paper. It may not be as bad as you think."

I poured him a cup of coffee. "I hope you're right. My mother is devastated. All she keeps talking about is how my father is looking down on us with a broken heart."

Noah took a sip from his mug. "Leila, I know you're blaming yourself for what happened, but this isn't your fault. What did the detective say about the pie—do they know which one contained the cyanide?"

"Not for certain, but it sounds like the one Emma dropped."

His mouth fell open. "The pumpkin pie?"

"Yes. And if it is, that means she saved my life."

Noah shook his head in disbelief. "This is unreal. You could have gone the same way as Mrs. Middleton—and so could have Em. Who would do such a thing?"

"It's obvious whoever did this didn't care who they killed." The more I thought about that fact, the more anxious I became. We needed a change of topic. "Does Emma know that I may be moving in with you guys after Christmas?"

Noah wrinkled his brow. "Not yet. And I didn't know it was a maybe. I thought it was already decided."

"Well, I wanted to make sure you didn't have a change of heart," I teased.

"You will never have to worry about that," Noah assured me as he brushed his lips against mine. "Speaking of telling people things, does your mother know?"

"Yes. Mom's been trying to talk me out of it, but I think she realizes the time has come for me to move on." I wondered what she would think about me taking Toast when I left, but was unsure of how to broach the subject. Mom was very fond of him, and he was the first pet either one of us ever had, due to my father's allergies. "What if Emma doesn't like the idea?"

Noah shook his head. "That won't happen." He wrapped an arm around my shoulders as we walked towards the entrance for the cafe. "I think the best thing is for you to move in, and then, after a few months, we'll tell her we plan to get married. We need to take it a little slow with Em, but she'll be fine."

The thought of being Mrs. Noah Rivers caused a tingling sensation to run through my body. I hadn't realized before how much I wanted my own family. After an emergency hysterectomy at the age of eighteen, I'd been forced to accept the cruel fate that I would never be able to have children. It hadn't helped when my ex-fiancé Mark backed out of our wedding because I could never give him a biological child. I thought true love was out of the question for me and spent many years convincing myself I didn't need a man in my life.

"I can't wait to start my life with both of you," I whispered.

"Same here." Noah tucked a stray curl behind my ear. "Look, I've got a few tap lines to repair out in the sugar bush. Then I need to finish up some candles for the gift shop. The holiday shopping rush is only a few days away. Let me know if it gets busy and you need some help in here, okay?"

"Will do. Thanks." I set my laptop up on the counter and waited for customers to arrive as I read emails. The website needed to be updated at least once a week, so I went to work on that next. One couple stopped in for coffee, but that was all.

When my mother arrived, it was after ten o'clock. She stared around at the empty café with a mournful expression. "How many people came in this morning?"

I hated to deliver the bad news. "Two people came in for coffee." On an average day, we might have had about fifty by now.

Mom bit into her lower lip. "What are we going to do?"

I answered with a shrug. "I'm not sure there's anything we can do. Hopefully it will blow over soon."

She started to wring her hands. "The holiday season is right around the corner. Do you know how much business we'll lose if—"

"We're not going to lose any business," I interrupted.

Mom shot me a doubtful look. "You can't really believe that."

I exhaled sharply and reminded myself that, like me, she was upset. This was no time to get into a war of words with her. "Yes, I do. And to prove my point, I'm going into my office right now to check Jenna's reference."

"Who's Jenna?" my mother asked suspiciously.

"The woman who I interviewed on Saturday." I picked up my laptop and cell. "If everything checks out, I'm going to hire her and see how soon she can start."

She gasped. "Leila, the farm can't afford to pay another employee right now."

"It's going to be fine. Please trust me, okay?" I kissed mom's cheek, which seemed to mollify her for the moment. "Call me if you need any help. Noah's outside in the sugar bush repairing tap lines."

She attempted a smile, but failed. I proceeded down the walkway and wasted no time shutting myself into the office. Once I was settled at my desk, the first thing I did was check the farm's email account for about the tenth time this morning, praying for some new syrup orders. There was still one pending from last week, but nothing else. It was rare not to see new orders arrive on a Monday morning, but I reminded myself that this was only a temporary lull.

On the spur of the moment, I decided to put together a quick newsletter, offering an extra ten percent off all products from now until Thanksgiving. We'd run a special promotion for Black Friday—fifteen percent off everything, which was our normal annual sale. Orders would be sure to flock in again this year with such a great discount.

I placed a call to Bagel Palace and asked to speak with the owner. After a minute, he came on the line, sounding impatient and busy. "Yes, can I help you?"

"Hi, Max, this is Leila Khoury calling."

There was a brief pause. "Leila, hi. Uh, how are you? Gee, I was sorry to hear about what happened at the farm on Saturday."

"Thanks." His voice was full of sympathy, but it left a bitter taste in my mouth. I didn't want people's pity. Instead, they needed to know this wasn't our fault, and Mrs. Middleton may have been targeted. "Everything is going to be fine."

"Of course, it is," he agreed. "So, what can I do for you? Do you need an order for an upcoming event at the farm?"

I shifted in my seat. "Not this time. I'm actually checking on a reference for Jenna Fleming."

"Oh, right," he said. "She was hoping that you might call. I'll be sorry to lose Jenna. She's one heck of a worker."

So far, so good. "Does that mean you would recommend her?"

Max cleared his throat. "Absolutely, without a doubt. Say, what would she be doing at the farm?"

"Working in the café with my mother," I explained. "Mom wants to go part time, so Jenna will eventually be running it by herself most days."

"She can handle it," Max said without hesitation. "Jenna's well organized. There's been plenty of days here when my other counterperson called in sick, and I was stuck in the kitchen making bagels. Jenna always took care of the busy storefront with no problems. She mentioned that she was a business major at college, so I'm guessing she'll eventually want to get into marketing."

My long-range plan for Jenna was to run the café. I did all of the marketing for the farm, which included newsletters, keeping our Instagram and Facebook pages up to date, and running monthly ads in the newspaper. I had no plans to step away from this type of work in the near future. "Is there anything else you think I should know?"

Max hesitated for a second too long. "Well, I don't know if this will matter to you, but she's a little overly sensitive. A customer yelled at her once because she gave them the wrong topping, and she went to pieces."

Uh-oh. I'd thought this sounded too good to be true. Mom was not exactly subtle when it came to her expectations in the kitchen, and I worried they would clash. I also knew there was no way that I could survive working in the kitchen with my mother.

"I'm sure that won't be an issue," I lied. "Thanks for your time, Max."

I clicked off and reminded myself to tell mom she needed to be a little more subdued while training Jenna. A warning sign flashed on and off in my brain, but I chose to ignore it. Jenna might be a little overly sensitive, but she seemed like a perfect match for the job in every other way. Mom needed a break, so maybe she'd cut down on the micromanaging a little bit. She needed to be realistic and understand it would be next to impossible to find someone else with her level of expertise.

I picked up the phone again and dialed Jenna's number. Her voicemail kicked in. "Hi, Jenna, this is Leila Khoury from Sappy Endings. I'd like to talk to you about coming to work for us. Please give me a call when you have a chance. Thanks."

While I was in the middle of putting together my newsletter with sale information, the intercom buzzed. I could never tell if it was Noah or my mother on the other end, so answering "Hi, sweetheart" was out. "Yes?"

"Leila." My mother's voice sounded strained. "Could you come out right away, please? Detective Barnes is here and would like to talk to both of us."

Uneasiness swept over me. "Sure, I'll be out in a second." I saved my document and hurried out of the office. A visit from Detective Barnes meant he had news. And if it were good news, I suspected that he would have called instead of coming all the way out here.

As I shut the door to my office, I saw Noah approaching from the opposite direction. His handsome face bore a serious expression. He reached out a hand and pulled me aside.

"Hey, I was just coming to talk to you about our standing order for Pancake Heaven. They aren't sure that—"

"Not right now," I interrupted.

Noah's jaw went slack. "What's wrong?"

"Detective Barnes is here to see me and my mother." I hated to sound like a damsel in distress, but in truth, I was terrified. "Will you come with me?"

He closed his hand over mine. "You didn't even need to ask. Now, don't think the worst, okay?"

It was difficult not to.

Detective Barnes was seated at a table in the otherwise empty café. When Noah and I entered, my mother was placing one of her famous lattes in front of him.

"Hello, Leila." Detective Barnes rose to his feet and then his gaze shifted to Noah. "Mr. Rivers, correct?"

"It's Noah, sir." Noah pumped his hand and then pulled out a chair for me. He remained standing, his hands resting lightly on my shoulders for moral support.

My mother took the chair on the other side of Detective Barnes. "What did you want to see us about, Detective?"

He glanced down at his iPad. "I wanted to come out here in person to give you the lab results."

"You have them already?" my mother asked in amazement.

"I had them put a rush on it," Detective Barnes explained. "A healthy dose of liquid cyanide was discovered in the pumpkin pie. It was enough to kill anyone who ate it."

My mother gasped. "Dear Lord. How could this have happened?" Her mouth dropped open as she stared into my face. "Oh, Leila, you almost ate that pie too!"

"What kind of a lunatic would do such a thing?" Noah wanted to know. "They might not have even known who they'd end up killing."

Detective Barnes mouth tightened. "It's hard to believe, but there are people who choose their victims at random. Just when I think I've seen it all, something even worse occurs." He stared thoughtfully at Noah. "Is it possible that I could speak with your daughter when she gets out of school today?"

Noah's grip on my shoulders tightened. "Why?"

"Leila said that she was the one who brought the pumpkin pie down from the café." Detective Barnes took a long sip of his drink.

"That's right," Noah said.

"Did she see who brought it?" Detective Barnes asked him.

"Not that I'm aware of," Noah said.

"The pie was left in the café," my mother explained. "I was busy behind the counter, so someone could have easily put it there without me seeing it. I was on the phone and making lattes."

"They even left the entry form and cash for the fee. The entrant's name was Sandy Sweets." That should have been a tip off.

Detective Barnes frowned. "Let me get this straight. No one saw the person drop it off, but you accepted the entry anyway?"

Maybe it wasn't his intention, but the detective made us sound like a bunch of trusting fools. In our defense, we had never thought for a minute that someone might try to kill one of the spectators with a poisoned pie. This was straight out of a horror movie.

My face began to warm. "There didn't seem to be any

reason not to accept it. People were leaving pies all over the place."

Detective Barnes crossed his right foot over the left. "I'd still like to talk to Emma, if you have no objections, Noah. Sometimes children pick up on things that adults don't."

Noah stroked his clean-shaven chin. "I guess that would be all right. As long as Leila and I can be present too."

"Of course," Detective Barnes said. "I'll drop by your house tonight after dinner. Would seven o'clock be okay?"

"That's fine," Noah said and recited his address.

Detective Barnes's sharp gaze shifted back to my mother. "I talked with some more of the spectators who were present at the farm on Saturday, specifically, a Callie Milson. She said she lives on your street, Mrs. Khoury, and that she too was friendly with the deceased."

"Oh, yes. Callie's a lovely woman and sometimes ran errands for Margaret if I wasn't available." Mom swallowed hard. "She went with Abigail to the hospital."

Detective Barnes glanced down at his iPad. "Callie said that she saw Margaret at the Jolly Green Grocer the day before the contest. The woman told Callie that she was going to be judging the entries."

"That doesn't surprise me." Then, I realized what the detective was getting at and shot up in my chair. "Holy cow. Do you think someone overheard her—maybe the person who baked the pie?"

"There's a good chance," Detective Barnes said. "But let's not jump to conclusions yet. First, we need to know why someone would have wanted to kill her. I talked to both of

Margaret's children yesterday. Her daughter Abigail said that she spoke with her mother almost every evening. She said that Margaret kept to herself most of the time."

"Yes, that's right," my mother agreed. "She was like a hermit in some ways. The only place she ever went was to the grocery store. There were many times she would ask me or Callie to go for her instead."

Detective Barnes typed something into his iPad. "Neither one of her children could think of any reason why someone would want to harm their mother."

I had wondered about that too. Something seemed off about Margaret's murder. Sure, the woman could be annoying, and she constantly took advantage of her neighbors' generosity, but that wasn't enough reason for someone to want her dead. At least, I didn't think so.

"Now what?" My tone came out sharper than I'd intended.

Mom frowned. "Leila, please don't be rude."

Detective Barnes scratched his head. "Without knowing who made the pie, I would suggest you be careful about what you tell your customers. The killer could be anyone."

I spread my arms out wide. "There's no need to worry, Detective. As you can see, we have no customers. There was an article about the contest and Margaret's death in the Maple Messenger yesterday. It's obvious no one wanted to take a chance on coming here for syrup and being the next one poisoned."

"Yes, I saw the article." Detective Barnes drummed his fingers against the iPad. "It's very unfortunate. People always seem to believe everything they read."

"Whoever wrote the article is the one who killed her," I pointed out.

"It's possible," Detective Barnes admitted, "but we don't know for certain."

I wanted to scream. What exactly *did* he know for certain? Perhaps I would pay a visit to Abigail myself and ask about her mother's acquaintances. Every day the killer continued to walk free cost my farm more business. It was a disturbing and terrifying thought to realize that we didn't know if or when this person might attempt to strike again.

"There's something else," Detective Barnes went on. "Now, this is strictly my own recommendation, but I feel it's best if you retained an attorney."

My mother's eyes widened. "What on earth for?"

He pursed his lips together. "There's an excellent chance Margaret Middleton's family could bring a lawsuit against your farm. They might try to take you for everything you own."

# CHAPTER SIX

**FORTIFIED WITH A CHANGE OF** clothes and food, I drove over to Noah's house at 6:30 that evening. He greeted me at the front door with a tender kiss while Emma waved happily at me from their kitchen table.

I loved Noah's home. It was a log cabin that he purchased shortly after relocating to Vermont from New York. The place had been neglected for a few years before he bought it, and Noah spent many hours re-staining the outside and making other repairs while working full-time at Sappy Endings.

There was a rustic feel to the place, complimented by the dark teakwood furniture and large wooden beams that supported the ceilings. The house only had two bedrooms, but both were larger than normal, and each one had a full bath. Noah hoped to turn the finished basement into a playroom for Emma when he had some free time. There was an eat-in kitchen and large family room with a woodstove that exuded warmth on cozy winter evenings. It was the kind of home that made you want to curl up on the couch with a good book and watch the snowflakes fly all winter long.

My parents' home never had a cozy feel to it. Mom was effortlessly and efficiently neat, and she'd instilled that trait in both my brother and me. Growing up, if Simon and I dared to leave our beds unmade before school, we would be sure to hear about it later. My father wasn't overly concerned with the neatness factor, but he considered the house my mother's domain and had towed the line as well.

Emma and Noah were finishing up dinner. Homemade chili and cornbread were on the table, and he invited me to join them.

"No thanks. I had a piece of kibbi and Syrian bread when I got home."

"The cornbread is from a box mix, but I have to say, it's pretty good. Just don't tell your mother. I'll bet that she never used a box mix in her life." Noah winked as he pulled out a chair for me.

"That's one bet you'd win," I agreed.

Emma paused in the middle of a bite, the spoon against her mouth. "I like kibbi. Especially the crunchy parts. Will you bring me some the next time you come to visit?"

"Those are the pine nuts." I laughed. "And of course, I'll bring you some." The reference to *visit* reminded me that Emma still didn't know I was planning to move in with them after the holidays. Noah was so nonchalant about the entire situation that it was easy for me to be optimistic as well.

Noah must have sensed there was something else on my mind because he reached for her empty bowl. "Em, if you're all done, go and take a quick shower. Hurry up because we have a guest coming."

"Who is it?" she asked.

"A friend of mine and Leila's," he said absently as she ran out of the kitchen. I picked up her glass and handed it to Noah, who moved over to the sink. He rinsed the items and set them in the dishwasher before turning to face me.

"All right, let's have it. What's up? Are you worried about Detective Barnes coming here tonight?"

I shook my head. "Not at all. He's a good guy and won't make Emma feel uncomfortable."

"Then, what's wrong?"

"I think we should tell Emma tonight about my moving in."

Noah calmly dried his hands on a dishtowel and placed them on my waist. "There's plenty of time. You're worrying over nothing. Em's going to love having you here."

"Maybe, but I'll feel better once she knows."

He hesitated, then wrapped his arms around me in a tight hug. "All right. If it means that much to you, we'll tell her after Detective Barnes leaves."

As he kissed me, a tap sounded on the front door. Noah glanced at his watch. "Hmm. He's five minutes early. Punctuality costs me again."

"Oh, go answer the door," I said, laughing as he opened it.

Detective Barnes stepped through the front entranceway and nodded at the both of us. "Hello, Leila. Mr. Rivers."

"Noah," he corrected. "Please have a seat. Can I get you a cup of coffee, Detective?"

"That would be great. Thank you," Detective Barnes said politely.

We sat in awkward silence until Noah returned a couple of minutes later. Detective Barnes accepted the mug with another "thank you." I watched as he typed something into his phone and Noah went into Emma's room and knocked on the adjoining bathroom door. "You about ready?"

"Coming, Daddy," she called.

Noah came out of the bedroom followed by Emma, who was wearing a pair of pink cotton pajamas with a ladybug design. She made a beeline for the couch, then stopped short when she spotted Detective Barnes.

"Hi, Emma," he greeted her.

"Hello," Emma said cautiously.

Detective Barnes patted the space next to him on the couch. "I'm Detective Barnes from the Sugar Ridge Police Department. Would you like to sit here?"

Emma glanced at her father, who nodded approval. She perched herself on the edge of the couch, as far away from the detective as possible.

"What grade are you in at school?" Detective Barnes inquired.

"First," she replied. "Mrs. Temple is my teacher. She's real nice."

"That's great." Detective Barnes grinned at her. "I'd like to talk to you about the pie contest at Sappy Endings the other day. The farm where your daddy works, right?"

Emma nodded and stuck her nose out in the air. "That's Leila's farm. But my Daddy does most of the work."

With great effort, I managed to hide my smile. The remark was not offensive to me, because I knew Emma associated work with gathering sap in the winter—not paying bills, updating websites, or dealing with vendors. We had about five thousand maple trees on the farm, and Noah took care of most of the tapping every winter. We usually hired someone on a temporary basis to help out, but the credit still belonged to Noah.

"I'm sure he's very busy," Detective Barnes agreed, "but I wanted to ask you about the pie contest. Did you have fun?"

Emma's curly head bobbed up and down. "Yeah, the clown was really good. He made me a balloon animal. But I didn't get to taste any of the pies. Heather took us to the gift shop and told us that an old lady got sick. And then she died."

Noah and I exchanged a glance. "Did Heather tell you that, Em?" he asked.

Emma twisted the bottom edge of her pajama top between her hands. "No. I heard my friends talking about it at school. Jacob Whitely said that Sappy Endings was a bad place, and no one should go there anymore because they poisoned the old lady."

My heart sank into the pit of my stomach. It was obvious Emma's classmates were only repeating things they'd overheard, most likely from parents or grandparents. That didn't make me feel any better, though. It was all terribly unfair since I had no way to defend our reputation.

"You know that the farm isn't a bad place, right, Emma?" I asked. "It was an accident that Mrs. Middleton died there."

Emma's brow furrowed. "You mean, like what happened with my mommy?"

"No, sweetie." I wanted to bite my tongue off. *Stupid, stupid.* I should have had more sense than to use the word accident around Emma, but I'd didn't realize she would associate it with her mother's death.

Noah spoke up. "Detective Barnes is here because we think someone might have wanted to hurt Mrs. Middleton on purpose. They may have put something in the pie to make her sick."

"Oh." Emma frowned. "Was she a bad lady?"

"No, of course not," Noah continued. "We don't know why they wanted to hurt her. You're going to hear a lot of things said about the farm in the next few weeks, Em. And they won't be nice things. Many people think it's our fault that the lady died, because Leila, her mom, and I work there."

Emma gave a small gasp. "Are you gonna go to jail, Daddy?"

Noah laughed. "No, baby. I'm not going to jail, and neither is Leila. The detective only wants to ask you some questions about the pie, since you're the one who brought it down to the sugar house."

Detective Barnes nodded. "That's right. You found the pumpkin pie in the café, right Emma?"

She nodded. "It was sitting on one of the tables."

"Was anyone else there when you found it?"

Emma relaxed and leaned back against the couch pillows.

"Selma was behind the counter, talking to someone on her phone when I came in. I saw the pie and asked if I could bring it to down to my daddy and Leila. She nodded and kept talking."

That explained it. Mom had clearly been distracted. I wondered why she would have allowed the little girl to carry a pie all by herself down to the sugar house when she could have easily dropped it. Mom never trusted me to carry pie or cake to the table until I was much older.

"You didn't see anyone else?" Detective Barnes asked. "Maybe someone was in the gift shop, or they walked out of the café right before you got there?"

Emma pressed her lips together and shook her head. "Nope. No one. Only Leila's mommy. But I did hear a funny noise outside."

Detective Barnes leaned forward. "Where outside?"

She yawned and rubbed her eyes. "From the parking lot. It was kind of like a banging sound."

Noah drew his brows together. "A banging sound?"

"Yeah, you know, Daddy. Like the noise your gun makes when you go hunting for deer."

Noah and I exchanged another glance. "Maybe it wasn't a gun?" I suggested. "Do you think it could have been a car backfiring?"

The child wrinkled her nose, having no idea what I meant. Emma was only six, after all. I tried again. "What I mean, is, maybe there was a car that had a problem getting started?"

"Em, do you remember that time last spring when

we went to see your grandmother?" Noah asked. "I was driving her car and when I started it there was this weird noise—"

"Yes, Daddy!" She bounced in her seat. "That's what it sounded like."

Detective Barnes tapped something into his iPad and looked over at me. "Wouldn't someone else have noticed a car leaving the parking lot that day? There were a lot of people around."

"Probably, but the contest didn't get started until after two o'clock," I remarked. "There's a good chance no one was walking around the parking lot at that time. And the gift shop was locked."

"What about the café?" Detective Barnes wanted to know. "Did your mother lock it after she left?"

"No There's not a separate door for it, like with the gift shop."

Detective Barnes looked embarrassed. "Oh, that's right. So, the main building door wasn't locked, only the gift shop?"

"Correct." I nodded. "We left the building unlocked in case someone needed to use the restrooms. We didn't worry about anyone going inside the café. There was always a chance mom would need to run up for something anyway."

"Did you see anyone go back up there during the contest?" Detective Barnes asked.

"Heather did. My mother asked her to grab some more spatulas. She's the one who told me Jenna was in the café.

This was after Emma brought the pie down and my mother followed her."

Detective Barnes cocked his head to the side and studied me. "Who's Jenna?"

"A new employee. She'll be starting at the farm this week and working in the café with my mother." Jenna had returned my call earlier in the day, thrilled with the offer.

"How long was the interview?" the detective asked.

I shrugged. "Maybe about fifteen minutes? I invited her to stay for the competition, but she had to leave. Then, I went back to the sugar house to help judge the pie contest."

Detective Barnes stared down at his iPad. "So, it's possible Jenna may have seen the person who brought the pie? She could have been out in the parking lot, on her way to see you, when they came out of the café."

I hadn't thought of that. "Yes, I suppose so."

The detective turned back to Emma. "Did another lady come into the café before you brought the pie down to the sugar house with Selma?"

"Nope, but I came down first. Selma was still on the phone in the café," Emma corrected him.

"Oh, that's right." Detective Barnes' face broke into a smile. "Well, thank you, Emma. You've been very helpful."

Emma took that as her invitation to leave. "Can I go play in my room?" she asked her father.

"Go ahead," he said. "Leila and I will come read to you in a few minutes."

She raced into the bedroom, not even giving the detective a backward glance. This was a relief because I worried that he might have frightened her with all the talk about Margaret's death. Fortunately, Emma didn't seem to realize she had almost tasted the tainted pie as well.

Detective Barnes rose from the couch and shook Noah's hand. "Thank you for letting me speak to her. She's a very bright child." He swiveled his head in my direction. "Where can I find this Jenna? What's her last name?"

"Fleming," I said. "I have her address, but you can stop by the farm sometime tomorrow to talk with her, if you like."

"I'll do that, thanks." Detective Barnes tucked the iPad under his arm. "Was she unemployed? It's usually a couple of weeks before people are able to start a new job."

"No, she worked at the Bagel Palace, but Max, her boss, said she didn't need to give notice. He has a niece that can fill in for her."

Detective Barnes nodded. "I see. Well, thank you both for your cooperation. Is there any special time I should stop by tomorrow?"

"No, of course not. Whenever you like." Dread settled in my chest as I wondered if tomorrow would be like today, with no customers. My mother may have been right—it wasn't the smartest idea to hire someone right now. No. I had to think positive. This would all blow over soon.

"Have a good night." Noah shut and locked the door behind him, then turned to gather me in his arms. "Why don't you stay here tonight?" He placed his lips over mine and didn't even wait for an answer.

"You do make it hard to say no," I confessed after we

broke apart. "Maybe for now I shouldn't make a habit of it, though."

"It's fine." Noah nuzzled my neck. "You worry too much. Emma adores you. She's going to be thrilled that you're moving in with us after the holidays, especially if Toast is part of the bargain."

Guilt surged through me. "I wish I could say for sure that he was, but I can't help thinking he should stay with my mother. She'll be all alone when I leave."

Noah kissed my hand and slipped it between his. "We'll worry about that later. Maybe you can work out some type of joint custody arrangement," he teased. "Now, come on. Let's go read Rapunzel for the fiftieth time this week."

We started towards Emma's bedroom, hand in hand. I was surprised to see her standing in the doorway, clutching her baby doll. She stared at us with a somber expression. Maybe the conversation with Detective Barnes had upset her more than I thought.

"What's wrong, princess?" Noah chucked her under the chin. "Are you ready for a story?"

Emma didn't reply. She turned and went into the room. We watched as she climbed into bed. Noah sat on the edge of it and thumbed through one of her fairy tale books. He began to read the story and acted out all the characters with perfection. Noah even used a high-pitched squeaky voice for the female roles while Emma giggled hysterically. I stretched out at the bottom of the bed, looking up at them.

"Now, how many more stories are you going to ask for?" he teased.

Emma's gaze met mine, and then she turned back to her father. "Why is Leila going to live here with us?"

I sat up with a start. Shoot. She must have overheard us talking. Her question had caught me completely off guard.

Noah stared over at me before answering. "Because we both want to be with you, and we want to be with each other." He kissed the top of her head, and she pulled away.

"But she has her own house," Emma pointed out.

"Yes, she does," Noah agreed. "But wouldn't it be nice if she was here all the time? Leila used to be a teacher. She can help you with your homework, and pick out your clothes, and maybe even make your lunch sometimes. She could even—"

"No." Emma folded her arms across her chest. "I don't want her to live with us."

# CHAPTER SEVEN

**LIKE A SUCKER PUNCH TO** the stomach, Emma's words left me breathless and in pain. I never would have imagined that she felt this way. I opened my mouth to say something—anything—but the words refused to come.

"That's rude, Emma," Noah said. "You're hurting Leila's feelings."

"But why is she gonna live here?" Emma asked. "She's a friend."

Noah's gaze shifted from his daughter to me, then back to her. "Leila's more than just a friend. I thought you knew that."

With bated breath I waited in silence, praying Noah didn't give her the "she's going to be your mother someday" speech, because I feared it would only make things worse.

I should have trusted Noah to say the right thing. He was her father.

He kissed the top of Emma's head. "Leila and I love each

other, and we both love you. We want to be together all the time. Like you and I are together." He hesitated. "Eventually, we'll be a family, when Leila and I get married."

Okay, maybe this hadn't been the right thing to say, after all.

Emma's eyes filled with tears. "But what about my mommy?"

Noah seemed dazed by her words. "I'll always love your mommy. That's never going to change. But she's in Heaven now, so it's okay for me to marry someone else who's not in Heaven. Leila will be your stepmother one day. She's not trying to replace your mommy."

The little girl stared at me with obvious contempt, making me feel as big as a pin. "Did you know that today was my mommy's birthday?" she asked in an accusatory tone.

I exchanged a horrified glance with Noah. Another punch to the gut. "No, honey, I didn't."

Emma's gaze, full of reproach, shifted to her father. "Daddy didn't remember either."

Noah looked stricken by her remark. "Of course, I remembered, sweetheart."

If I had known today was Ashley's birthday, I never would have asked Noah to tell Emma about our cohabitation. Emma lifted her nose in the air, as if she smelled something pungent. "Leila's not going to be my stepmother—*ever*."

Before I had a chance to recover from the latest stinging remark, Emma grabbed her doll and jumped out of bed. Noah and I watched, mystified, as she ran into the adjoining bathroom and slammed the door. I waited to see if Noah would go after her, but he didn't. Resigned, he walked into the living room with me following.

"She needs a little time to get used to this," he said.

"Maybe I should leave." My voice shook.

Noah placed his hands on my arms and rubbed them gently. "Leila, I'm sorry. I never thought that she would react this way."

"It's okay." We both stood there, trying to deal with the awkward situation as best we could. Noah reached out his arms and pulled me into them. I rested my head on his shoulder, willing myself not to cry.

But the tears came anyway.

"Hey." Noah swiped the pad of his finger under my eye. "Don't worry. Em will come around. I didn't handle this right."

"It's not your fault."

Noah heaved a long sigh and moved towards the living room window. "Yeah, I don't know about that. I thought she understood. You and I have been going together for a year. It's been two years since her mother died. Maybe I thought she'd put it behind her. The nightmares stopped over a year ago." His shoulders sagged as if a heavy burden had been placed on them. "She's not even seven yet, so I figured it would be a little easier—for her—at least."

I understood what he was saying. Noah might never fully get over Ashley's death, but that didn't mean he couldn't love someone else. I went up behind him and placed my arms around his waist. "It's okay. I'm sorry I pushed you to tell her, and today, of all days."

Noah nodded to show that he acknowledged my comment but kept staring out into the night, as if answers were hidden in the darkness. "How could I have been so stupid. I didn't even think she remembered today was Ashley's birthday. She's so young. My mother gave her a birthday book last summer, because Em wanted to know when everyone's special day was. She wrote down everybody's birthdays in there—yours too. That's probably why she got so upset—because I didn't mention it today. I figured if I brought it up, she would be sad."

My heart broke for Noah and his daughter. "Kids have better memories than we give them credit for. It sounds like Emma's made the decision for us. We need to wait before moving in together."

Noah turned to face me and wove his fingers through my hair. "It's over a month away. She'll feel differently by then."

"Maybe." Or maybe not. An enormous lump grew in my throat, making it difficult to speak. I didn't want to force anything on the child. Defeated, I picked up my purse from the coffee table. "You should go to her. I'll see you in the morning."

Noah opened the front door and walked me to my car. "It's all going to work out, Leila. I love my daughter and you more than anything else in this world. Everything will be fine. Trust me."

---

When I arrived at work the next morning, Jenna was already behind the café's counter, listening intently to my mother's instructions. After I dropped my purse in the office, I entered the café to grab some coffee. "Don't let her work you too hard on your first day," I teased.

Jenna laughed good-naturedly. "Oh, I'm not worried about it. I'm so excited about everything that I'm going to learn from your mom. I never knew she made the baklava here. My mom brought some home a few weeks ago. Oh my gosh, it's to die for."

My mother's cheeks flushed, and she waved off the compliment. "Oh, surely you've had better."

I looked away so she wouldn't see me smile. There was no doubt in my mind that Jenna's comment had pleased my mother. Maybe Jenna was trying to kiss up to her, but whatever the case, it looked as if she'd already had my mother figured out. Mom liked nothing better than when someone praised her culinary skills.

"When will the customers start coming in?" Jenna asked.

As she adjusted the ties on her apron, I noticed the blouse that she had on underneath. It was a purple floral print with a square neck and puffy sleeves. "I have a blouse almost exactly like yours. Purple's my favorite color."

Jenna stared down at the blouse and then flashed me a smile. "It's mine too." She turned back to my mother. "Shouldn't people be here by now?"

My mother's smile faded. "Well, dear, it looks like this will be a good day for us to focus on your training. Since the pie competition on Saturday, people have decided that they—uh—might need a break from the farm for a while."

Jenna folded her arms across her chest. "That's terrible. I

heard about what happened, but it's ridiculous people would stay away for that reason. They must realize you guys aren't the ones who killed that poor woman."

"Sometimes people will believe only what they want to believe." My father had been famous for uttering this phrase when I was a child. A pang of sadness filled my heart. I wished that he was here. He would have handled the lack of business situation way better than me and had some wise words of comfort to offer about Emma.

Mom studied my expression. "Leila, is something bothering you?"

"Not a thing." I plastered on a smile. "Now, if you both will excuse me, I have a lot to do in the office. Jenna, when you get a chance, stop in later to see me, and I'll have you fill out your paperwork."

Jenna grinned. "Sure thing. Thanks, Leila."

I didn't waste any time returning to my office. It was obvious my mother knew something was troubling me, but I didn't want to get into it with Jenna around.

Noah had a tour scheduled this morning with some out-of-state guests who most likely hadn't heard about the fatal pie competition. The loneliness in the office was more palpable today. When it was noon, I picked up my phone and called Heather.

She answered on the third ring, sounding distracted. "Hey, what's up?"

"Sorry, did I catch you at a bad time?"

"I'm just finishing up a set of extensions. Hang on a minute, okay?"

When Heather came back on the line, she sounded more like her usual self. "Phew! Those took longer than I expected. What's going on? You sound upset."

"No, I'm fine." I took a few deep breaths in an attempt to keep the tears at bay. *Stop this now.* I felt sorry for myself and had no right to. Emma was the one I needed to worry about. The poor little girl was still grieving for her mother. Her happiness had to come before mine.

"Oh my God, you're crying." Heather's tone turned anxious. "Did something else happen with Margaret's murder?"

I blew my nose into a tissue and told her about the incident at Noah's last night. When I had finished, Heather sucked in a deep breath on the other end of the line. "Oh my gosh, Lei. That must have been horrible for everyone. What are you going to do?"

"What is there to do? I can't think about marriage if she won't accept me."

"She'll come around by then," Heather said, echoing Noah's sentiment.

I pulled up the email account for the farm while we talked. "And what if she doesn't? Emma clearly thinks I'm trying to replace her mother. I would never do something like that."

"I know you wouldn't." Heather's voice was soft and reassuring. "Give her some time, okay?"

The memory of Emma's stony little face flashed through my mind. "Heather, if you could have seen the way she looked at me last night. It felt like she hated me. I wanted to crawl under a rock."

"She doesn't hate you," Heather insisted.

"Yeah, well, I don't know anymore. If only—" I stopped in mid-sentence while scrolling through the farm's email account and let out a gasp.

"What is it?" Heather asked. "Are you okay?"

An email with the subject *Pie or Die Contest,* caught my attention. Great. Why did people feel compelled to poke fun at someone's death? I was tempted to delete the email but opened it instead and began to read.

*Have you figured it out yet? Better hurry, before it's too late for you.*

My breath caught in my throat. What the heck was going on here? If this had been sent by the person who made the cyanide-filled pie, were they planning to strike again?

This was clearly one sick individual. Margaret's death had only been a game to them. With my heart pounding, I tried to respond to the email, but the *Send* address was protected with no way to access it.

"Lei, are you still there?" Heather wanted to know.

"Sorry. I-I just got an email that m-may have come from the person who poisoned Margaret." I couldn't stop shaking, but managed to draw a breath and tried to steady myself. "I need to phone Detective Barnes and tell him what happened." How had everything managed to go wrong so quickly? A couple of days ago, I had been sitting on top of the world, safe and secure in my relationship with Noah and looking forward to moving into his house so we could all become a family. I'd also been excited about the pie-baking contest and anticipated that business at the farm would pick up during the holiday season. There was no way of knowing when the bottom might fall out of your life. Everything could change in the blink of an eye.

A new sense of determination filled me. Maybe I couldn't do anything about Emma's feelings towards me, but I was going to do whatever I could to ensure the farm's livelihood.

"This settles it." A surge of anger shot through me. "I've decided to have a talk with Abigail Middleton tonight. The farm and I can't wait for the police to find Margaret's killer. Something has to be done as soon as possible. What kind of person are we dealing with here?"

"A dangerous one," Heather remarked. "Want me to ride shotgun?"

Her comment made me smile. No matter the situation, we always had each other's back. "There's no one else I'd rather have with me."

# CHAPTER EIGHT

**HEATHER WAS WAITING FOR ME** when I arrived home from work. She and my mother, who had left the farm shortly before me, were involved in a serious discussion about decorating Heather's living room. Heather and Tyler had bought a house last April, shortly before their wedding. She was so busy with work and relocating her hair styling business to the new home that there hadn't been much time for her to do any decorating.

"It's too late now," Heather complained as she savored a bite of the delicious meat pies my mother made for dinner. "Mom wants me to host Christmas Eve at our house. There's no way I'll have everything done in time."

"Nonsense." My mother scoffed. "All you need are a couple of modern paintings to hang on the walls and some throw rugs for the floor. What about the curtains I told you to order?"

"They were out of stock but will be in next week," Heather said.

"Good," my mother said approvingly. "When they arrive, I'll come over and help you set them up."

Heather's face lit up like a Christmas tree. "That would be awesome. Thank you, Mrs. Khoury. You have such an eye for decorating."

My mother stood there as she spoke, proud as a peacock. Mom did enjoy strutting her feathers when people paid her compliments, and deserved every single one. She started to clear the table and turned her attention back to me. "As for you, my dear daughter. I don't think it's a good idea for you to go see Abigail tonight. Don't involve yourself in this mess."

"But Mom, I'm already involved," I told her. "We all are. A woman died at our farm, and now people are sending us threatening emails."

"It's horrible enough that Margaret died, but even worse that this person is gloating over it," Heather added.

I grabbed a sponge to wipe down the table. "They're gloating because they're the one who killed her. I'm certain of it."

"What?" My mother nearly dropped the dish she was holding. "When did this happen?"

Quickly, I explained about the message. She closed her eyes and let out a small gasp. "I don't believe it. Did you call Detective Barnes and tell him?"

"Yes, and I forwarded him the email. He confirmed there's no way to trace it." Whoever this psycho was, they had managed to cover their tracks in an efficient manner.

"It's such a tragedy," my mother lamented. "I still can't believe Margaret is gone. What I can't understand is why someone was targeting her. Sure, she could be a bit annoying at times, but that's no reason to kill someone. It doesn't make any sense."

Heather reached down and picked up Toast from the floor. She cuddled him in her arms as he closed his eyes in contentment, his head nudging her hand for more pats. "Maybe Margaret led a double life that no one else knew about," she said.

I rolled my eyes at her. "That's a little hard to imagine. From what Mom told me, Margaret lived a pretty mundane life. It sounds like she didn't have any friends besides Mom and Callie and stayed home all the time. Maybe if I talked to Abigail, she would remember a person Margaret had a disagreement with. Or something like that. I know Detective Barnes already spoke to her, but sometimes people get nervous when they talk to the police and forget to mention things."

Mom rinsed a plate and set it in the dishwasher. "Well, that girl definitely is the nervous type. But what if Eric is there? Won't it be kind of awkward for you?"

"Won't what be awkward?" Heather's brows drew together.

I took Toast from Heather and set him back down on the floor. My mother placed a paper plate with some meat pie scraps in front of him. "Mom once tried to get her son Eric and I together."

My mother waved a hand in dismissal. "All right, so I

once thought he would make a nice boyfriend. But you didn't tell me back then that he was harassing you."

"That makes two of us," Heather murmured. "How come you never said anything?"

"It wasn't a big deal. He texted a few times and called me, even though I kept telling him that I didn't want to go out."

"I thought it was a good match. Eric is a lawyer and he makes great money," my mother said.

"He gave off weird vibes, Mom." She'd always told me to go with my gut when faced with uncertainty. "And so what if he's a lawyer? Mark's a lawyer. Need I say more?"

She threw up her hands and sighed. "All right, you win."

*You win.* I glanced over at Heather, who had a small smile perched on the corners of her mouth. After sixty years, my mother was finally starting to mellow. Miracles could happen after all.

My mother chewed her bottom lip. "If I had known that he was bothering you, I never would have tried to push the two of you together." She turned to Heather. "When Leila finally told me about the flowers and the weird note he sent with them, I wished that she had gone to the police back then."

"Why didn't you?" Heather asked.

I sucked in a deep breath. "Because that was when Mark and I started having problems—prewedding jitters. You know, the beginning of the end. Anyway, I had other things to worry about and decided to let it go."

"Margaret didn't seem that enthusiastic about you dating Eric the one time I brought it up," Mom mused. "I always wondered why. Maybe she thought you weren't good enough for him. I doubt she knew about the flowers or the note either."

"What did the note say?" Heather asked.

My mother went over to the walnut desk in the corner of the room and opened the top drawer. She fished through some papers, and then produced a square pink message card, the same size as a Post-it Note. She handed it to Heather.

"You kept it?" Disbelief filled my tone.

"Of course, I kept it." My mother's mouth hardened into a fine, thin line. "If he ever tried anything again with my daughter, I was going to be ready for him."

Her statement touched me deeply. Back then, my mother and I were having problems and soon stopped speaking to each other after my breakup with Mark. It was comforting to know that she still had my back through it all.

Heather squinted at the card. "*Dear Leila, Roses are red, Violet are blue. By the end of this evening, I will be with you. Forever.*"

"He has a great way with words, doesn't he?" I quipped.

"Oh, Lei, you should have gotten the police involved." Heather rubbed at the goose bumps forming on her arms. "Eric sounds like some kind of whack job."

"It's been five years since he wrote the note," I said. "Margaret mentioned to Mom recently that he was dating someone. It's all in the past now."

Heather gave me a doubtful look but didn't say anything further.

Mom handed me an apple and maple strudel covered

with plastic wrap. "I made this for the café, but why don't you take it over to Abigail instead. People should bring food when they're visiting relatives of the deceased. It probably won't get used tomorrow, anyway."

"Don't say that Mrs. Khoury," Heather said. "I'm sure things will get back to normal soon."

My mother didn't answer.

"We won't be long," I called over my shoulder and followed Heather out the front door, balancing the strudel between my hands.

The sun had already disappeared from the sky, and the Middleton house was enshrouded in darkness. One lone light shone in an upstairs window. I'd never realized how gloomy our neighbor's home was before with its dark-brown vinyl siding. The lawn was overgrown with leaves, and the front wood steps were cracked in several spots.

"This place gives me the creeps," Heather said, echoing my sentiment.

We climbed the steps, listening to them creak and groan underneath our weight. I tapped on the door and waited. A minute later, the front porch light came on and the door opened. Abigail peered out at us from the dimly lit house. She smiled when she realized who it was. "Hello, Leila. Heather."

I held out the plate with the strudel. "My mother sent this. We wanted to let you know that we're here if you need anything."

Abigail blinked back a tear as she took the plate from my hands. "That's so thoughtful. Please thank your mother for me."

"Is it all right if we come in for a minute to talk?" I asked.

Abigail hesitated as she considered my question. "I guess it would be okay. Eric flew back to New York City this morning. I don't expect him to return until tomorrow."

"Would Eric prefer it if we weren't here?" The words fell from my lips before I could stop them.

Abigail switched on the interior light, and we followed her into the small living room area. The entire house was overcrowded with boxes full of trinkets, piles of old books and magazines. It was a fire hazard waiting to happen.

A narrow path in the room led to an outdated flowered sofa overstuffed with pillows. A burnt orange recliner nearby had seen better days. The room smelled of mildew and cooked cabbage. There were rumors throughout the town that Margaret had hoarder tendencies, but I never dreamed it was as bad as this.

"Eric—uh, is having a hard time dealing with mom's death." Abigail set the strudel down on a coffee table covered with books and dirty coffee cups. The color rose in her cheeks as she moved a cup aside to make room and it fell on the floor. "Please excuse the mess. I haven't gotten around to cleaning up the place yet. Mom never liked to throw anything away."

Or do dishes, it seemed. From the couch, a good portion of the adjoining kitchen was visible, and I easily spotted a huge pile of dirty ones on the counter. My mother must have found this house tough to take. She was so neat and tidy that I could imagine her running from the place in screams. I had to give her credit. Mom had come over to see Margaret at least two or three times a week and never once mentioned to me that the place was a disaster zone. I couldn't recall an occasion when she or my father had ever looked down their noses at other people and their circumstances. It only made me admire my parents more.

I decided to be honest with her. "Does Eric blame Sappy Endings for your mom's death?"

"No, of course not." Abigail's tone was adamant, and she refused to meet my gaze.

What would stop the man from suing our farm? A vision of my father appeared in my mind. He had been so proud of Sappy Endings and devoted his entire life to the art of creating artisanal maple syrup. Would this be the end of his legacy?

*No.* The farm was not going anywhere. I would do whatever was necessary to save our livelihood.

"Abigail, we're here because we want to help," I said. "We want to find out who's responsible for your mother's death. Did she have an argument with someone? Maybe she mentioned it on the phone to you?"

"I can't recall anything." Abigail's mouth tightened. "Mom never really interacted with anyone except for your mother and Callie down the street. I don't know how she would have managed without them."

My mother knew Margaret was lonely and starved for attention, which is why she put up with her. Mom knew what it meant to be a good neighbor.

"To tell you the truth, I was surprised when Mom asked me to come with her to the pie contest," Abigail admitted.

"She said she'd heard someone at the supermarket mention it, then decided to go too. It made me happy that she wanted to be outside in the nice weather with me. She'd been so depressed ever since I moved away."

Abigail stopped to wipe her eyes. Always the more sympathetic one of us, Heather rose from the couch and went over to pat her on the shoulder. Abigail stifled back a sob and stared up at her with a grateful expression.

"You said that Eric is coming back tomorrow?" It didn't seem right that Abigail's brother had left her here alone with their mother's house. Anyone who had to stay here by themself was bound to be depressed. "When was the last time he saw your mother?"

"Oh, it's been at least a year. But Eric loved mom," she added quickly. "I think on some level he may have blamed her for our dad's death. They did everything together. After dad died, Eric couldn't wait to get away from—I mean, get away."

It was obvious to me what she meant.

"Is Eric seeing anyone?" Heather asked casually.

I had a feeling that she was fishing around to see if Eric might still be infatuated with me, and I had no desire to know the answer.

Abigail shook her head. "Not for at least a year. Funny thing about my brother—he's so successful at work. It only took him three years to make partner at the firm. I love him, but Eric's never been good at personal relationships. Every time he dates someone, it never lasts longer than a few weeks."

Uneasiness washed over me. Margaret had lied to my mother that Eric was dating someone. This was the last thing I wanted to hear. Abigail might not know about Eric's past infatuation with me. I'd never told anyone the details except for my mother.

"Getting back to your mom," I said. "Did anyone else know that you both were going to the pie contest?"

Abigail pursed her lips. "Yes, Eric knew. I texted him earlier in the week and told him."

"How often did your mother talk to Eric?" I asked.

"She called him every Friday like clockwork. Eric wasn't good at making calls himself. The last time she called, he was in some kind of bad mood, and it got her all upset. He yelled at her a lot. Sometimes he doesn't think." Abigail quickly changed the subject. "Will you be coming to the wake tomorrow?"

"Of course. We'll be there, won't we Heather?"

Heather's mouth dropped open, but she quickly shut it and plastered on a smile. "We wouldn't miss it."

Abigail dabbed at her eyes with a tissue. "I'm so glad. To tell you the truth, I'm worried there won't be much of a crowd, since mom didn't have any friends—besides your mom and Callie, that is."

Margaret might not have had any friends, but I was more concerned with her enemies. The wheels kept turning in my head, and I had to wonder if Eric's resentment towards his mother might have extended to plotting her death. "When was the last time your brother was in town, Abigail?"

She looked surprised by the question. "Oh, it's been a few months."

This didn't make any sense. "I thought you said that your mother hadn't seen him in a year."

"Uh, he didn't see Mom. Eric came to visit an old friend. He was only here overnight but never told her that he was coming." Abigail's head shot up. "I don't understand why someone would want her dead. My mother had no enemies. Why would someone do this?"

That's what I wanted to know too.

# CHAPTER NINE

**AS I SUSPECTED, BUSINESS DID** not improve the next day. A few people stopped in for their morning caffeine fix, but it was nowhere near what we usually received. With Thanksgiving coming up quickly, the gift shop and café should have been bustling with customers. I was already starting to worry about turning any kind of profit for this year.

My mother and Jenna somehow managed to stay busy in the café. Mom showed Jenna how to make our all-day breakfast sandwiches, which consisted of scrambled eggs, sausage or bacon, Vermont cheddar cheese, and a spoonful of our syrup—all on a toasted English muffin. When I went in to get coffee, Jenna was laughing at something my mother had said.

"You have such a great sense of humor, Mrs. Khoury." She giggled.

My mother smiled at her fondly. "Please, call me Selma."

I almost went into cardiac arrest. My mother was known for a stiff, professional tone with her employees. None of that seemed to exist any longer. It was already obvious to me how well she and Jenna were getting on—far better than I had hoped.

"Leila." My mother turned to me expectantly. "Did you want to come to the wake with me? It's from four to eight tonight. Since Jenna is here, I figured I'd leave a little early and go right at four, because I have dinner plans. I have every confidence that Jenna can handle the café for an hour."

Sure, Jenna could handle the place for an hour. Even Toast could run the café. It wasn't a difficult process when there were no customers around.

"Thanks, Mom, but I have some things to take care of in the office, so I'll stay until closing. Heather's car is in the shop, so she'll get dropped off here, and we'll go to the wake together." My curiosity had been piqued. "What kind of dinner plans do you have?"

"I'm going to Simon's." An unmistakable note of pride filled her voice.

I blinked. There must be some mistake. Simon had never invited my mother or me over for dinner before, and there was a good reason why. His culinary skills rivaled mine—nonexistent.

"Simon's cooking dinner?" I stole a shortbread cookie off the tray she'd removed from the oven. Sweet scents of maple and vanilla mixed together in the air and permeated through the room, making my stomach growl. The cookie melted in my mouth. "Oh, these are so good."

"Simon isn't cooking, silly," my mother explained. "Tony is starting culinary school in a few weeks and wants my recipe for grape leaves. So, it's a bit like a tutorial session."

"Who's Tony?" Jenna inquired.

"Simon's new roommate." Mom's eyes twinkled with mischief. "I'll have to arrange for you to meet him, Jenna. Tony's handsome and unattached. And he's going to make a wonderful chef someday. Why, he'd be perfect for you."

The smile on Jenna's face faded. "Thank you, but I'm already seeing someone."

"Be sure to bring me back some grape leaves," I teased.

My mother acted like she hadn't heard me. "Oh, that's too bad. You'd make an attractive couple. How long have you and your boyfriend been dating?"

"About a year," Jenna said. "He's a terrific guy and treats me great."

My mother nodded in approval. "I'm glad to hear it. That's so important in this day and age."

"What time do you think you'll be home, Mom?" I asked.

"I'd love to meet your boyfriend," my mother said to Jenna, ignoring me. "You should bring him by the farm sometime."

The entire conversation threw me for a loop. This was so unlike my mother. She'd never even tried to make small talk with our last employee, but now she was already attempting to fix Jenna up with my brother's roommate?

I gave up and started towards the office. As I walked away, the two of them kept chatting about how much syrup to add to lattes. Oh well. At least they were getting along. My original fears had gone unfounded. This was a positive sign, I reminded myself, but regardless, a small twinge of apprehension ran through me. Was it possible that after many years of a strained relationship with my mother, I could be jealous? No, that was simply ridiculous.

---

"Okay, what's with you?" Heather glanced up at me worriedly, then turned back to study her reflection in the compact mirror as she applied a fresh coat of lip gloss. As far as I was concerned, Heather didn't need lip gloss or any kind of makeup to make her look beautiful. With peaches and cream skin, wavy blond hair, and a curvy figure, she had everything going for her. Growing up, I had often thought of myself as a dandelion next to a rose bush, but to her credit, she'd never done anything to make me feel that way. Heather always made everyone around her feel special.

"Nothing. I'm fine." I parked my car in front of the funeral home. As Abigail had worried, there were only a handful of cars surrounding the place, even though the wake had started two hours earlier. "I was thinking about how well my mother and Jenna are getting along."

Heather put the compact back in her purse. "Really? Your mom never gets along with any of the coworkers—besides Noah, that is."

"Tell me about it. Maybe she's turning over a new leaf."

"Nice pun," Heather quipped.

"Well, at least my mother's trying. I can't put my finger

on it, but it's surprising how well they're getting along. You know how she is. It usually takes mom an awfully long time to warm up to someone."

"Jenna seems nice," Heather observed. "Funny, there's something about her that reminds me of you."

"Really? I guess I can't see it."

"Is she married?" Heather asked.

"No, but she has a boyfriend. My mother wanted to set her up with Simon's roommate."

"Now, that sounds more like your mother. She isn't happy unless she can play matchmaker, which reminds me, I can't believe that she once wanted you to go out with Eric. I always thought no one would ever measure up to Mark in her eyes."

I gave a snort. "Let's face it. Mark was always her first choice, but dating another lawyer might have made her happy too."

Heather jabbed me in the side playfully. "What is it about you and lawyers? I know Eric was a few years ahead of us in school, but I don't remember much about what he looks like. He always seemed a bit creepy to me."

We stopped to sign the register, and I gestured at a man in the viewing room. "There he is."

Eric Middleton was standing in the receiving line next to his sister and another woman. He was about six feet tall and slender to the point of being gaunt. His gray suit was expensive and clearly a designer name, but it hung off his skinny frame. His dark eyes were too large for his pinched, narrow face while his black hair was slicked back with a massive amount of gel.

"Creepy *and* greasy," Heather added, as if she'd read my mind. "Kind of like he belongs on the other side of the law. What type of attorney is he?"

"Criminal."

She nodded. "Yeah, that sounds about right."

While Abigail was timid, I remembered Eric as being high-strung and always ready to put someone in their place. If you told Eric that the sun was yellow, he'd insist it was orange. His career as an attorney definitely suited him well.

We moved slowly into the room, our gazes fixed upon Eric. He was shaking hands with a white-haired gentleman. "What exactly is the deal with him?" Heather whispered. "How long has he had this major crush on you?"

"I wouldn't call it major, and I'm sure he's moved on. He asked me out while Mark and I were engaged." As soon as it got around Sugar Ridge that my wedding was off, Eric had tried again, but without flowers this time. There was no official mourning period for a wedding cancellation, but I didn't appreciate his asking me for a date less than forty-eight hours after the breakup, while I was nursing my fresh broken heart.

Heather clucked her tongue against the roof of her mouth. "I still can't believe you never told me this."

"At the time, I was too upset about Mark to think much about it." That wasn't entirely true. Talking about it would have implied that there was a serious problem. All I wanted to do was to forget that Eric existed.

"But he asked you out several times, right?"

"Yes, why?"

She stared at me like I had corn growing out of my ears. "Isn't it obvious? He could still be obsessed with you, Lei."

My body grew numb. "That's crazy. He has a whole other life in New York City now. It's all in the past. *I'm* in his past."

"You hope," Heather added. "Does he know that you and Noah are dating?"

"I'm sure he does. Margaret knew, so she must have told him." At least I hoped so.

Eric and the white-haired gentleman were turned away from us. My mother had told me last night how Margaret once mentioned that when her time came, she wanted to be cremated. Her children had honored her request. The silver-colored urn was displayed on a small wooden table next to Abigail. Heather gave a visible shudder as we passed it.

Abigail gave us each a quick hug. I noticed that she kept looking over at her brother, as if willing him to turn around. Eric was still chatting with the same man. They appeared to be deep in discussion, and the elderly gentleman took a business card out of his pocket and handed it to him.

"How are you holding up?" I asked.

Abigail shrugged. "Okay, I guess. It still doesn't seem real." She glanced over at her brother again and lowered her voice. "Eric is having a difficult time. He was rude to your mother when she stopped in earlier. Please apologize to her for me."

Maybe Eric felt guilty for never coming to visit his mother? "It's okay. I'm sure Mom understands."

"Of course she does," Heather agreed. "It's expected that he would—"

She stopped mid-sentence, and I followed her gaze. Eric had come up behind his sister, his dark eyes pinned on me. I forced a smile to my lips.

"What are you doing here?" Eric's tone was cold and stiff.

I lifted my chin and met his eyes. "Hi, Eric. We wanted to let you know how sorry we are about your mother."

His features looked as if they had been carved out of stone. "Save it."

"Excuse me?" Was it possible that he was still nursing some type of grudge against me? Or was his resentment directed at the farm because of what happened to his mother?

"You aren't welcome here." Eric fastened his hateful glare on Heather. "And neither is your friend."

The murmur of voices around us came to a sudden halt. Heather's cheeks bloomed a bright red as heads turned in our direction.

"Eric, I'm sorry if you're still upset with me, but maybe this isn't the right time—"

"Oh, get over yourself," he said with a sneer. "That has nothing to do with it. Seriously I don't know how you have the gall to show your face here. You killed my mother."

Gasps punctuated the air. Heat rose through my face, and I found myself looking away from his piercing angry gaze. "That isn't true. My family feels awful about what happened, but you must realize this isn't our fault. We didn't make the pie, and no one was supposed to taste any of them until after the judges had sampled them."

A vein pulsed in Eric's neck. "That doesn't matter. She died at your farm, so that makes you responsible."

"Eric!" Abigail was wringing her hands in desperation. "Please don't do this. You're making a scene."

Eric brushed past his sister and stuck his face next to mine. The smell of stale coffee on his breath invaded my nostrils. "I mean it, Leila," he spat out. "We'll see you in court. You aren't going to get away with this."

His words shocked me to the very core. I had expected Eric to be upset, but nothing like this. He was a lawyer, after all, so I should have known he'd play the lawsuit card. When I thought of all the things my mother had done for Margaret over the years, I'd hoped that he might be a bit more understanding. "Please, Eric. You have to know that—"

"Get out!" he screamed.

The silence in the room was so deafening that you could have heard a mourning card drop. People were whispering and nudging each other as they stared over at me. I cringed under the reproachful gazes. Abigail started to sob, and the woman standing next to her put an arm around her shoulders.

Heather reached out and clutched my hand in hers. "Come on, Lei. Let's go."

We turned and walked out of the viewing room with everyone staring at us. Although I could no longer see Eric, I sensed his eyes on my back, burning a hole through my shirt until my flesh ignited.

The undertaker averted his eyes as he opened the door for us. Heather and I walked in silence to my car, but when I fumbled and dropped my keys, she reached down and picked them up off the ground. "Let me drive, love."

"No, that's okay," I managed to choke out.

Heather ignored me and got behind the wheel. Having no choice, I went around to the passenger side and got in. She started the ignition and then turned to me, patting my arm as she talked in a gentle tone. "It's okay, hon. Let it all out."

Loud, ugly sobs filled the car as I cried into my best friend's shoulder. Heather stroked my hair and made soothing remarks. The sad part was that I didn't even know what exactly I was crying about—the sheer embarrassment from Eric screaming at me, the thought of Sappy Endings being destroyed, or Emma's sudden distrust of me.

Or maybe it was a combination of all three.

# CHAPTER TEN

**ONCE WE HAD REACHED HEATHER'S** house, I felt comfortable enough to drive myself home, but she remained unconvinced. "Why don't you come in for a while?" she suggested. "Have a glass of wine with me and destress."

"No, thanks." I settled myself behind the wheel. "I'm pretty tired. Maybe I'll just head home and fall into bed."

"Are you sure?" Heather's mouth twisted into a frown. "I can call and order a pizza. Ty's going to be starved when he gets home. Come on, we'll have a great time. I really want you to stay."

It was obvious that she was worried, so I tried to set her mind at ease. "I'm okay, really. I'll grab a bowl of cereal when I get to my house."

"What's this?" Her eyes widened as she leaned over my side window. "None of Selma Khoury's famous cuisine tonight?"

I managed a smile. "Nope. Mom didn't have time to cook."

"Stop it," she teased. "We are talking about *your* mother, right? She always finds time to cook."

"She left work early to go to the wake, then ran Toast over to the vet to get a cortisone shot," I explained. "We think he has allergies. Anyway, she was running late, so she took Toast with her to Simon's for dinner."

"That cat eats better than most people," she joked. "And what's up with your brother making dinner? He can't cook. Your mom must be having cereal too. Neither you nor Simon can boil water."

"Would you stop?" I laughed, although we both knew she spoke the truth. I realized Heather was trying to make me feel better about the incident with Eric, and it was working. "No more insults about our cooking skills. Didn't I tell you that Simon's new roommate was going to culinary school? Tony wants to learn how to make grape leaves from the best cook in Vermont. Yes, those were his own words."

Heather winked. "Wow. It sounds like someone knows how to score points with your mother."

I started the engine. "I was counting on her bringing some grape leaves home for my dinner, but they do take a while to make. Oh well. At this rate, I'll be asleep before she gets home."

Heather reached for my hand. "Lei, I know that things look bad right now, but they'll get better. Have faith."

My eyes started to fill, but I managed to blink the tears away. I'd mistakenly thought there weren't any more to shed.

"Thanks for being there for me tonight. This is no time for me to feel sorry for myself. I need to find out who killed Margaret and keep my fingers crossed that Emma will eventually come around."

"She will," Heather assured me. "That little girl loves you. She's confused right now. Maybe she never really made the connection that Noah and you were in a relationship like the one her parents had."

"She's seen us kissing before."

"Yes, but that doesn't mean anything," Heather said. "She's what, only six? I'm sure you and Noah are discreet around her."

I stared at my friend in amazement. "Jeez, when did you learn so much about kids?"

Heather grinned. "I've been getting prepared, for when my time arrives."

"Oh my God." I squealed. "Are you pregnant?"

She shook her head. "Not yet, but hopefully soon."

"I'm so excited! Wow, I didn't even realize you guys were trying for a baby." I squeezed her hand. "That would make me a soon-to-be aunt—sort of."

"Not sort of," Heather insisted. "You know you're the sister I never had."

"Right back at you."

She winked. "And since you'll be the child's favorite aunt and godmother, that means I'm entitled to free babysitting, right? Only kidding."

"You don't even have to ask. I'd love to babysit little Leila anytime."

We both laughed, and the weight on my chest started to ease. Even though I couldn't have children of my own, it would be pure joy to surround Heather's with love. I'd hoped to do the same for Emma, but wasn't sure when I might get that chance.

———————————

The house was dark and eerily quiet when I arrived home. I started to call Toast, and then remembered he was with my mother. He always settled himself by the front door, waiting for me to walk through it. My mother and I joked all the time that Toast must think he had been born a dog.

I kicked off my shoes and stretched out on the sofa. The day had been long, exhausting and extremely stressful. After a couple of minutes, I wandered into the kitchen and peeked in the fridge. My mother always had leftovers on hand. There was kibbi and some vegetables, but for once none of it held any appeal. I was about to go upstairs and take a hot bath to unwind when my phone buzzed. I glanced down at the screen. *Noah.*

"Hey, gorgeous. How's everything?" he asked.

"Just fine," I lied.

"You don't sound fine." His husky voice filled with concern. "Leila, I'm so sorry about what happened last night."

I flopped back down on the sofa. "Please don't apologize. It's not your fault. How's she doing today?"

He hesitated. "Em's okay. We got home from her dance recital a little while ago. She did a super job."

"I knew she would." I had been looking forward to seeing Emma dance. I'd even helped to pick out her outfit. The theme had been Disney, and Emma decided that she wanted to go as Cinderella. We'd chosen a sparkly blue leotard and tiara for her to wear. "I'll bet she looked beautiful."

"I tried to read the Cinderella book you bought her, but she told me she wanted to skip it tonight," Noah said gruffly.

"What? That doesn't sound like her."

Noah cleared his throat. "It's not like her. Em loves books. Maybe I'll call her teacher tomorrow and see if she can shed any light on what's wrong."

"We know what's wrong. She thinks I'm trying to replace her mother." I blew out a breath. "I realize she has to come first. If this means we have to wait to be together, I understand."

"I appreciate your saying that, and I know it's because you love her too," Noah said quietly. "But I know my daughter better than anyone. There's something else causing her to behave this way. Once I figure out what it is, she'll accept you into her life again."

*But what if she doesn't?* I decided not to say the words out loud. It would sound as if I didn't trust Noah, and nothing could be further from the truth.

Noah cleared his throat. "Now, tell me about your night. How was the wake?"

This was Noah's attempt to change the subject, and I went along with it. "Awful. Eric Middleton threw Heather and me out of the funeral home."

"You've got to be kidding me."

Noah breathed heavily into the phone after I told him what happened. "Unbelievable. I guess he's not going to be happy until he tries to take you to court," he said.

"I can't lose the farm. No. I *won't* lose it."

"Whoa. Hang on a minute," Noah interrupted. "No one said anything about you losing the farm."

I bit into my lower lip. "My father and mother worked too hard for too many years, and I'm not going to let it happen. I'm sorry Margaret is dead, but I'm going to fight for what belongs to my family."

"I'll be with you every step of the way, because I love the farm too."

My heart warmed at his words. "Thank you. That means so much to me."

"I still can't believe Margaret's family would do such a thing," Noah mused.

"I don't think it's Abigail. I doubt she'd want anything to do with a lawsuit, but she'll go along with whatever Eric says. He's definitely head of that household."

Noah was quick to reassure me. "Don't worry. There are many people in Sugar Ridge who will support your family."

"Well, if they want to support us, why aren't they coming to the farm?" I couldn't keep the irritation out of my tone, and Noah didn't deserve that. "Sorry. I didn't mean to snap at you."

"That's okay, sweetheart. I know how upset you are. Don't worry, the police will figure out who did this."

Frustrated, I closed my eyes. "By the time they find out, it may be too late."

"Leila." Noah's voice became sharp. "Don't do this."

He'd already guessed my thoughts. "Noah, I don't have any choice. Maybe if I do some more snooping around in Margaret's life—"

"Please don't get involved in this mess."

I sucked in some air. "I'm already involved, and so are you. My father's business is on the line here, and I'm going to do whatever it takes to save it. We're not going down without a fight."

Noah was silent for so long that I started to wonder what was going through his head. "You know my feelings on this. I don't want you to be in any danger. You've already been involved with two murder investigations in the past year. But I do understand and admire what you did to bring your father's killer to justice." He heaved a long sigh. "And I'll continue to support you, no matter what."

Like a fountain, tears began to run down my cheeks. "How did I get so lucky to find you?"

"I wish you were here with me tonight." Noah's sensual voice exuded warmth and sent a tingle through me. "Em's supposed to go to a sleepover at a friend's house this weekend, but tonight she said that she didn't want to leave me." He paused. "If she changes her mind, we'll have some alone time together."

"That would be wonderful." I missed being in his arms while we sat together on the sofa as we watched TV or listened to the crackling of the woodstove. "But she needs you more than I do right now." All I wanted was for us to be a family someday.

"Okay, sweetheart. I'll see you in the morning. And don't worry, everything's going to be fine. I love you."

"I love you too. Good night." Noah had no idea how much I had needed to hear him say those words. We were going to be together. Maybe it would take longer than we'd anticipated, but if I was patient, things would eventually work out.

The phone call had zapped the last of my energy. I glanced at my watch. 7:30 p.m. My mother probably wouldn't be home for at least another hour. I leaned in against the overstuffed pillows and clicked the TV remote. There was nothing interesting to watch, but the house was too quiet, so I left it on, barely listening to the familiar sounds from *Jeopardy*. I grabbed the afghan my mother had knitted off the back of the couch and wrapped it around me. It was freezing in here. The weather had been so unseasonably warm for the past couple of weeks that we hadn't even turned on the furnace yet. Well, there was no time like the present. The forecast had predicted frost for tonight.

I roused myself from the couch with the afghan wrapped around my shoulders and flicked the switch on the wall. The furnace quickly rumbled to life, and I laid back down on the couch, content to stay there all night. I clutched the blanket tightly around me and immediately fell into a deep slumber.

Sometime later, a loud beeping awakened me. My eyelids flickered open, and I lay there in confusion, trying to determine where the noise was coming from. Did the fire alarm go off? There was no smoke, but breathing had started to become difficult.

A succession of four beeps sounded, followed by a brief pause, and then the beeps started again. My brain became muddled with confusion, and I couldn't think straight. How the heck could I turn that blasted noise off if I didn't know where it was coming from?

As I sat up, nausea began to build in my stomach and my head ached. When I went to stand, my legs wobbled, and almost buckled underneath me. My entire body felt weak. For a moment, I worried that I might pass out. Panic overwhelmed me as I desperately tried to make sense of the situation. What was happening?

Slowly, I moved across the room on legs that would not stop shaking. I took several deep breaths in an attempt to clear the sudden cobwebs from my brain, but it only seemed to make my condition worse. The air was stagnant, and I quickly became lightheaded. The beeps continued until I thought they might split my head in two. When I reached the staircase, I stared up at a flash in the ceiling.

A bright red light flashed across the surface of the carbon monoxide detector.

*Dear God.* In a stupor, I glanced around for my phone. I needed to call for help, but couldn't remember where I'd left it. An inner voice screamed at me. *Get out. Get out of here as quickly as you can.*

There was no time left to go back and look for my phone. Spots began to dance in front of my eyes as I staggered towards the front door. Desperately, I tried to fight against the blackness that threatened to consume me. I threw open the door and was vaguely aware of falling forward across the *Welcome* mat. The next second, my world, like the night, went dark.

# CHAPTER ELEVEN

**"MA'AM? CAN YOU HEAR ME?"**

A man I had never seen before with ash-blond hair was bending over me, a concerned expression on his face. He placed an oxygen mask over my nose and mouth. "You're going to be all right. Try to stay calm, okay?"

I didn't know what I had to be calm about. I felt light-headed and weak, and for the life of me, couldn't remember what had happened. When I noticed I was on a gurney being placed inside an ambulance, anxiety spread across my chest. Maybe the stress of the past week had caught up with me and I collapsed?

Someone gently touched my shoulder. I turned to see Noah next to me in the ambulance. He took hold of my hand between his two strong ones, massaging it gently.

"You're okay, sweetheart." His voice was husky with emotion. "Everything's going to be fine. Thank God you got out in time."

"What—what happened?" The words must have sounded gurgled to Noah because of the mask. I still had no recollection of anything that had occurred after I spoke to Noah on the phone earlier. It was as if someone had taken an eraser and wiped my mind clean.

"Your house is filled with carbon monoxide." A vein bulged in Noah's forehead. "After I got off the phone with you, my mom came by for a surprise visit. I asked if she'd mind staying with Em for a while so that I could come by. It was obvious to me that you were upset."

He stopped and drew a deep breath. "When I drove up in the driveway, I saw you lying on the porch, with the front door wide open." His deep-set blue eyes filled with unshed tears. I had never seen Noah in such a state before. "Leila, I don't know what I would have done if something had happened to you."

I didn't know what I would ever do without Noah and needed to tell him so. My hand went to my face to remove the mask, but Noah guided it away.

"Leave it on, Leila. There will be plenty of time to talk later."

"The mask is necessary, ma'am," the EMT said. "Your body's oxygen level has to get back to normal."

There were so many things that I wanted to say, but it was impossible. Noah must have sensed my overwhelming urge to speak because he pressed his soft lips against my forehead. "I called your mother. She and Simon will meet us at the hospital."

He kept talking, but his words started to garble together,

and I drifted back into an unconscious state. The next time I awoke, I found myself lying in a hospital bed. When I struggled to open my eyes, an unfamiliar male voice floated towards me.

"Leila should be able to go home in the morning," the man said. "We've elevated her oxygen level for the past four hours, and she appears to be symptom free. Of course, I don't want to take any chances. With your consent, I'd like to conduct a neurological exam before she leaves."

"Yes, that's fine. Do whatever has to be done. I need to know that she's going to be okay." My mother hiccupped back a sob.

Noah and my mother were standing with a man wearing a white doctor's coat. Noah happened to glance in my direction and noticed that I was awake. Relief broke out across his face, and he strode across the room to me.

"How are you feeling?" He lifted my hand to his mouth and kissed it.

"Much better." I sighed. "It doesn't hurt to breathe anymore."

My mother crossed over to the other side of my bed and kissed me on the cheek. "Oh, my dear. You gave us such a scare." She gestured at the man in the white coat. "This is Dr. Andrews. He said that you're going to be okay."

"Hello, Leila." Dr. Andrews smiled down at me. "Are you having any pain?"

I shook my head slowly. "My head hurts a little."

"I still don't understand," my mother said. "How could this have happened?"

Dr. Andrews shrugged. "There're many ways that carbon monoxide can leak in a house. It's hard to say offhand. The fire department might have a better idea by morning."

"Almost any appliance can cause it," Noah explained. "A gas dryer or stove, or the furnace. And yours runs on propane."

Dr. Andrews nodded in agreement. "There's always a chance it can happen with a furnace that runs on propane."

"Yes, and especially if was installed incorrectly or damaged somehow," Noah added. "You should have all of your appliances tested. I can check them for you, Selma."

My mother appeared grateful by his offer. "Thank you, Noah. I appreciate that."

Dr. Andrews patted my arm. "Leila should try and get some rest."

"Excuse me, doctor." A woman in pink scrubs stuck her head in the doorway. "There's a Detective Barnes outside who would like to see Miss Khoury."

Dr. Andrews scratched his head and frowned. "Are you up to talking with him, Miss Khoury?"

"Yes, he can come in."

"All right," Dr. Andrews conceded. "But I'll tell him he can only stay for a few minutes."

He left the room and after a few seconds, Detective Barnes appeared. He looked very different from his usual attire and was dressed in jeans and a New York Giants sweatshirt.

Detective Barnes shook hands with Noah and greeted my mother as he sat down in the chair next to my bed. "You're smiling. That's a good sign."

"It's your outfit," I said. "I've never seen you dressed so casually."

He winked. "I was off duty tonight and went out to meet some friends for dinner. Don't tell anyone because remember, I'm not allowed to have a personal life. But there isn't any chance of that happening with you around, right?"

Noah stuffed his hands in his jean's pockets. "She likes to keep the police department busy."

"I've noticed," Detective Barnes said. "After the call came in, I went out to your house to talk with the fire department and have a look around."

"It was very nice of you to come out, Detective," my mother said gratefully. "Especially at this late hour."

"What time is it?" I asked weakly.

"Almost midnight." Noah kept hold of my hand, but his gaze was focused intently on the detective.

Detective Barnes checked his watch. "Well, Leila and I are old friends, so when I recognized the address, I wanted to make sure that she was okay."

Uneasiness swept over me. While I appreciated Detective Barnes's concern for my well-being, I knew there was another reason why he was here. "There's something you're not telling us."

"That's one of the things I like about you, Leila. You always believe in being direct with people." Detective Barnes removed a small notepad from his sweatshirt pocket. "As I said, I went out to your house and had a talk with the fire investigator to see what may have caused the sudden increase of carbon monoxide in your home." He paused, as if for effect. "The results are very interesting."

Tiny wrinkles appeared at the corners of my mother's mouth. "What did you find out, Detective?"

Detective Barnes folded his arms across his chest. "Someone stuffed a towel in the vent outside—the vent that leads to your furnace. This is what led to the build-up of carbon monoxide inside the house."

Noah cursed under his breath. "You're saying that some-one deliberately did this?"

Detective Barnes shifted in his seat. "I'm afraid it looks that way."

A horrified expression came over my mother's face. "But why? Who would do such a terrible thing to us? To Leila?"

"It's hard to say," Detective Barnes admitted. He studied her expression. "Has anyone threatened either one of you lately?"

"Of course not," my mother said. "Leila, do you know of anyone?"

Eric's angry face flashed through my mind. "It wasn't exactly a threat, but Eric Middleton practically threw Heather and me out of Margaret's service tonight."

My mother gasped. "What?"

I quickly explained what had happened. "Abigail said that he was rude to you when you stopped by earlier."

My mother waved a hand in the air, as if swatting at a fly. "He was a bit short with me, yes. When I said I was sorry about his mother, he just grunted and turned to the next person in line. But I chalked it up to stress. I couldn't stay long because I'd made the appointment for Toast at the vet, and then had to get over to Simon's. So, I chatted with Abigail for a couple of minutes, and then left."

"He's going to try and sue us," I mumbled.

My mother shook her head. "No. I can't believe he would do such a thing."

Detective Barnes spoke up. "I talked to Eric the day after his mother died. He said that he was sorry it had to happen at Sappy Endings because he'd always considered the Khoury's like family."

"You're kidding." Nothing could be further from the truth. The only contact I'd ever had with Eric was when he asked me out. Did Eric have a split personality, or was he deliberately trying to throw Detective Barnes off?

Noah massaged the bridge of his nose between his thumb and forefinger. "Maybe after Eric thought about it, he decided there was an opportunity for him to make some money by suing you."

Detective Barnes drummed his fingers on the chair. "That's possible, but Eric and his sister both stand to inherit money from their mother."

"Margaret didn't have any money," my mother insisted.

"She inherited a substantial sum of money when her husband died." Detective Barnes studied his iPad. "From what I've learned, she lived frugally and had close to a million dollars in savings. Abigail said that Margaret never mentioned her finances to anyone because she was afraid people would try to take advantage of her."

My mother's eyes widened. "Margaret was rich? Why,

that's—my goodness. I had no idea. She was always counting her pennies and acted like she didn't have enough to make it through the day."

How ironic. Margaret had constantly complained about a lack of money when she had more than everyone else. "Do you think Eric may have killed his mother for an early inheritance?"

Detective Barnes thought for a minute. "Anything is possible. I did some checking on flight records, and Eric was already in Sugar Ridge the day his mother died. He never flew into town for his mother's death."

I couldn't believe my ears. "Abigail said that he came to town after Margaret's death. You're saying that he was already here before she died? How is that possible?"

"That's exactly what I'm saying. Plane records don't lie," Detective Barnes remarked. "Perhaps Abigail didn't know he was in town, either."

The look of hatred on Eric's face from the wake was still vivid in my memory. I blinked, and his image disappeared.

Detective Barnes's sharp eyes closely examined my face. "I get the feeling there may be another reason why he verbally attacked you at the funeral parlor. Maybe something that didn't have to do with the farm or his mother's death."

The man was more perceptive than most people. "He—he asked me out a couple of times in the past." I went on to tell the detective about the note that accompanied the flowers. "But I'm sure he's over that by now."

"Not necessarily." Noah's mouth hardened into a fine, thin line. "The guy sounds like a stalker to me."

"He was a little infatuated with Leila," my mother admitted. "But I find it hard to believe Eric had a hand in his own mother's death."

Detective Barnes didn't reply. Uneasiness swept over me. "Is there something else you're not telling us, Detective?"

His sharp gaze met mine. "You're a smart woman, Leila. It was only a few months ago when you figured out who killed the woman at Heather's bridal shower. From what I've learned, you also uncovered your father's murderer last year. It's entirely possible that Eric could have been behind his mother's murder. We haven't been able to find anyone else who had a vendetta against her. Money is a powerful motivator. But…" He paused.

"But you have your doubts?" I asked.

"Well, given what's happened to you…" The detective didn't finish. He didn't need to, because at that moment, a lightbulb clicked on in my head. From the look of amazement on Noah's face and my mother's sharp cry, I knew they had drawn the same conclusion as me.

"Oh, my God," I whispered. "Is it possible that Margaret wasn't the one they wanted to kill? Do—do you think someone wanted to poison me instead?"

Detective Barnes paused. "Yes. That's exactly what I'm thinking."

# CHAPTER TWELVE

**"I DON'T BELIEVE THIS." HEATHER** took a long swig from her coffee cup. "Once again, you're in danger. Why would someone want to hurt you?"

Her attempt to cheer me up wasn't helping. I finished my coffee and set it next to the uneaten breakfast tray the nurse had brought me two hours earlier. "Thanks for bringing me the coffee and breakfast sandwich from the farm. The food in this place is totally inedible."

"That's because you're spoiled," Heather teased. "Anyone who had your mother for a cook wouldn't be able to eat hospital food, either."

"You do have a valid point."

She wrapped her hands around her cup, as if for warmth. "I wish someone had called me last night to tell me what was going on. When your mom phoned this morning, I couldn't get over here fast enough. Did they say what time you can go home?"

"The nurse said that Dr. Andrews was making his rounds, so hopefully soon."

"I can bring you home," Heather offered. "My first client isn't until one o'clock today."

I roused myself out of the hospital bed and rummaged through the tote bag filled with clothes Heather had brought. "Thanks, but Noah's coming to get me."

The corners of Heather's delicate mouth turned upwards. "I'll have to tell him to behave himself. You're in no condition for a romantic interlude."

"Oh, please." I made a face at her. "It's not like we're running away to Hawaii together. He's taking me back to the farm. I have some work to catch up on."

Heather's mouth dropped open. "Are you crazy? For goodness' sake, someone tried to kill you last night. You need to rest!"

"All of my tests came back negative," I said. "The doctor told me there's no trace of carbon monoxide left in my system. I was very lucky."

"Beyond lucky," Heather put in. "Someone was watching over you last night."

"If I had been exposed to it for a few more minutes, I could have had all kinds of issues." I blew out a shaky breath. "Dr. Andrews said I might have had brain damage."

Heather brought a hand to her mouth. "Or you could have been killed."

Yes. There was that too.

"Dear God," Heather murmured. "Why would anyone want to hurt you?"

It was a good question, but I didn't have an answer. I'd laid awake most of the night, thinking about what Detective Barnes had said. Someone knew I was inside the house and deliberately plugged the vent. This was no accident.

I was far from perfect. Sure, there must be people who didn't like me. I'd had disagreements with some before, but nothing significant enough to stand out in my memory.

Detective Barnes seemed to think there was a slight chance my mother could have been the intended victim, but I didn't believe it for a second. No, someone had wanted me out of the way, but who and why? "Whoever did this knew that I was home alone last night."

Heather gave me a stricken look. "They could have been following you all evening. Maybe even all week or for months."

As she talked, I went into the bathroom to get changed. I threw on jeans and a turtleneck sweater in record time. "Heather, do you know how awful this makes me feel?"

"You see?" she shot back. "I knew you were rushing things. Lay back down for a while."

"No, that's not what I meant." I emerged from the bathroom with the hospital gown in hand. "I'm talking about Margaret. It's my fault she's dead. The pie she ate was meant for me, not her."

"You don't know that for sure. This isn't your fault, Leila. Yes, the article Simon wrote said that you were the only judge, but that doesn't mean you're responsible for Margaret's death. Anyone else could have tasted that pie too." Heather tossed her cup in the waste basket. "Whoever laced it obviously didn't care if anyone else got hurt besides you."

Emma had wanted to taste the pie. Bile rose in my throat. What if I had let her have a bite before I did? The possible outcome was too awful to imagine.

Heather sat down on the edge of my bed and rummaged through her purse. "Okay, we need to consider all the possibilities here. Time to make a list."

"A list of all the people who want me dead?" I asked in disbelief.

"Not necessarily." Heather shook her head. "We can start with maybes for now."

"Gee, thanks." This could not be happening. "I've only been back in Sugar Ridge for a year. There hasn't been a lot of time for me to make enemies."

With a determined look on her face, Heather pulled a notepad and pen from her purse. "Can you remember any customers you've had a disagreement with?"

Part of me wanted to laugh out loud at the serious expression she wore while the other part was paralyzed with fear. I'd made a similar list about a year ago when my father had been killed. If there was one person who I never thought of as having enemies, it had to be him. My father was the kindest, most generous man on the planet, but someone had still plotted his demise anyway. I was nowhere near as likeable. If it could happen to him, then it could happen to anyone.

"My mother deals with most of the customers in the café—you know that. And I've never had any kind of disagreement with our clients."

"You mean the businesses who buy syrup from the farm?" Heather asked.

"That's right."

"Let's go further back in time," Heather suggested. "Can you recall anyone who might have been holding a grudge against you for years?"

We both drew the identical conclusion at the same moment. Heather gave a muffled shriek. "Oh my god. How could we forget about Taylor? She was at the farm for the pie contest!"

A cold chill swept through my body. "But that was nine years ago. I can't believe she'd wait all this time to get back at me."

Heather shook her pen at me. "Time doesn't matter. Remember how Taylor was in here a few months ago? You called me up afterwards and told me about it. Say what you want, but I could tell you were upset."

It had been an awkward encounter, that was for sure.

Heather scribbled something on the pad, and I leaned over her shoulder for a better look.

*Leila's Enemies*
*Taylor*
*Eric*

"Eric's a creep." Heather drew a circle and stars around his name. "I could see him as a killer."

"It's hard for me to believe that he'd be behind this." Then again, why not? If Margaret had been the intended victim, her inheritance was an excellent motive. I relayed the details of Margaret's wealth and how her son had been in town the day she died.

Heather blew out a long, shaky breath. "Wow. I didn't know Margaret had any money."

"That makes two of us."

"It doesn't matter." Heather tossed her head. "Eric is clearly full of anger and animosity, and that puts him at the top of my list. If he was out to get you, can you imagine how he must feel right now, knowing his mother died instead of you? And that it's his fault?"

I didn't want to imagine. If anything, this would make Eric even more bent on revenge, and at my expense. "He doesn't exactly strike me as the type who would make a pie, though." I snapped my fingers. "Darn. I forgot to look at the entry forms. Maybe there's something in the pumpkin pie that could lead us to the killer."

"I thought the police had the forms," Heather remarked.

"They made photocopies in my office for me and took the originals."

Heather frowned. "Maybe whoever brought the pie didn't even bake it. They could have bought it from one of the bakeries in town. Or somewhere else in Vermont. Maybe we should call all the bakeries in the area and see if they have records of selling pumpkin pies that weekend."

"That's quite a long shot," I observed. "There's a ton of bakeries around, and this is their busiest time of year."

"Oh yeah, I forgot about that. Did you see anyone else at the contest who might have had it in for you?" Heather asked.

She certainly didn't believe in mincing words. "Maybe I should try and talk to Cameron. I thought I saw him there."

"Your former student, right? Do you want to talk to him?" Heather asked.

"Not really." I went on to tell Heather about the last time I'd spoken to Cameron. It wasn't one that I cared to remember. After he'd handed in his test, I'd asked him to accompany me to the principal's office. I doubted that he'd want to remember the incident either.

Heather's eyes grew large in her face. "Do you think he's still holding a grudge?"

"I honestly don't know what to think. If he was at the contest, then why didn't he speak to me? Was he going to try and hurt me, after all these years? I find it hard to believe that he only came for the pie contest."

Heather drew her brows together. "There's one more thing I don't understand. If Cameron was living in Florida with his family, what's he doing in Vermont? Did he travel two thousand miles to settle the score with you after all these years?"

"Cameron's family is originally from Vermont," I explained. "When I first met him in Florida, he told me he'd been born in Bennington. His grandfather had recently passed away, and he said that his parents were considering a move back to Vermont."

"He must have been the teacher's pet, since he came from Vermont too," Heather teased.

I snickered. "Very funny. You know that I would never play favorites with any of my students. It was a comfort to find one that I had something in common with, especially the first year. I was missing my father terribly. And you as well."

"Yes, I remember," Heather said softly.

"Cameron was fun to talk to," I went on. "We spoke about maple syrup and lots of other things in Vermont. His parents had been to Sappy Endings a couple of times and knew my father. It's another reason I took a personal interest in his situation."

Heather raised an eyebrow. "What situation?"

I hated to relive this part. "A fellow teacher who had Cameron's brother as a student asked me one day how he was doing in my class. His parents were sticklers about perfect grades and denied the boys privileges if they didn't toe the line. Cameron was nervous and jumpy all of the time. I figured the pressure was mounting for him."

"The poor kid," Heather murmured.

I sucked in some air. "And that's why he resorted to cheating on his final exam. There was no reason for him to do it. Cameron was a straight-A student in all of his classes, except mine. He confessed that he'd never liked history and had trouble remembering certain dates. It started to affect his performance. I offered him extra help after school on more than one occasion, but he always refused."

She shook her head. "Maybe he was afraid his parents would find out."

"That's what I thought too. The sad part was that he didn't need to cheat. No one does." In the worst-case scenario, Cameron would have wound up with a C, but he'd been highly sensitive, and the grade might have felt like the end of the world to him.

"His parents must have been furious when they found out about the cheating."

I bit into my lower lip. "They weren't furious with Cameron—at least not at first. They accused me of lying."

"No way."

It had been one of the most difficult things in my life to turn Cameron in. He'd denied the cheating, even though two other students and I had seen him. "It's the truth. Cameron's parents came to school to meet with the principal and accused me of lying. They even wanted the school to fire me. Obviously, I wasn't fired, but after that day, many of my students started to regard me in a different light. It was like they didn't trust me anymore."

Heather gave me a sympathetic look. "You poor thing. I wish you had said something to me at the time. I mean, I vaguely remember you talking about some kid who you caught cheating, but I didn't realize the rest. It must have devastated you."

"I learned to live with it." The following year had become easier when I'd welcomed in a new class. I had been determined to stick it out in Florida, even though I was never happy there. Instead, I had remained on the staff for three more years, until my father's death called me home. That was all in the past now. I was happy in Sugar Ridge. I belonged here.

"Do you know where he lives?" Heather asked.

"No, but I can find out." I pulled out my phone and did a quick search on Google. "Here it is. He's on Elmwood Road in Bennington."

"I know where that is!" Heather practically bounced on the bed. "There's an adorable little antique store on the same road. My mom and I have been there several times."

"What do you think about going there tonight after Sappy Endings closes?"

"Sure. We can go anytime you want," Heather said. "I picked up my car before coming over here. And for some reason, Thursdays are always slow for me. Please don't push yourself too fast, okay? It's not good for your health."

"I'm fine. Besides, I don't have a choice. The sooner I find out who's doing this, the sooner my life can get back to normal."

Because if I didn't find out who was responsible, I might not have a life for much longer.

# CHAPTER THIRTEEN

**NOAH ARRIVED AT THE HOSPITAL** a few minutes later to escort me back to the farm. After I had signed the release forms and gathered my things, I couldn't get out of the place fast enough. I hated hospitals and in the past year had spent way too much time in them. Heather followed us to the farm in her car since she no appointments scheduled for a while.

Once we were in Noah's truck, he leaned over and ran a gentle finger down the side of my face. "How are you really feeling? Are you having any trouble breathing?"

"No, I'm fine." Except for the fact that someone was trying to kill me.

"Good." Noah took my face between his hands and kissed me passionately. When we broke apart, I was breathless, but couldn't have cared less. The kiss had been well worth it.

"I don't want to let you out of my sight, not even for

a minute." Noah started the engine. "It's not safe for you anywhere."

"You can't be my bodyguard twenty-four hours a day," I protested. "Besides, I can't live like this forever. I'm not going to hide under my bed."

Noah pulled out of the parking lot. "You're welcome to stay at my house. We can drive back and forth to work together every day."

"It's a tempting offer." I smiled at him. "But I'll pass."

"I don't want you to be alone," Noah said. "And if you're worried about Em, don't be. She'll come around."

"Everyone keeps saying that." I sighed. "But what if she doesn't?"

He hesitated for a second too long. "I told you, there's got to be something else that's making her upset. Don't worry, I'll find out what it is. Either way, my offer still stands."

"Thank you, but I can drive back and forth to work by myself. And I don't want to make Emma feel even more uncomfortable. Like I said, I'm not going to let this person dictate my every move."

Noah pulled his truck up in front of Sappy Endings. "You are so stubborn."

"But that's why you love me, right?" I teased.

"Leila!" He gathered me in his arms. "This is serious. I love the fact that you're so independent, but this is no time to play detective. We're talking about your life."

A lump rose in my throat, making speaking difficult. "I promise not to take any unnecessary chances."

Noah turned his head as Heather pulled up next

to us. "Are you two planning on going somewhere this afternoon?"

Shoot. He knew me too well. "A little road trip."

He cursed under his breath. "Where to?"

"There's an antique store she wants to check out in Bennington." I told myself that it wasn't really a lie. Heather had mentioned that she wanted to go there again—but maybe not today.

Noah shot me a look that said I wasn't fooling him. He got out of the truck and came around to my side to help me out, placing a supportive arm around my waist. We walked towards the front door, which Heather held open for us.

I glanced around the empty lot with a sigh. "Still no customers I see."

"Come on, love," Heather assured me. "Things will get better. The holidays are bound to help."

My mother and Jenna were in the café, trying out a new recipe and laughing together. As we walked in, Heather whispered in my ear. "Jenna's hair is styled like yours today."

"Of course, you'd notice her hair first," I teased. But she was right. I took a closer look and noticed that instead of the usual ponytail, Jenna's hair was loose around her shoulders, with the same bit of curl at the ends like mine. Maybe she had simply wanted a change.

Mom leaned over the counter to hand Noah and me coffee, then served Heather a warm latte. "How are you feeling, dear? Would you like something to eat?"

"No, thanks. The breakfast sandwich Heather brought

filled me up." I took a sip of my coffee and then decided to ask the million-dollar question. "Any customers today?"

The look in my mother's eyes said it all. She turned away to remove a tray of baklava from the wall oven. "A few." She disappeared into the small kitchen work area and out of my sight. I didn't attempt to follow her. My mother and I understood each other these days. She was having a tough time dealing with this and had moments when she needed to be alone.

Jenna's gray eyes clouded over. "Your mother has been so upset this morning. Only four people came in for coffee. I keep telling her that things will get better. Don't worry, I'll go see how she is." She smiled at Noah, nodded to me, and then followed my mother into the work area.

"Jenna," I began, but she either didn't hear or chose to ignore me. My mother disliked people invading her turf when she needed a private moment. Oh, well, Jenna might as well find out for herself.

Noah rubbed his hands up and down my arms. "I'm going to head out to the sugar house and bottle up some syrup. We're still getting online orders so that's a good thing at least."

"Really? How many?"

"Ten so far, and all out of state." He tweaked my nose playfully. "Please be careful, okay? I'll see you when you get back." Noah smiled at Heather and went down the walkway towards the back door. After he left, I placed my head in my hands.

"What is it, hon? Are you feeling okay?" Heather asked anxiously.

"Physically, yes, except for a headache. But mentally, no." I stared up at her. "Someone's trying to kill me and ruin my farm at the same time. I need to find out who's behind this."

Heather tapped her fingers against the side of the cup. "You will. And once the killer is found, customers will start pouring back into Sappy Endings. It's only temporary."

"I hope you're right."

"We need to stay positive." Heather glanced at her phone. "My one o'clock cancelled, so I'm all yours. We can leave now if you want. Did you tell Noah where we're going?"

"I said you wanted to check out an antique store in Bennington. That's not actually a lie, right?"

"Of course not." Heather winked. "I do want to find a vase for my living room. It might not be today, though."

"Perfect. That's what I'm going to tell my mother when she comes back out here." I rose and shifted my handbag onto my shoulder. "Well, *if* she comes back out before we leave—"

A peal of laughter startled us both. We watched, mystified, as my reserved mother emerged from the work area with Jenna's arm around her shoulders. Jenna was staring at her with a look of pure adoration that took me by surprise. She acted as if my mother was the most beautiful person on the face of this earth. Had I ever looked at my mother like that? I didn't think so.

"Thank you, Jenna. I'm feeling much better now." Mom turned to me with a pleased expression. "Leila, the best thing we ever did was to hire this lovely young woman."

# CHAPTER FOURTEEN

**"OH, COME ON." HEATHER BEGAN** to laugh as she drove towards Bennington. "You're making a big deal out of nothing."

"What? That someone could be trying to kill me?" It was a horrible feeling to know someone wanted me dead, and even worse that a woman may have died because of me. I told myself I wouldn't take any unnecessary risks. We were only going to talk to Cameron, and Heather had appointed herself as my protector. It was a job she'd been very good at her entire life.

"No, silly. I'm talking about Jenna. If you dislike her, why did you hire her?"

"I don't dislike her," I said. "But there's something about her that rubs me the wrong way. She's only been working for the farm for a couple of days, and it's like she's already part of the family."

A small smile played on the corners of Heather's mouth. "You don't have to worry."

"About what?"

"Your mother's still going to like you best," she joked.

Oh, for crying out loud. I knew Heather was only joking, but it made me stop and think about what she'd said. My mother and I had finally gotten past our rocky relationship and were both on common ground. We loved and respected each other. It wasn't like she was going to adopt Jenna and give her a home, like we'd done with Toast. So, why did this thing bother me?

I struggled to find the right words. "I guess I'm just surprised at how my mother's acting. She always told me you can't be friends with your employees."

Heather made a left-hand turn onto a narrow, winding road. "Well, I'm glad that didn't stop you and Noah," she laughed.

"Very funny."

"You should be glad that she's getting along with Jenna," Heather pointed out. "The last thing you need to worry about right now is more friction at the farm."

"Yeah, that's true."

"Besides," Heather continued, "maybe Jenna is looking for a substitute mother in her life right now. She might have a rocky relationship with her own mom—like you once did."

"I hadn't thought about that," I admitted.

"Or Jenna's trying to suck up to her boss." Heather glanced slyly at me.

"Ha!" I laughed. "My mother can spot a suck-up a mile away."

The colonial home on Elmwood Road had seen better days. We got out of Heather's SUV and walked up the stone-filled driveway. The white paint on the outside frame was chipped in several places and needed a good pressure washing.

I thought of my own mother, who prided herself on her home's appearance. Every summer she tended to her vegetable garden and azaleas with loving care. Because of her work schedule, she hired one of the neighborhood teenagers to mow the lawn, but I would occasionally do it on Sundays. Since my father died, she did everything else by herself, with the exception of snow removal in the winter. I had to admire her strength and determination. She wasn't getting any younger, and I knew that working in the cafe, no matter how much she enjoyed it, exhausted her most days.

Heather was talking. "Sorry, what did you say?" I asked.

She pointed at the dirty pane of glass on the front door. "Do you think he's home? What are you planning to say to him?"

"The truth. I want to know why he was at the farm the other day."

Heather swallowed nervously as I tapped on the door. After several seconds, the dingy white curtain moved and a woman about my mother's age peered out at us. She opened the door and smiled, but her eyes narrowed when she met mine.

"What do you want?" she asked in a gruff tone.

Oh, shoot. She did remember me, after all. I knew I

hadn't changed much in five years, but Eileen Wilton had. Her face was leathery and lined with wrinkles, as if she'd smoked two packs a day her entire life. She was dressed in a green bathrobe and flip-flops, even though the temperature hovered in the forties today. Her once-black hair was lined with gray and piled high on top of her head, reminiscent of the popular seventies' beehive hairdo.

I summoned up my courage and gave her a brave smile. "Hello, Mrs. Wilton. My name is—"

"Yeah, I know who you are," she interrupted. "You're that teacher of Cameron's. The one who accused him of cheating in your class."

The hatred in her eyes was so vivid that sweat began to pool on my forehead. What could I say? Any denial on my part would only anger her further. I tried another tactic. "This is my friend, Heather."

Heather gave the woman her most radiant smile. "Hello."

Mrs. Wilton grunted in return and swiveled her head back in my direction. "What are you doing here?"

I swallowed hard. "Um, I wanted to know if Cameron was home. I'd like to speak with him."

"He's not here right now, and even if he was, you're the last person he'd want to talk to. Because of you, he ended up losing out on a full scholarship." Mrs. Wilton began to close the door.

"Please wait." I waved my hand in the air. "I don't understand. How could something like that happen? He was a freshman in high school when—uh, the unfortunate incident happened."

Mrs. Wilton paused, her hand on the doorknob. "It went on his permanent record, that's how. I would think a teacher like you would be aware of the consequences."

She was right. I should have been more aware but at the time, I never thought that the incident would mess up Cameron's entire academic state. Would I have done things differently if I'd known this would be the result? No. Despite the fact that I'd felt sorry for him, his actions had been unfair to the other students.

If I kept trying to avoid the subject, it would sound like I didn't care about Cameron, and that couldn't be further from the truth. My heart went out to him when I'd discovered his home situation. Anytime he received a grade less than an A, he looked like he wanted to burst into tears. "What's he doing these days?"

"Don't pretend you care," Mrs. Wilton spat out, "because that's a lie. If you must know, Cameron's going to community college here in Vermont. We moved back home after what happened. Didn't you realize that?"

"But I thought that you were already planning to return to Vermont." I had known it would be no picnic coming here to question Cameron, but wasn't prepared for the tremendous guilt trip that had come over me. "Mrs. Wilton, I—"

She cut me off. "He's managed to succeed, despite what you've done to him. Cameron's always been so good at science." There was an unmistakable note of pride in her voice. "He's studying to be a pharmacist at Vermont Mountain College. When he finishes there, he'll transfer to a four-year school."

"VMC is a great school," Heather remarked. "I have a friend who went there."

Mrs. Wilton ignored her comment. "Yes, he's learned to persevere. My son is a true Wilton. And now, I'll ask you to please leave my property. Cameron's put the past behind him and has moved on. He doesn't need any more reminders, especially from you."

"Then why was he at Leila's farm the other day?" Heather burst out.

Mrs. Wilton looked at Heather as if she had two heads. "What are you talking about?"

I closed my eyes in frustration. It hadn't been my intention to tell Mrs. Wilton about Cameron's visit, but the cat was out of the bag now. "Cameron was at Sappy Endings on Saturday."

She shook her head. "No, you're mistaken. He would never go there."

"It was a pie-baking contest," Heather explained. "Maybe he wanted to submit an entry?"

"Are you deaf?" Mrs. Wilton wanted to know. "I already told you he wasn't there. He went out with friends that day."

"I'm not trying to upset you," I said gently. "But I'm almost positive that I saw him there."

Mrs. Wilton's nostrils flared like a dragon's. She took a step forward and stabbed me in the chest with a sharp acrylic fingernail. Fear shot through me, and I moved out of her reach.

"Don't you dare touch her," Heather shrieked. She reached out and put a hand protectively on my shoulder.

"Get off my property," Mrs. Wilton yelled. "Both of you. And don't ever come back."

With no other choice, Heather and I retreated down the driveway, back to her SUV. As we drove away, I turned for one last look at the house. Mrs. Wilton was still standing on the porch. She made an obscene gesture in the direction of the vehicle, then went back inside.

"That woman is a lunatic," Heather declared.

"Yeah, I figured she'd be like that. She'll defend him until her dying day. Sometimes parents refuse to believe their child is capable of doing something dishonest." I'd seen it a few other times during my teaching career but this situation was by far the worse. Cameron had seemed to be the complete opposite of his mother. Despite my qualms, I needed to talk to him again and try to uncover his true feelings.

Heather interrupted my thoughts. "Where to now?"

"Let's head on over to the college. There's always a chance we might spot him." A very small chance.

Heather's eyes grew round like dinner plates. "What will you say to him?"

"I'll ask why he wanted to see me." There had never been a chance for me to talk to Cameron after the cheating incident occurred, although I would have liked to. All I'd wanted back then was to help him, but everything had gone wrong. "I have to say that I'm glad you're here with me."

"You know you can always count on me." She smiled, but it couldn't mask the concern in her eyes.

Our drive to the campus only took about fifteen minutes. There were about a dozen different brick buildings scattered along one street. It was a glorious autumn day, with vibrant orange and red leaves decorating the ground. We parked in the visitor's lot and then studied the nearby directory.

Heather ran her finger over the markings. "Do you think he lives here?"

"I don't believe they have on campus housing. And from the way his mother talked, it sounded like Cameron lives at home." I glanced at my watch. "It's after two o'clock. Most of the classes are over with by now."

"Maybe he's hanging out in the library," Heather said. "As long as we're here, we might as well walk around and see what we can find out, if anything."

"Sounds like a plan."

She pointed at a nearby building. "Maybe the admissions office will tell us something."

"Heather, I don't think they—" My words fell on deaf ears. Heather had already started up the steps of the building. I sighed and followed her, having an idea of what was going to happen.

Less than five minutes later, Heather followed me outside and turned to flash the building a look of contempt. "They didn't have to be so rude."

"No one was rude to us," I reminded her. "The woman said that they couldn't disclose personal information about a student."

"Well, it was worth a try." Heather sighed.

We crossed the street to a gray building with a sign mounted on the front that read VMC Science Building. A bronze statue of Albert Einstein sat on the lawn.

"Check this out. Mrs. Wilton said that he was interested in science," I mused. "Let's go inside and have a look around. I doubt we'll be lucky enough to see him, but stranger things have happened."

"True." Heather followed me up the front steps. "And you've had a lot of practice with strange in the past year."

"Very funny."

Heather pulled her coat tighter around her and shivered. "Maybe we could follow him tomorrow morning—from his house, I mean. Then, once he gets to the campus, we'll confront him."

"But we don't know what time he leaves in the morning or what days he even has classes. Besides, we both have businesses to run." *Yeah, right.* Some business. Everything that my father worked so hard for all his life was quickly falling to pieces.

As Heather reached the door, it was pushed open from the other side by a young man. The sudden movement pushed Heather backwards. She grabbed for the railing and managed to stop herself in time before falling down the steps.

An expression of horror crossed the young man's face, and he rushed to Heather's side.

"Gee, I'm sorry. Are you all right?"

Heather nodded. "I'm fine—you just surprised me."

The wind whipped the young man's dirty-blond hair around his face. He stopped to push it out of his eyes. He was over six feet tall with a brawny build and shot us both a genuine smile. "I don't think I've seen either one of you on campus before. Are you students?"

A triumphant smile crossed Heather's face. We both would turn thirty in a few short months, and she was flattered by the compliment.

"No, we're not students," I said. "We're looking for a friend who goes here. Are you a science major by chance?"

"Yep, Troy Foster. I'm a chemistry major. "Who's your friend? Maybe I know her."

"Him," I corrected. "His name is Cameron Wilton."

Troy's wide grin disappeared. "Oh, sure. I know Cam. He's in one of my classes. The dude doesn't talk much to me. No offense, but I didn't think Cam even had any friends."

"Really?" From what I could remember, Cameron had been a loner in high school and not friendly with other students. I couldn't recall one instance of him chatting with a classmate, so this made sense to me.

Troy's cheeks flamed. "Um, it's just that, well, he never talks to anyone, except the professor. Cameron stays after class with him a lot. The other guys say he's a suck up, but I don't think so. You don't need to suck up when you have the highest grade in the class."

"Is he a chemistry major too?" Heather asked, forgetting what Mrs. Wilton had relayed.

Troy shook his head. "Nah, I heard him tell Professor Green that he wanted to be a pharmacist. I guess that's why he's so into toxicology."

A wave of uneasiness passed over me. "Did you say toxicology?"

"Yep." Troy swung the bookbag onto his back. "That's the class we're in together. I'm only taking it for fun—and the credits. I swear though, Cameron should be teaching it instead of Professor Green. He knows everything there is about different poisons."

# CHAPTER FIFTEEN

**"OKAY, THIS IS WORSE THAN** I thought," Heather admitted as we drove away from the college campus. "I think we should call Detective Barnes as soon as we get back to your house."

My headache was back in full force. I didn't know if it might be a lingering affect from the carbon monoxide last night or the shock that Cameron might have been plotting to poison me. "I can't believe he's behind this."

"Jeez, weren't you listening to anything that Troy said?" Heather asked in disbelief. "Cameron showed up at Sappy Endings during the pie-baking contest, and with an axe to grind. To top it all off, the guy's a toxicology major. If that doesn't sound suspicious, I don't know what is."

Despite how much I wanted to believe that my former student had nothing to do with the incident, there was no way I could ignore the evidence we'd found. "Carbon monoxide is a poison too."

Heather sniffed. "Yeah, and I bet they talk about all kinds of poisons in that class, including ones you can put in a pie. Now, will you please call Detective Barnes? There's no need to wait until we get back to the farm."

"All right, I'll call him." I pulled my phone out of my purse. "When we get back to the house, I'm going to look through all the entry forms for the pie contest again. Maybe there's some clue that I missed."

"There was a form attached to the pumpkin pie, right?"

"Yes, and the cash fee. I wouldn't have entered the pie without it."

Heather shrugged. "It seems weird that they'd go to all that trouble, but I guess it had to look realistic."

I dialed the detective's number, but the call went straight to his voicemail. "Detective Barnes, it's Leila Khoury. I wondered if you could give me a call about Margaret Middleton's murder. I might have another suspect for you to consider."

As I clicked off, Heather pulled into the driveway. My mother's car was parked on the left side. I stared at my watch in disbelief. "It's not closing time yet."

Heather offered me a sympathetic glance as she got out of the SUV. "Maybe everyone decided to pack it in early today."

If this kept up, we would be packing it in on a permanent basis.

When I opened the front door, the mouthwatering smell of my mother's meat pies, or *Sfeehas* as they were also known in Arabic, floated through the room. I always marveled at how my mother managed to make the diamond shape of the bread in such a perfect contrast to display the meat mixture in the center. The pies were made with lamb, pine nuts, and tahini. Tahini was a spread my mother created from hulled sesame seeds, oil, and salt. The hulled sesame seeds were toasted, then ground and emulsified with oil to create a smooth, creamy seed butter with a pourable consistency.

We followed the scent to the kitchen. Mom looked up with a smile as she placed a salad bowl on the table. Toast was sitting on a chair, waiting patiently for his share. My mother set a paper plate down on the floor with some of the meat from the pie, and he immediately jumped down and raced over to the plate. She sighed and patted his head wistfully as he ate. "I'm going to miss him when he leaves."

I opened the cupboard, collecting plates for the table. "Where's he going?"

She looked surprised. "I figured you'd want to take him when you move in with Noah and Emma."

Fearful that I would drop the plates, I quickly set them down on the table. "But I never told you it was for certain."

Mom shot me an amused look. "You didn't have to tell me. I know more than you think, dear."

I glanced over at Heather, who gave me a shrug in return. Apparently, I didn't give my mother enough credit.

After I washed my hands, I sat down at the table between Heather and my mother. Everyone was silent for a time as we devoured my mother's delicious food. I washed down some of the meat pie with a glass of water and decided to speak up. "First off, I figured you'd be upset if I took Toast with me."

My mother sipped at her glass of limonada. "Don't you want to take him with you?"

"Of course I do." Toast was like a best friend in some ways. He was always there for me to tell my troubles to. There were many days when I preferred his companionship to that of humans. Plus, he asked for so little in return—food, water, care, and chin scratches. "I'd miss him like crazy."

"Well, then it's settled." My mother forked a bite of salad into her mouth.

My voice began to tremble. "But you love Toast too. And you'll be all alone. I don't think it's right to—"

She waved me off impatiently. "I'm not five years old, Leila. You found Toast, and I know how much he adores you. He sleeps with you every night and is more attached to you."

Her expression seemed forlorn, and it made me sad to see. She must have guessed what I was thinking because she reached over and patted my arm. "Don't worry about me, dear. I love Toast, and do hope you'll bring him to visit sometimes. But I've already decided that the best thing I can do is adopt another cat so I can have my own companion. I may even get a senior cat. There are so many of them out there that need good homes and get overlooked."

Heather clapped her hands. "That's a wonderful idea!"

Mom looked pleased. "I thought so too. And hopefully he or she will get along with Toast since they'll be seeing each other on a regular basis."

I pushed the tabbouleh around on my plate with a fork. "Thanks for the offer, Mom, but this might be premature. I may not be moving in with Noah and Emma after all."

Mom listened, wide-eyed, as I told her about Emma's

recent reaction. "Well, that's to be expected. She may have never fully realized the extent of your relationship with her father. Be thankful that it happened now, before you moved in. She's a little girl and this is very hard for her."

I tried to keep my voice on an even keel. "I know it is, and she has to come first. That's why I don't think I'll be going anywhere for a while."

"It will all work out." Mom passed the tabbouleh to Heather. "Could there have been something that might have triggered her sudden dislike of you?"

My mother never believed in pulling any punches. "Her mother had a birthday the other day," I explained. "Noah didn't think Emma remembered the date, so he didn't say anything, but that made things even worse because she took it as a sign her father didn't care."

"Children are a great deal smarter than we give them credit for," Mom said. "They're also very resilient. No, I'm thinking there must be another reason why she's suddenly acting like this. In time, you'll figure it out, and Emma will come around."

"That's what I told her too." Heather helped herself to some more salad. "She adored Leila before, and she will again."

Their remarks helped to cheer me up some, and I wanted to believe what they said was true. I knew Noah wouldn't stop loving me if his daughter didn't approve, but what would happen if Emma never came to accept me? It was bound to affect our relationship, and maybe even our plans to wed someday.

After Heather and I had cleared the table and my mother

put the leftovers away, I went up to my room and brought down the photocopies of the entry forms. I tried to conjure up a visual image of each pie as I read through the descriptions.

"I meant to take a photo of all the pies ahead of time," Heather said regretfully, as if she read my mind. "But I never got around to it because I was busy with the kids."

"Me too." Things had been so hectic that day. If only I had let my mother handle the details like she'd offered.

My phone screen lit up at that moment. I picked it up from the table and saw a text from Noah. The two little words filled me with both joy and sadness at the same time.

*Miss you.*

I quickly typed back, *Miss you too. Can we find some time to hang out tomorrow night?*

His answer was a while in coming. *I'll try. Let me see what I can do.*

Noah's response told me everything that I needed to know, without his coming right out and saying it. Emma still didn't want to see me, especially at her house. I closed out of the text and searched through my phone for the picture of Emma and me from a couple of weeks ago. She had dressed up as Cinderella for Halloween. The little girl was obsessed with the Disney princess these days. I stood at her side, wearing overalls and a big straw hat, which had made her giggle. My heart ached. We'd both been so happy that day. If I could understand what was running through her head, maybe we could work through this.

When I absently thumbed through the rest of the photos,

I noticed that there was a new row I hadn't seen before. I gasped out loud when I realized what they were.

My mother and Heather looked up from the entry forms they were studying. "What's wrong?" Heather asked.

"Look!" I held the phone out to her.

Heather squinted down at the photos. "Oh my God—it's a picture of the pumpkin pie! I thought you said you didn't take any."

"I didn't."

She stared at me with a puzzled expression. "Then how did it get there?"

I thought back to Saturday when I had hurried over to the café to meet with Jenna. "I left my phone on the table with the pies."

My mother's face brightened. "Yes. I remember. Emma was holding it while you were up at the café. I didn't think much about it and figured you wouldn't mind. Margaret was—" She stopped to make the sign of the cross on her chest. "I hate to speak ill of the dead, but she was driving me bananas. She kept asking if she could fill in for you. I was so distracted that I couldn't think about anything else."

"Emma must have snapped the pictures by accident," Heather observed.

"Kids love to play with cell phones." I glanced through the photos again. There were several images that Emma had taken—some blurred, a couple of the grass, one of some-body's foot, and several of the pies. "She knows how it works, because she asked me one day if she could take a picture of Toast with my phone. Her aim is getting better."

Toast, who was curled up on the other remaining kitchen chair, looked up expectantly at the mention of his name. He offered us a sleepy squeak.

Heather laughed and leaned over to stroke his fur. "Too funny. My cousin's little boy is only eight, but he knows how to work her phone better than she does."

I increased the size of the photo and examined the pumpkin pie as if it was the first time I had ever seen it. "Check this out. I forgot how pretty the pie was, with the maple leaf design on the crust. Could someone have done this by hand, Mom?"

My mother put her glasses on and took the phone from me. She studied the photo with a critical eye. "They can be done by hand, but this one definitely wasn't. The person who made the pie used a mold or stamp."

"How can you be so certain?"

Mom raised an eyebrow at me. Whoops. I'd almost forgotten who I was talking to for a minute. "I think *I* would know, Leila. If the design of the leaf had been done by hand, it would be much less uniform."

I took my phone back from her. "I wonder if we could somehow manage to trace where the mold came from. Didn't Max make bagels in the shape of a maple leaf during Open House Weekend last March?"

"Yes, he did. You should ask him where he got his mold from." She frowned. "I've seen this mold before."

"In a store, you mean?" Heather asked.

Mom shook her head. "No. Someone I know has one, but I can't think of who it is. There are cake and pie supply stores that sell these all over Vermont. We don't have any in Sugar Ridge, though. It may be like searching for a needle in a haystack. The person who made the pie might have even gone out of state to buy it, or bought it online."

Since Vermont was famous for its maple trees, I figured it must have come from somewhere in the state, but decided not to argue with her. "It's the only real lead we have to go on right now." I typed "cake supply stores" into Google on my phone. "The nearest one is in Bennington."

Heather stared up from the entry form she was examining with a shocked expression. "Holy cow. It's near Cameron."

"Who's Cameron?" my mother asked.

I'd never told my mother the story of how I'd turned a student in for cheating on his exam. There were many things I had never shared with her from my teaching days, mainly because we were barely on speaking terms back then.

She put a hand to her mouth after I finished telling her the sordid details. "Oh, Leila. Do you think he would really want to hurt you?"

"I didn't think so at first, but now I'm not so sure. If I did ruin his life, like his mother said, it's entirely possible."

Heather waved the entry form in her hand. "Did you guys look at the name on this form? There was only one pumpkin entry, right?"

"There was also a pumpkin cheesecake entry," my mother said, "and a pumpkin pie with pecans. But I figured there would be more, especially with Thanksgiving right around the corner. We had five or six apples, though, a couple of chocolate, and—"

"What's funny about the name?" I interrupted. "Oh, wait a second. Wasn't it something like Candy Sweet?"

"Sandy Sweet. If that's not phony, I don't know what is," Heather declared. "And there's no address."

I studied the form again. "I wish I had taken a closer look at it during the contest. That name should have been a tipoff something was definitely wrong."

"Don't blame yourself, dear," my mother said. "It was our first time organizing it, and we were all going in twenty different directions."

Hopefully, it wouldn't be our last time. I took my time reading through the entire entry form. Underneath the email address was a blank space for the recipe to be written out. If unusually long, the recipe could be stapled to the form, or we would have accepted a printout. The pumpkin pie recipe had been neatly printed in the space provided. Its crust had been created from scratch. The filling consisted of standard ingredients—fresh pumpkin, maple syrup, vanilla, milk, and maple sugar.

I flipped over the form. We had included an optional area if the baker wanted to tell us why they'd chosen to make this particular pie. I hadn't read any of these the day of the contest, but assumed there would be various reasons, such as the pie was a family favorite or had been carried down through generations, etc. The idea had been my mother's brainchild. All I cared about was the taste. This part of the form was not mandatory, and the baker could have skipped over it if they wanted to.

To my surprise, the baker of the aforementioned killer

pie had chosen to fill this portion in. I half suspected the answer to be something common like, "I made pumpkin pie because it's almost Thanksgiving," or "this is the traditional pie everyone serves with their turkey."

But I was dead wrong.

In the space for the response, the killer had written:

*I made this because it's Leila's favorite.*

# CHAPTER SIXTEEN

**"WHOEVER DID THIS MUST KNOW** you well," Noah observed. "I mean, how else could they find out that your favorite kind of pie is pumpkin?"

Noah and I were in the sugar house making maple sugar. It was a product I'd been wanting to offer to customers for a while, along with syrup and maple candy, but we'd been so busy there hadn't been time before.

How things changed. We had ample time for it now. In fact, all we had was time.

I watched as Noah poured maple syrup into a large stainless-steel pot with high sides. He set it to boil over medium high heat on the small gas stove we kept in the sugar house. "It's creepy," I admitted, "to think that it's someone who I've been in contact with before."

Noah added a spoonful of butter to the pot which reduced the foam. He then inserted a candy thermometer to check the temperature. His handsome face grew stern when he stared up at me. "Don't think I haven't thought about that as well. For all we know, it could be a customer. Another reason for you not to be here."

"No. That's not an option. I'm not going to stay hidden in my house all day. I have a responsibility to the farm, and to my father's memory."

He didn't answer—probably because he knew that he would never get me to change my mind on the topic.

For the next ten minutes, we waited for the syrup to boil, saying little. Noah checked the temperature again. Satisfied with the result, he turned off the burner underneath the pot to prevent scorching.

"The liquid is extremely hot," Noah warned. "Stand back while I stir. I don't want you to get splashed."

We were both wearing aprons and heat-resistant gloves to avoid burns. I did as Noah asked but kept peeking over his shoulder, since the entire process intrigued me. The texture began to change as Noah continued to stir the contents. This made the process more difficult, but he handled it like the pro he was. Once the sugar was granulated, Noah stopped stirring and poured it into a stainless-steel mesh strainer to remove the larger chunks.

"Should we package the sugar and take it over to the gift shop?" I asked.

Noah shook his head. "It needs to air-dry overnight," he said. "The humidity is lower in the sugar house, so we'll keep it out here. But if you want to go ahead and sample some, that's fine. It's perfectly okay to eat. Once it dries, I'll separate the sugar into bags for sale in the gift shop."

"Sounds good to me." It was exciting to have another product available for public consumption.

"Hmm." He gave me a shrewd look. "Did you know that maple syrup is one of the few wild crops left on our planet?"

"Yes, I did."

He cocked an eyebrow. "No fooling?"

"Why are you so surprised?" I laughed. "My father told me. One more reason why he was so proud of his farm."

Noah pushed the hair back from my face. "He'd be proud of you and all the great changes you've made in the past year, if he could see them."

"He sees them," I said with confidence.

Noah held out the wooden spoon to me, and I took a taste. Maple sugar was much sweeter than granulated sugar. "Yum. I should dip my Oreos in this."

Noah barked out a laugh. "You're a sugar addict, that's for sure. Just like Em."

There was an awkward pause, and Noah quickly changed the subject. "I've made over a hundred candles for the gift shop this week."

"All holiday scents?" I asked.

"Mostly," he replied. "There's vanilla maple and evergreen. It seemed like a good thing at the time, but now I'm starting to wonder if they'll sell. Last winter, we couldn't keep enough on hand during the holiday rush."

It was difficult not to be depressed by everything going on in my life. With each day that passed, it was getting harder for me to believe that customers would soon be back at the farm, making purchases for the holidays and enjoying the benefits of our artisanal maple syrup.

At the same time, though, I tried to focus on all the positives in my life, and one of them was standing next to me, pouring more sugar into the strainer. "I'm so glad you're here with me." He was a huge source of strength, more so than he knew.

Noah put down the bucket of maple syrup he was holding and wrapped his arms around my waist. "I'll always be here for you. Don't ever forget that." He kissed me lightly on the lips. "I know things seem kind of bleak right now, but once the police find Margaret's killer, everything will get back to normal."

He didn't pose the question that both of us were thinking. What if we didn't find out in time? What if this maniac got to me before the police found him?

As if on cue, my phone buzzed from my jeans pocket. I glanced down at the screen. It was Detective Barnes.

"Sorry I didn't return your call last night," he apologized. "I had another homicide to investigate."

I told him about the visit to Cameron's house and college while giving him the backstory on our relationship. "He probably has nothing to do with it, but—"

"We'll bring him in for questioning," Detective Barnes said. "We have to check out every possible angle."

"There's another reason I called—one that concerns me more." I told him about the pumpkin pie recipe, and the message included.

Detective Barnes coughed on the other end. "Is there any chance you mentioned that pumpkin pie was your favorite kind? Maybe for the Maple Messenger article?"

"No, I'm sure I didn't." There were a million items jostling for space in my brain right now, but I knew Simon wouldn't have asked me about my favorite kind of pie. The only person I remembered telling it to was Emma.

"Can you think of anyone else who might have a grudge against you?" Detective Barnes asked. "By the way, I'm not ruling out Eric Middleton."

"It seems crazy that he'd want to kill me because I refused to go out with him."

Detective Barnes paused, as if to consider. "Well, not as crazy as you might think. And who knows—maybe he hoped his mother would taste the pie first. That way, when she died, he could sue the farm."

"And get his inheritance at the same time," I said. "That's sick."

"Whoever did this *is* sick," Detective Barnes remarked. "There's no way that the person who made the pie knew you'd taste it first, even if pumpkin is your favorite. They simply didn't care if anyone else died. We're looking for someone unstable who may also have some culinary skills."

"According to the card, the crust was homemade, but that still doesn't mean it wasn't made by a bakery." Taylor's face flashed through my mind. "Oh God. I did think of someone else. My old college roommate was at the farm for the contest. She went to culinary school."

"And she has a grudge against you?"

Detective Barnes voice sounded a little too eager to me. *Jeez, try to control your excitement.* "I wish this was all behind us, but maybe not. When we were in college, I suspected that she was stealing money from me. I asked her about it one night, and she went crazy. A couple of days later, I caught her in the act. It turned out that she was using the money to help support her drug addiction, which was even more of a shock. Taylor got expelled from college, and I know she still blames me for it."

"I see." Detective Barnes paused. "What's her full name? And did you speak to her during the contest?"

"Taylor Hudson, and yes. She was pretty rude to me, but I'm used to it."

Detective Barnes mulled this over for a minute. "I don't remember seeing her name on any of the entry forms. I'm looking through them again now to be certain."

"Taylor made fun of our contest and said that she was entering the Pillsbury Bake-Off. She told Heather and me that she was there to check out the sugar house, but I suspect her real interest was in checking Noah out."

Noah nearly dropped the strainer when he heard me.

"So, this isn't the first time you've seen her since college?" Detective Barnes inquired.

"Taylor came in a few months ago to purchase maple syrup. I don't think she's ever going to forgive me for what happened."

A faint tapping sound could be heard on the other end of the line, and I figured Detective Barnes was busy capturing my comments for his iPad. "Does she live in Sugar Ridge? Is that why you ended up rooming together?"

"No, but she's not far away. Her family is from North Adams, and I think she's still there as well."

"I wish you had told me about her sooner," Detective

Barnes said. "Taylor's name is not among those we inter-viewed on Saturday, so she must have left the farm before we got a chance to talk to her. I'll look into this further. If you think of anyone else in the meantime, please let me know immediately. I don't care how improbable it might sound—I will be the judge of that. Please be careful, Leila."

"Thank you, Detective, I will." I clicked off.

Noah was busy moving the covered pans of maple sugar to a shelf in the corner of the sugar house. He looked at me expectantly. "Any new developments?"

I removed the apron and threw on my denim jacket. "Nothing."

His brow wrinkled. "Where are you going?"

"I'm in the mood for a bagel and thought I'd run over to Bagel Palace. What should I bring back for you?"

"Nothing." A muscle ticked in his jaw. "You don't even like bagels that much."

I couldn't look at him. "Well, I want one now."

Noah sighed in frustration. "Leila, I thought you were taking this seriously. Someone is trying to kill you. I don't want you going anywhere by yourself."

"Look, I promise to be careful. I need to ask Max about a baking mold that he owns, and it has to be done in person. If Heather doesn't have an appointment, I'm sure she'll come and meet me."

He cursed under his breath. "I've got someone coming for a tour in five minutes and really can't—"

"But I don't want you to drive me, I want to drive myself." I tried to make him understand. "Noah, I can't live my life like I'm in a box. The police don't have any concrete leads and aren't making much progress. You don't know how crazy this is making me. I feel like I'm suffocating."

Noah's features softened. "I do know, but—"

"Please." I silenced him with a kiss. "It's only for a few minutes."

"You are so stubborn." He shook his head. "Okay, on one condition."

"Which is?"

He fished a set of keys out of his back jeans pocket. "Make sure Heather can meet you there, and I want you to take my truck."

"That's two conditions," I teased.

Noah didn't laugh. "You need to drive something other than that purple Nissan you bought last spring."

"You don't like my choice of vehicles, Mr. Rivers?" I'd been forced to buy the car when mine had been totaled in an accident. I loved the color purple, and no one around here had a car like it.

"No, I don't. As far as I'm concerned, it only makes it easier for that nutcase to find you." He traced a finger over my lips before kissing them. "Do you have any plans for tonight?"

"What'd you have in mind?"

He nuzzled my neck, the day-old stubble from his face brushing against it. "I thought maybe you could come over."

Surprised, I stared up at him. "I don't know if that's a good idea. How—how will Emma feel?"

"Don't worry, she's fine."

He couldn't fool me. The doubt in his tone was evident.

"No, she's not. I can tell by the way you're acting. Has she said anything about me?"

Noah shook his head. "She's quieter than usual. I wish she would open up to me. She won't even tell my mother what's going on, and they talk about everything under the sun. It's just going to take some more time, I guess."

"Sure, that's understandable." A stab of regret shot through me. Emma was still upset, and now it sounded like she was unhappy with her father as well. "I never wanted to cause any kind of rift between you two."

"Hey, I'm not going to have you talking like that. This is only temporary." Noah stared at me thoughtfully, and then snapped his fingers. "Here's a thought. Maybe she'd welcome a visit from Toast. He's got to be her favorite male right about now."

"That's a great idea." The cat might help break down the barriers between us. I should have thought of it sooner.

He pulled me close and kissed me passionately. "Em has a dance lesson tonight. Tomorrow after work, let's stop over at your house to get Toast, pick up some takeout, and then head over to my place. How does that sound?"

"Wonderful." I dangled the keys from my hand. "Okay, I should be back within the hour."

His expression turned sober. "Please drive carefully."

"Always." I thought about telling my mother that I was leaving but chickened out. Like Noah, she would not be happy. I went directly from the sugar house to the parking area and unlocked Noah's truck. Seven minutes later, I pulled into the small parking lot that adjoined Bagel Palace.

A young woman with light brown hair cut in a chin-length bob smiled at me as she placed a tray of cinnamon raisin bagels in the display case. "Hi, can I help you?"

"Is Max here?"

The woman closed the case. "He's in the back room. Was he expecting you?"

I shook my head. "Would you please tell him that Leila Khoury is here? I'd like to talk to him if he has a couple of minutes."

"No problem." She disappeared behind the swinging doors. Less than a minute later, she returned with Max behind her. He looked surprised but pleased to see me. "Hey, Leila. How's it going?"

"Fine, Max. Do you have a minute to talk?"

Max's bushy gray eyebrows rose slightly, as if he'd only now realized this was more than an average bagel run. "Sure." He turned to his coworker. "Beth, can you take that tray of pumpernickel out of the oven for me in two minutes?"

"Of course, Uncle Max." Beth smiled at me, and then disappeared behind the swinging doors.

Max folded his arms across his broad chest. "How's Jenna working out for you and your mom?"

"She's—fine. My mother's very fond of her."

He watched me closely. "Are *you* fond of her?"

My body stiffened. "Why do you ask that?"

A huge grin spread across his face. "No reason. Jenna likes to lap up the attention at times. I think it's because she doesn't have many friends."

That seemed a strange thing for him to say. "Have you met her boyfriend?"

Max looked surprised. "I didn't know she had one. Has he been out to the farm?"

"Not yet." I cringed slightly, thinking about how my mother would probably fawn over him as well. *Oh, so what. Stop acting like a jealous schoolgirl, Leila.* Mom adored the fact that Jenna liked to bake and was a fast learner. It had always been a bone of contention between us that I didn't like any of the same things she did. We'd never had much in common.

"Jenna's working out fine, but I didn't come here to talk about her." I showed him the picture of the pumpkin pie with the leaf on my phone. "Last March, when we had our Maple Syrup Open House Weekend, you made bagels in the shape of maple leaves. Did you use a mold for those?"

"Sure did." Max examined the photo. "It looks like the same size as the one on this pie."

"Do you still have it?"

"Of course." Max opened one of the drawers under his cash register and fished around inside it for a few seconds. He held up the mold for me to see. "Here you go."

I looked at the mold, and then back at the photo. They did appear to be the same. "Is there a supply store in town that sells these?"

Max shook his head. "Not around here. But I didn't buy it from a store."

"Where did you get it from?"

"One of those traveling salespeople," Max explained. "You know the kind I mean. They come in here like once a month, trying to get you to buy new equipment—anything from stainless-steel pans to bagel slicers. But hey, I'll try anything once. And my sales went up quite a bit that weekend. I'm going to use it again next year."

"Do you happen to remember the salesperson's name or the company they represent?" I asked. "Maybe it will help me to find out who made the pie." It was a longshot, but I had to try.

"Hmm." Max frowned. "I can't remember her name, but she did bring me a catalogue." He opened another drawer and sifted through a bunch of papers. "I think I still have it—Aha! Yep, here it is. Her name's on the back cover."

I took the catalogue from his hands and examined it.

Max kept on talking. "I've been meaning to place another order. There's a lot of good stuff in here. But you know how it is when the holiday season begins to creep up on you. There's never enough time for anything."

I was no longer listening to what he said. Underneath Gismo's Restaurant and Kitchen Supplies was printed the name of the salesperson who had visited Max.

*Taylor Hudson.*

# CHAPTER SEVENTEEN

**"LEILA, ARE YOU OKAY?" MAX** asked. "You look kind of pale."

"Um, no, I'm fine." There was no way I could share with him that Taylor might be a killer. For one thing, I didn't have any proof. And if by some chance Taylor was guilty and the accusation found its way back to her, she would hightail it out of Vermont as soon as possible. "How often does Taylor stop by to see you?"

He paused to consider. "Oh, every couple of months, I guess. Why do you ask?"

"This is a funny coincidence, but I went to school with Taylor," I explained.

"No kidding?"

"No kidding. I've been trying to catch up with her for a long time, but we keep missing each other," I lied.

Max gestured at the sales booklet. "Her number's underneath her name. Why don't you give her a call?"

"But it would be so much more fun if I could surprise her." My heart began to thump wildly against the wall of my chest. "Is there any chance you could call and see if she has time to stop by now? I'd really appreciate it."

Max shifted from one foot to the other. "Well, sure. I guess I could do that. But she may not be around. The only way Taylor would come out here this minute is if she's in the area and knows for sure that I'm going to place an order. And I can't think of anything I need right now."

"Don't worry about that," I assured him. "I'd be glad to order a few things from her." I didn't care if it cost me a hundred dollars. The expense would be well worth it to get Taylor here.

Max rubbed his hands together. "Okay. I guess there's no time like the present." He drew his cell out of his apron pocket and punched in a series of numbers. "Taylor? Yeah, hi. It's Max over at Bagel Palace in Sugar Ridge." There was a brief pause. "Fine, thanks, and you?" Another pause. "Hey, is there any chance you could come out here with those new bagel trays you were telling me about?"

Taylor's garbled voice could be heard on the other end. "That would be great," Max replied. "Okay, see you in a half an hour."

I had to refrain from clapping my hands. "She's coming over now?"

He nodded. "You were lucky. Taylor's working remote today and said she'll be here in a half an hour."

"Thanks so much for doing this," I said. "I don't want to keep holding you up, so I'll go back out to my truck and make a couple of calls until she arrives."

"Yeah, sure. Whatever works." Max nodded and disappeared into the back room.

I wasted no time leaving the shop and heading back to Noah's truck. After locking the doors, I tried to phone Heather, but the call went straight to her voicemail. She must be with a client. I quickly sent a text. *Call me as soon as you can.* At the last second, I added, *I'm okay.* After I hit *Send*, I hunched down in the seat, out of anyone's view. It seemed ridiculous, but I had promised Noah to be careful.

For several minutes I sat there and wondered if Taylor could be capable of murder. I had to admit she did fit the mold to perfection. *Ugh. Mold.* Time to stop with the puns.

Taylor had sold a maple leaf mold to Max that he used for his bagels—the same type that was used on the cyanide-loaded pumpkin pie. She liked baking competitions and had mentioned the Pillsbury Bake-Off. Plus, Taylor hated my guts. Yes, she definitely had more of a motive than either Cameron or Eric.

My phone buzzed, startling me out of my thoughts. "Hello."

"What's wrong?" Heather asked. "You sound upset."

I blew out a shaky breath. "I'm sitting in the parking lot of Bagel Palace."

"*Alone?*" Heather made it sound like a dirty word.

"Yes, alone. There's no harm in that, right? I'm not breaking any laws."

"Please be careful," she murmured.

"I had to go for a drive to try and clear my head," I explained. "And I wanted to ask Max about the mold. Don't worry. I've got Noah's truck, and no one followed me."

"How can you be so sure?" Heather wanted to know.

I loved Heather dearly, but her questions were starting to grate on my nerves. "I promise you that I'm fine. That's not what's freaking me out." I went on to relay what Max had said about Taylor.

"Are you insane?" Heather burst out. "You're a sitting duck for that psycho. Why would you even want to see her?"

"Calm down," I said.

Heather breathed into the phone like an obscene phone caller. "Oh my God. See? I was right. She never got over how you turned her in, just like Cameron never got over it."

"Heather," I began.

She was on a roll now. "Stay right where you are. I'm coming over now. My other appointment cancelled, so I have plenty of time."

"You don't have to." Secretly, I was relieved that she had offered.

Heather didn't even bother to answer as she continued with her tirade. "Taylor could have died if you hadn't told on her. But, hey, that's the thanks you get, right? Do someone a favor and they try to shoot you in the back to reciprocate."

The visual image made me cringe. Slowly, I lifted my head in the seat to look around. I didn't see anyone but slouched back down.

"Do you think she could have been the one to poison the pie?" Heather asked.

"It's possible. Taylor was quite the baker, even back in college. Plus, she had access to the mold since she sells them.

But it doesn't make any sense. Why would she wait so long to get back at me? The same goes for Cameron."

Heather was silent for a minute. "Okay, let's think about this timewise. She was in recovery for a while, right?"

"Yes, from what I know, about two years." I double-checked the door locks. "Then she went off to culinary school in California for a couple of more years."

Heather's voice escalated with excitement. "Okay, now we're getting somewhere. And when she finished school, she came back home to Vermont, right? Where were you at the time?"

I paused for a moment to reflect. "I would have left for Florida around then. Yeah, that's right, because I ran into her mother—who liked me, thank goodness—a few weeks before I left. She told me Taylor was coming back to Vermont the next month."

"Wait a second. This is very important. Did you tell her mother you were moving to Florida back then?" Heather asked.

All those Nancy Drew books Heather had read as a child were starting to pay off for her. I resisted a snort. "No, I didn't mention it. I was still a little preoccupied with the fact that my fiancé had left me at the altar, and my mother and I weren't speaking to each other."

"Good. I mean, it's good you didn't tell her," Heather added. "That must be it then."

"What are you talking about?"

"Don't you see?" Heather asked. "Taylor decided to wait until you returned to Vermont. She must have been biding her time all these years. I'll bet she figured out that if she waited this long, no one would ever suspect her. It's her. I *know* it's her. The woman isn't playing with a full deck. She should have been grateful to you for saving her life, not the opposite."

Oh, brother. The urge to roll my eyes was great, but I managed to stop myself in time. Heather's conclusion was so far-fetched that even Nancy herself would have laughed out loud. "Well, either way, I need to talk to Taylor. This has gone on for way too long."

"You can't talk to her alone," Heather objected.

"She's on her way to Bagel Palace as we speak."

Heather let out a loud breath on the other end of the line that sounded like she'd been holding it forever. "Okay, I don't care if she shows up before I do. Promise me that you will *not* go inside to confront Taylor until I get there."

"She's not going to pull a gun on me in front of Max," I protested.

"All right, let's say Taylor isn't the one trying to kill you," Heather said. "What if there's someone else watching your every move and waiting for their opportunity to finish you off?"

Uneasiness settled over me, and I rose up in the seat again to take another look around. There was a duplex across the street from Max's store. For all I knew, Heather was right, and the pumpkin pie lunatic who had tried to asphyxiate me might be stationed at one of the windows with a shotgun. "All right, I promise."

"I'll be there in less than ten minutes." Heather clicked off.

Two minutes later, I heard the sound of a car approaching. Hopeful, I rose up in the seat and peered out. A candy-apple red sports car was parked a couple of spaces away from me. The driver had long, blond hair and wore sunglasses. I ducked back down before she saw me and glanced at my watch. Taylor must have driven here at record speed to arrive so quickly.

I waited a few seconds and stole another look in her direction. The sports car appeared to be a new model. Life as a saleswoman of kitchen products must be very good. Taylor was headed towards the front entrance, dressed in a full-length brown leather coat with matching boots.

Heather had made me promise to stay in the truck until she arrived, but Max would be wondering why I hadn't come back inside yet. Hopefully he wouldn't mention me to Taylor. If he did, the jig was up.

Five minutes later, I was getting ready to climb the sides of the truck when Heather's SUV pulled into the lot. She hurried over and stood in front of me as we made our way to the entrance. "Sorry. I hit some construction at the last minute."

"You don't have to act as my bodyguard," I said.

Heather shielded her eyes from the bright sun. "Someone has to watch out for you. God knows where that psycho is lurking. Come on. Let's get inside."

She held the door open for me to enter first. Beth was behind the counter, waiting on a customer, and Max was seated at a table in the far corner, thumbing through a catalogue. Taylor sat across from him, writing something on an order pad. She didn't even glance in our direction.

"You can't go wrong with those bagel trays," she told Max. "They're an excellent choice."

"Okay," Max sighed. "I'll take one."

"Shall I put you down for three of them?" Taylor asked eagerly. "We have a fabulous sale going on this month—buy two and get one free. And you'll get a bagel slicer at half price."

"Sure, why not. I've already got one, but the blade's getting dull." Max himself appeared bored by the subject. He happened to look up at that moment and noticed me. Taylor turned to see what had caught his attention. I watched the color drain from her face as our eyes met. She placed the order form back in the briefcase and stood, her chair scaping loudly against the tiled floor. "You can pay me on delivery. I need to get going."

I took a step forward. "Taylor, I'd like to talk to you for a minute."

Her nostrils flared. "Well, I sure don't want to talk to you. I was done talking to you nine years ago. Now, if you'll please excuse me."

Max jabbed his thumb in the direction of the kitchen. "Um, I'll be in the back room, if anyone needs me." He quickly went behind the counter and said something to Beth, who had finished waiting on her customer. She wasted no time and followed him through the swinging doors.

"They didn't have to leave." Taylor tossed her head. "Because I have nothing to say to you."

"I think there's a lot left to say." I moved in front of the door, blocking her escape, and hoped that a customer wouldn't choose to enter at that moment. "You've avoided me for nine years, but then you suddenly show up at my farm for a pie-baking contest you didn't even enter."

"So what?" Taylor asked. "It's a free country."

I tried another tactic. "All I want to know is why you were really there."

Taylor's eyes widened in disbelief. "Do you honestly think I came there to call a truce? Well, think again. You're the reason I had to leave school. I had to start my life all over again, thanks to you."

Heather folded her arms across her chest. "You should thank your lucky stars that Leila was there to help. You might have died!"

"Oh, please." Taylor's eyes were cold and frigid as they stared into mine. "I didn't have a problem. I knew exactly what I was doing. But thanks to you, I got expelled, and my parents made me go to rehab. They didn't think I was ready to go back to college after that, so I worked in the family grocery store and had to live at home with them. Finally, I was allowed to go away to culinary school. You pretty much ruined my life."

Even though I suspected she felt this way, it was disturbing to hear it. I didn't expect to be thanked for what I'd done all those years ago, but I certainly hadn't expected her to still be carrying so much resentment towards me.

"I'm sorry you feel that way." My voice started to quiver. "We had some good times together. I thought maybe—"

"You thought what? That we could go back to being friends? Maybe get together and chat about college days over a drink? Or go on a shopping spree?" The bitterness in Taylor's tone spewed out like venom. "Please. All I want is to forget that I ever knew you." She reached out a hand and shoved me out of her way. I lost my balance and fell towards a table.

"Hey!" Heather gasped. "Don't you dare touch her!"

Taylor ignored Heather's protest and turned her hateful glare back on me. "It's really too bad you didn't eat any of that pie the other day. It would have been the best thing that ever happened to me."

Without another word, she stomped out of the shop.

"Oh my God." Heather helped me to my feet. "Are you hurt?"

My entire body went numb. "No, I'm all right."

"Did you hear what Taylor said? She practically admitted to being the one who killed Margaret!"

I struggled to pull myself together. "No, that's not what she said. Taylor said she wished that I had died. She didn't say she poisoned me."

"Well, it sounded like the same thing to me," Heather remarked.

I glanced out the door in time to see Taylor's sports car flash by. She zoomed down the street at a speed way too high for the town's thirty mile per hour zone. Thankfully, no one besides Heather had witnessed our altercation, unless Max and Beth had been peeking out the kitchen door. "I guess we're done here."

Heather held the door open and walked me back to Noah's truck. She seemed more relaxed now than when we'd first entered the shop. I chalked it up to the fact that she suspected my killer had driven away a few seconds ago.

"Where are you going?" Heather's tone was full of suspicion as I got into the truck. "Please tell me you're going straight back to the farm."

"Yes, that's exactly where I'm going, Mom." I tried to make light of the situation, even though my throat had become tight with tears. It was horrible to realize someone hated you so much that they wished you were dead. "If we don't start getting customers soon, we'll have to close down—at least on Saturdays." *And maybe the rest of the week as well.*

She reached through the open side window and squeezed my hand. "Don't worry. Things will get better. Do you want to call Detective Barnes and tell him about Taylor or should I?"

"No, I'll call him when I get back to the farm. But we still don't know for sure she's the one—"

Heather held up a hand. "Oh, it's her. I'd bet my life on it."

My phone buzzed at that moment. *Noah.* "Great. Noah's checking in to make sure I'm okay. I'll call you later."

"You'd better. And please be careful." She jogged back to her SUV and then blew me a kiss as she drove out of the parking lot. Heather had already made up her mind about the culprit. I only wished that I could be so sure.

"I wanted to see if you were all right," Noah said. "I was getting worried."

"Sorry. Everything's great," I lied.

Silence stretched between us for several seconds. "What's going on?" he asked.

I decided to come clean. "I ran into a blast from my past at Bagel Palace. Don't worry, Heather was with me, and I'm on my way back to the farm now." My hands were still shaking from the encounter. I went to put my sunglasses on, and they slipped out of my grasp and fell to the floor of the truck. "Hang on a second."

"Leila? Where'd you go?"

"No, I'm still here. I dropped my sunglasses." As I reached down under the glove compartment to grab the glasses off the floor, a loud popping noise startled me. For a minute, I thought a car had backfired. "Okay, all set." I stared up at the windshield and stifled a gasp.

"What's wrong?" Noah asked worriedly.

Noah's windshield had multiple cracks in it. At first, I had no idea what might have caused it, then spotted a small, round hole in the middle of the glass. A bullet hole, to be more specific.

The blood roared in my ears as the words of the recent email played over and over in my head.

*Better hurry, before it's too late for you.*

# CHAPTER EIGHTEEN

**NOAH CONTINUED TO PACE BACK** and forth across the wooden floor of the café. "Okay, that settles it. Please, Leila. No more going any place by yourself until this person is caught. Promise me."

"I promise." I took a long sip of the tea my mother had brought me. It had a strong, bitter flavor, and I suspected that she'd added a bit of brandy. I wasn't a big fan of alcohol, but I needed something to calm my nerves.

Detective Barnes nodded in agreement. "I have to say that I agree with Noah. This was too close of a call."

"I never should have left you by yourself." Heather's face was filled with misery. "This is all my fault."

My mother placed a plate of maple shortbread cookies on the table in front of us. "Stop saying that, dear. It's not your fault."

"It isn't anyone's fault. I thought I'd be safe in Noah's truck." And I had never expected someone to shoot at me.

Noah gripped the back of my chair. "Someone wants you dead at any cost. I hate this. I hate that you're in danger. All I want to do is keep you safe."

I knew Noah had to vent his feelings, so I refrained from comment. It was still hard to believe that someone was out there, watching my every waking move. "I can't live like this."

At first, I didn't realize that I'd said the words out loud, until everyone stared at me.

"Noah's right." Heather reached for her second cookie. She always ate more when she was nervous. "This person has to be stopped. Are there any leads, Detective?"

Detective Barnes accepted a container of to-go coffee from my mother and tucked his iPad under his arm. "I'm afraid we don't have much to go on right now, other than what Leila has told us, and she's experienced firsthand. Do you think Taylor could be behind this?"

"Without question," Heather insisted. "Detective, she was absolutely horrible to Leila. She shoved her into a table and then said she wished Leila had been the one to eat the pumpkin pie!"

My mother placed a hand over her chest. "How could she say such a thing? What kind of monster is this woman?"

"She would have run us down with that sports car of hers if she had the chance," Heather added.

An important detail nagged at my brain, but the constant chatter made it difficult for me to think straight. "Wait a minute. Taylor has a newer model sports car."

"What about it?" Heather asked.

I turned to Detective Barnes. "Emma said that she heard

a strange sound coming from the parking lot the day of the contest."

He nodded. "We thought it might be a car backfiring."

I took another sip of my tea. "So, that makes me think Taylor wasn't the one to drop off the pie. Older cars backfire, not brand-new ones."

Noah placed his hands on his hips. "That's unlikely, but it can still happen these days. Most modern fuel-injected cars don't backfire because of the way their onboard system is designed."

Heather raised an eyebrow. "Whatever that means. Car talk is foreign to me."

"You didn't see where the shot came from?" Noah asked. "Could another car have pulled up next to yours?"

"I don't think so, but I was on the phone talking to you and didn't pay much attention."

"We determined that the shot came from a further distance," Detective Barnes said. "At least a ten-foot range."

"This isn't Leila's fault," Heather broke in quickly. "I thought for sure Taylor was the one who tried to kill her. Leila probably thought she was safe after that psycho woman left."

She was right about that. "It doesn't matter. I shouldn't have assumed everything was okay. I have only myself to blame."

"Did anyone see what happened?" Noah asked. "Someone who passed by or maybe a customer going into the bagel shop?"

Detective Barnes shook his head. "So far, we haven't been

able to locate anyone. But we're hopeful a witness will still come forward." He smiled at my mother. "Thanks for the coffee, Selma. Leila, if you think of anything else, don't hesitate to contact me."

Noah walked with him to the main entrance while my mother sat down next to me and Heather. Still stressed, Heather popped another cookie into her mouth.

"You need to let the police handle this," Heather said. "I know you're worried about the farm, but your life is more important."

"Heather is right," my mother said. "Who else besides Taylor could have killed Margaret?"

"Cameron," Heather said. "And Eric is a person of interest as well."

My mother shook her head. "I still refuse to believe it. Do the police honestly think Eric could have killed his own mother?"

"Not on purpose, Mom. Remember, I was the intended victim." The fact that Margaret had died instead of me might have enraged him even more. "But I would like to talk to Abigail again."

"It's not safe. Don't even think about going to see her," Heather warned.

She didn't have to worry. I wasn't that foolish. I decided not to mention my plan to call Abigail later.

Noah reappeared. "I need to check on the maple sugar," he said. "I'll package it up and then bring it over to the gift shop."

"Do you want any help?" I asked.

He shook his head. "No, stay here with your mother. I won't be long, and when we close up, I'll drive you home."

"What about your truck? Will you be able to drive with the windshield like that?" I asked.

"It'll be fine," Noah assured me. "I've already called my insurance agent. A glass company is coming out first thing in the morning to replace the windshield."

This was a relief. I bit into my lower lip. "I'm so sorry this happened."

"Hey." Noah reached out and lifted my chin with his finger. "I couldn't care less about the truck. When I think about how you might have been—"

He stopped in mid-sentence, but we all knew what he had been about to say. An awkward silence filled the room as Heather and my mother discreetly moved behind the counter.

Noah placed his arms around my waist and kissed me. "I don't know what I'd do if something happened to you," he whispered.

"Nothing's going to happen to me," I insisted.

Noah released me and smiled reassuringly. "I'll be back soon."

After he had left the café, Heather came back over, munching on another cookie. She gave me a playful nudge in the side. "I've never seen him kiss you before."

"That's because he likes to keep those type of things private."

My mother appeared at the counter. "That's how it should be. I've never been one for public displays of affection myself. Your father and I always believed that they belonged behind closed doors."

This wasn't news to me. My parents had been brought up in a certain way in Lebanon. "Times have changed, Mom."

She stuck her nose out in the air. "Perhaps, but good manners never go out of style. I hope that you two are careful around Emma as well."

"Of course we are." The mention of the little girl reminded me there was another subject I wanted to talk to my mother about. I glanced around the cafe. "Where's Jenna?"

My mother folded a dish towel in half and set it on the counter. "There hasn't been much for her to do in here today. She's been in the gift shop all afternoon, cleaning the shelves."

Heather finished her cookie and smacked her lips. "Delicious as always, Mrs. K. I think I'll take one with me for the ride home."

"You don't have to leave yet, dear," my mother told her.

Heather gave me a hug and kissed my mother on the cheek. "Thanks, but I get the feeling there's something Leila wants to talk to you about in private."

"What are you, psychic?" I teased.

"Absolutely." She gave me a wink. "Besides, Tyler and I are going out to dinner tonight. This is the only evening he's had off all week, so I'm really looking forward to it. But if you need anything—anything at all—call me, okay? And please don't go anywhere by yourself. I'm worried enough already."

"That makes two of us," my mother agreed.

Although the situation was dire, it comforted me to know there were so many people who cared about my welfare. At times like this, I'd learned to count my blessings. It was awful to feel confined, but I had no choice. My attacker wouldn't be happy until I was six feet under.

After Heather had left, my mother brought two mugs over to the table and sat down next to me. I picked up a mug and cupped my hands around it for warmth. The delightful scent of maple and pumpkin spice wafted through the air. I gave in to temptation and took a small sip. The drink was both spicy and sweet, and I took time to savor the liquid on my tongue. "Wow, this is delicious. What is it?"

"A spiced pumpkin maple latte," my mother asked. "It's a mixture of pumpkin butter, vanilla, and coconut milk that I added to coffee. Then I topped it off with maple cream."

"Maple cream—like the pie that was entered in our contest?" I asked.

She wiggled her hand back and forth. "Sort of. Not as many ingredients, though. I used a mixture of whipping cream and maple syrup."

I took another sip. The drink was pure heaven in a cup. "This is exactly what I needed to calm my nerves. It's even better than the brandy. Thank you."

My mother twisted her hands in her lap. "Margaret's funeral was early this morning. It doesn't seem right that I wasn't there. I've been friends with her for so long."

The sad look in her eyes tugged at my heart. "You already paid your respects at the wake, Mom."

"That doesn't matter," she insisted. "I should have been at the funeral too."

"There's no law saying that you couldn't have gone."

Tears welled in her eyes. My mother never cried, and this only made me feel worse. "No, it would have been impossible. Look what Eric did to you and Heather at the wake. He might have behaved worse and I didn't want to make a mockery out of Margaret's death. If it is true that Eric's the one who's been trying to kill you—" She stopped to catch her breath. "I think it was best to stay away."

We both sipped our drinks in silence for a couple of minutes. "Have you talked to Abigail?" I asked.

She shook her head. "I've left a couple of messages, but she hasn't returned my calls."

"Let me try her later," I offered.

Mom raised an eyebrow. "As long as you don't go over there in person. You can't afford to trust anyone, dear."

"I realize that." There was more that I wanted to ask Abigail. Did she know Eric's whereabouts the day of his mother's death? How could I ask her tactfully? Did she have any idea that Eric might have killed his own mother?

"There's something else bothering you." Mom set her mug down on the table. "What is it?"

I shifted in my seat. "I was wondering how you really felt about me moving in with Noah."

She shrugged. "I would prefer that the two of you were married first, but in this day and age, no one seems to think twice anymore about a couple living together. You're an adult, Leila. It's your decision to make, not mine."

"Who are you and what have you done with my mother?" I asked.

She laughed out loud.

"Well, there's a good chance it might not happen for a while," I admitted. "I can't move in if Emma is still uncomfortable with the situation."

Mom reached over and patted my hand. "I think it's wonderful that you're putting her first, especially after all that poor little girl has been through." Her eyes began to mist over again. "It's the right thing to do, Leila. Don't rush her. This is traumatic for Emma, but she adores you and you'll be a wonderful stepmother to her."

"Thanks, Mom. That means a lot to me."

She waited for me to continue. "What else? Come on now. I know you have something else on your mind."

I blew out a long breath. For several months, I had been slowly working up the courage to ask my mother a personal question—ever since I realized that Noah and I were destined to be together. It was obvious she adored Emma, but I still had to know the truth. I swallowed hard. "Mom, it's no secret how much you've always wanted grandchildren. I realize that I can't give you any, but I still need to know if—"

She broke in, looking shocked. "Leila, I'm surprised that you would even ask me such a thing. I hope you know that I would love Emma as if she were my own biological grandchild."

"Thank you," I said gratefully. "I just needed to hear you say it."

Mom brought a tissue to her eyes. "I understand why you had to ask. It's because you believe I've always favored Simon over you."

She had never come right out and said this to me before. "Mom, it's okay. That doesn't matter anymore."

"Let me finish," Mom said firmly. "Growing up in Lebanon, there was a lot of pressure placed on a married woman to bear a son who could carry on the family name. Oh, I realize this isn't exclusive to our culture, so it's no excuse. You never knew your father's parents, but believe me, they weren't the friendliest sort of people."

"Dad told me," I said with a chuckle.

My mother stared down at the table. "When your father told them that he planned to marry me, they were very upset."

"Why?" This struck me as odd. How could they not see that my mother would be the perfect wife for him?

Mom closed her eyes and sighed. "Because I am not of full Lebanese descent."

Her words hit me like a slap to the face. "You never told me this. But it doesn't make sense. You had an arranged marriage."

My mother stirred her drink. "It was *supposed* to be an arranged marriage. Once my in-laws to be found out that my father was not one hundred percent Lebanese, they no longer wanted your father to marry me. Your maternal grandfather was only part Lebanese. He was also of Indian descent. Even though my mother was one hundred percent Lebanese, your grandparents always looked down their nose at me."

"Does Simon know?" I asked in disbelief.

She shook her head. "I never told him. And believe me, I never planned to tell you either, but after everything I put you through with Mark, and practically ordering you to marry a man of our culture—"

My mother broke off and stared out the window. "I was ashamed of how I behaved, so I figured I owed you the truth. It's taken me a long time to work up the courage and tell you."

I had a sudden urge to pinch myself to see if I was dreaming. "How did Dad react to all of this?"

Mom's face broke out into a radiant smile. "Your father told his parents off. And let me tell you, my dear daughter, that was something one did not do back then. It was a pure sign of disrespect. Your father announced that he was marrying me, and he didn't care about my background or what they thought. In return, your paternal grandfather told your father that he was cutting him off for good and to not ask for anything after we wed. Your father and I married in a private ceremony and left Lebanon the next day for our honeymoon to America." She paused. "Your grandparents didn't know we never planned to return."

I could barely take it all in. "They must have been devastated."

She nodded. "They adored your father, so I imagine it was very difficult for them. When he stood up to them, I knew I had found my soul mate. The same way that you know Noah is yours."

I squeezed her hand, unable to speak.

"Getting back to our talk about children," Mom continued. "There was still the pressure of having a male child, and I knew how badly your father wanted a son. Of course, when you were born, he fell head over heels in love with you." She smiled, as if remembering. "He thought that you were the greatest thing since maple syrup."

This made me laugh. "But you were disappointed that I wasn't a boy."

She glanced at me with a sheepish expression. "That doesn't mean I didn't care about you, Leila. Perhaps I am not good at showing it, but I have always loved you very much."

A lump formed in my throat. "I know."

My mother went on. "I'm not trying to make excuses, but when you were born, I felt as if I had disappointed your father, even though it was plain to see how much he loved you. Then, two years later when Simon was born, I was so happy that I'd done what was expected of me, and I showered him with more attention. It wasn't fair to you, and I'm sorry."

Her words left me speechless. There was so much that I had never known about my parent's love story, and the first time I could remember ever having such an intense heart-to-heart with my mother.

In the days that had followed my broken engagement with Mark, I'd longed to talk to my mother about our breakup, but knew it was impossible. She'd been so cold and angry and insistent that it was my fault. If I had known what she had gone through many years ago, it would have brought us closer much sooner.

"That's okay, Mom. It truly doesn't matter anymore." I threw my arms around her, and we embraced for several seconds. When she released me, I was struck by a lone tear that had fallen onto the table's surface, glistening in the light from above. I didn't know if it belonged to my mother or me, but that wasn't important. My only regret was that we had wasted so much time to get to this point in our lives.

"I love you, Mom." It was the first time I ever recalled saying the words out loud to her.

She smiled at me through her tears. It was as if she'd read my mind. "I know that, dear. But it's always nice to hear."

# CHAPTER NINETEEN

**MY MOTHER AND I WERE** still talking quietly in the café when Noah returned. The look on his face caused a nervous tremor to run through me. "What's wrong?" I asked.

"One of our main vendors has permanently cancelled their weekly syrup order." Noah's voice was hollow. "They said they'll be in touch if they want more."

*If.* That didn't sound very promising to me.

My mother pushed back her chair from the table and gathered up our mugs. She said nothing and quickly went behind the counter. I knew she was thinking of my father. Everything he had worked so hard for his entire life was starting to disintegrate before our eyes.

"This is crazy," I burst out. "What's the matter with these people? Do they actually think we'd poison their syrup?"

Noah rubbed a hand over his face. "Hard to say. Folks believe what they want to believe. I'm betting you that

Sappy Endings is the most popular topic in Sugar Ridge right now."

"And you would be correct."

I whirled around at the familiar voice. Simon was standing in the doorway of the café. He came over and wrapped his arms around me. "Mom called earlier to tell me what happened. Are you okay?"

"Yes, I'm fine, thanks. You didn't have to come out."

"Are you kidding?" he asked in surprise. "I've been worried about my big sis. Besides, I wanted to let you know I've been trying to keep the farm's name out of the newspaper."

"You're their head reporter," I said. "Doesn't that count for anything?"

He snorted. "Not really. It means that I'm one step above the rest of the staff, which in my field means nothing. I think it's time for me to find another job. The Bennington Journal has been after me for a while. I need a change of pace."

My mother stared at him with a stricken expression. "But you'd have to relocate."

Simon and I exchanged a smile. Despite the earlier conversation with my mother, I knew that Simon would always continue to be her favorite. Whatever feelings of jealousy and insecurity I might have experienced while growing up had vanished. I knew my mother loved me, and that was all that mattered.

"I don't want you to move away," she blurted out.

"Relax, Mom." Simon patted her cheek. "It's not like Bennington's on the other side of the country. It's less than an hour from here. I'll still come by every weekend—as long as you promise to make me *Emu* every couple of weeks," he teased.

*Emu* was a favorite dish of mine and Simon's. The hearty soup was prepared with kofta meatballs, vermicelli, and rice, cooked in a rich tomato sauce. It was delicious anytime of the year, but even more so during cooler weather.

Mom forced a smile to her lips. "Are you trying to bribe your mother?"

He laughed, and then his expression turned serious. "I stopped by to see if you had gone to Margaret's funeral today."

My mother's smile faded, and she lowered her eyes to the floor. "I didn't think it was a good idea, especially after the way Eric treated all of us at the wake."

Simon listened with interest as my mother explained what happened. "Wow. I had no idea. What a jerk."

"He's grieving," my mother said as way of explanation.

"I don't know." Simon accepted a latte from my mother. "He never seemed to like his mother very much."

My mother gasped. "Simon Victor Khoury, that is a terrible thing to say!"

He took a long sip of his drink. "Sorry, Mom, but it's the truth. I remember this one time when I was standing near him after the church sermon was over. We were both waiting for you and Margaret to get done talking with the priest, and I said something like, 'Parents are so embarrassing.' I was only a teenager, so don't take it personally, Mom."

My mother rolled her eyes at the ceiling but said nothing.

Simon continued. "Then Eric went on to say something

like, 'My mother is the worst. Why couldn't she have died instead of my father?'"

We were all stunned into silence. My mother sat down heavily in a chair. "You never told me this before."

"I didn't want to upset you," Simon admitted. "Then, for a long time, I forgot about it. But after her death, I started thinking about it—a lot."

"It sounds like he had a lot of resentment built-up towards his mother," I said. "Plus, he was in town the day that she died. What if he did have something to do with her death?"

My mother's eyebrows rose. "Are you saying that maybe you weren't the intended target after all?"

"No, I think with the other attempts on my life, it's pretty clear someone wants me dead. Eric didn't like me or his mother very much, so who knows what he could have been thinking?"

"Death changes people," Simon added. "He was never the same after his father died."

We were all quiet, thinking of my father. Our lives had changed drastically after his murder. At least his death had brought us all closer. It had done the opposite for the Middletons.

"There's no way Eric could have baked a pie," Mom huffed. "Margaret always said he was totally helpless in the kitchen. Eric might be a good lawyer, but he doesn't have any culinary skills. Abigail loved baking with her mother, but that man never lifted a finger around the house to help with anything."

"That's not important," I said. "He could have bought

the pie from a bakery or had a friend make it and then put the cyanide inside."

"Good point," Simon agreed.

"Oh, Lord." My mother gasped out loud. "I remember where I saw that maple leaf mold. Margaret used to have one."

Simon and I exchanged a glance. "Does she still have it?" I asked.

Mom rubbed her arms, as if the subject chilled her. "I don't know. I'm trying to remember when I saw it at her house. It had to be a few years ago, when I helped her put new shelf paper in her kitchen cabinets."

"It's worth telling Detective Barnes about. I'm going to call him tonight." I wondered if the police could search the Middleton home. If they didn't find the mold after sifting through all the junk Margaret had, what would it mean? That the mold had been disposed of long ago? Or was it in Eric's possession?

My mother exhaled sharply. "I don't want to talk about this anymore. It's all too upsetting. Leila, it's closing time. I want to get home and put dinner on the table. Are you coming with me?"

"No, thanks, Mom. Noah's going to bring me home."

My mother nodded and turned her attention back to Simon. "You're coming for dinner, right?" The question was merely a formality. Simon knew he was expected at the house and that our mother would never take no for an answer.

Simon kissed her on the cheek. "Sounds great, Mom. Sure, I'll follow you over."

"What about you, Noah?" my mother asked. "Can you join us for dinner?"

He shook his head with regret. "Thanks, Selma. I wish I could, but my babysitter's not available tonight, and I need to take Emma to dance class."

"Oh, that's too bad," Mom said. "Leila, do you want to go with me, then?"

Had she not hear what I had said? My mother was a smart woman, but at times, her actions still surprised me. Didn't she realize Noah and I never had any alone time anymore, which was why he drove me back and forth to work? "No, thanks, Mom. I'll see you back at the house."

A flicker of understanding crossed her face and she nodded. "Oh, of course. Okay, see you there."

---

I slept badly and tossed and turned so much that even Toast became annoyed with me. Sometime during the night, he abandoned his spot at the bottom of my bed and went in search of a place where he would not be disturbed. He returned promptly at 5:30 a.m. and sat on my chest until I pushed him off. Toast wanted his breakfast and would not be ignored. I finally gave up and went downstairs to feed him while he meowed plaintively behind me.

After a shower, I dressed quickly and went into the kitchen. My mother had *Ahweh* ready, which was a relief, because I could barely keep my eyes open. She had retired upstairs to shower and dress for the day. I was pouring myself a cup when the screen of my phone lit up on the table. Heather.

*Are you awake? If so, call me. I need to talk to you about something.*

Heather never texted me this early in the morning. She liked to sleep in as late as possible and usually scheduled her clients after ten o'clock. Something was definitely wrong because no one could get her up at this hour.

The phone rang twice before she picked up. "Hey. How's everything?"

"Well, I'm still here," I joked. "So, I guess it's a good day so far."

"That's not funny."

I sipped my coffee. "Why are you texting me at this hour? This is way too early for you."

She hesitated before answering. "If you must know, I couldn't sleep last night."

*Join the club.* "Didn't you and Tyler have a good time?"

"We had a wonderful time," Heather said. "After dinner, we went to the movies. It's been ages since we had a date night. Sometimes it feels like Tyler's been working evenings forever."

"Cheer up. That will change soon."

"I know." Heather lapsed into silence for so long that I started to wonder if she had hung up. Finally, she spoke again. "There's something I need to tell you."

"Please, no more bad news," I groaned. "I'm not sure I can take it."

"It's not *that* bad," she said. "I mean, at least it doesn't have to do with anyone dying."

"Well, that's a good start. Okay, spill it."

She hesitated. "Last night, when I left the farm, I forgot that Noah had put aside a bag of maple sugar for me. After I said goodbye to you and your mom, I started to get into my car, then remembered, so I went over to the sugar house."

I still didn't understand what she was getting at. "Go on."

Heather lowered her voice. "I never went inside, because Noah wasn't alone."

"Was there a customer with him?"

She blew a long breath into the phone. "No."

I was starting to lose patience. "Heather, what exactly are you trying to tell me?"

"Jenna was in there too." Heather spoke quietly. "I over-heard her talking to Noah."

"So?"

She gave a loud groan. "Jeez, Lei, will you let me finish? Jenna thanked him for recommending her for the job at Sappy Endings."

I gave a mental shrug. "Yeah, so? He used to talk to her all the time when he went into Bagel Palace."

"Well, that wasn't all she said." Heather sniffed.

"Heather, will you please get to the point? This isn't high school drama club."

She sighed. "All right. Jenna asked him if they could go out to dinner."

"Dinner?" I asked in surprise.

"You know," Heather said. "The meal that people eat in the evening. It comes after lunch."

"I don't understand."

Now Heather was losing patience. "She asked him out. On a *date*."

I threw back my head and laughed. "No, you must have heard her wrong. Jenna knows that Noah and I are practically engaged."

"It doesn't matter," Heather insisted. "She wants him, Leila."

Neither one of us said anything for a minute. Finally, Heather spoke again. "See? You're not laughing now, are you?"

I tried to shake off the shock. "Well, it's not a big deal. Lots of women are attracted to Noah. He's a good-looking guy, and he's sweet and kind—"

"Look," Heather interrupted. "You don't have to sell me on Noah. I know what a terrific guy he is. I'm only telling you to watch out for Jenna. She's lusting for him."

I cringed at her choice of words.

"It probably wouldn't even matter if you guys were married. Jenna wants him for sure." Heather paused. "I didn't want to say anything before, but I've noticed the way she looks at him."

"Get out. I haven't seen anything."

"No offense, but you've been a little preoccupied lately," Heather remarked. "Between worrying about your farm going under and the fact that someone's trying to kill you, there's not a lot of spare time to notice who's checking out your boyfriend."

"When did you notice this?"

"The day you came back from the hospital," Heather said. "Remember, when your mother got upset and went into the café's work area? Jenna kept looking at him before she followed your mother into the kitchen. She had this weird expression in her eyes—like one of intense longing. I suspected she wanted him, but didn't want to tell you since you just got out of the hospital."

My mouth went dry. "I don't believe this. Why didn't Noah tell me?"

"Maybe he was worried you'd get upset and fire her on the spot," Heather offered.

"No, I wouldn't do that." I wasn't that fickle. Of course, Jenna had a crush on him. That didn't come as a big surprise. Noah had been nice to her, and he helped her find a job. She had probably mistaken his intentions for something else. I trusted Noah, so that wasn't the problem.

The problem was that Jenna had been doing little things to irritate me ever since I'd hired her, and now she was interested in my boyfriend. "Maybe we're making too much of this. What happened after she asked him out?"

"Not much," Heather said. "I couldn't see their faces, but to Noah's credit, he seemed to handle it fine. Noah told Jenna he was flattered but committed to you, and he hoped they could still say friends."

Bless his heart. Noah always knew exactly the right thing to say, unlike me.

"What are you going to do?" Heather asked.

"What can I do? I can't fire her because she has a thing for my boyfriend."

Heather gave a loud snort. "Then you need to find a different reason. This is going to make your work relationship awkward. Are you going to be able to pretend everything is fine when you see her? I know you, Lei. Your face is like an open book. She's going to know something's up."

"Honestly, if business continues to sink, I'll have to fire her anyway." Jenna would think it was because of Noah, though, and that would make things even worse.

"Give her that as a reason, then," Heather suggested. "And, for what it's worth, I think you ought to watch your back. Jenna might make another play for him. You don't need any more headaches in your life."

"It's going to be fine," I said.

Heather's tone was full of disbelief. "How can you be so nonchalant about this?"

"Trust me," I said. "The last few days, I've learned that there's more important things in life to worry about."

# CHAPTER TWENTY

**THE NEXT DAY WAS SATURDAY,** which meant that Noah wasn't available to drive me to the farm because he had to drop Emma off at her babysitter's house. After Amelia finished up some personal chores, she would take Emma to dance class, and then they would return to Noah's house until he arrived home—with Toast and me in tow.

Even though I kept telling myself Emma would come around, I felt myself growing more concerned with each day that passed. The death of her mother would undoubtedly affect the poor child for the rest of her life. Maybe I should ask Amelia to stick around in case she needed to give me a ride home.

I had wanted to get to the office early to rearrange my files and pay a few bills. That should keep me busy for most of the day. The morning did not get off to a good start when I suffered another restless night of sleep. I didn't doze off until almost 5:00 a.m. and was dead to the world when my mother shook me awake.

"Leila," she bellowed in my ear. "We're going to be late!"

Mom had mistakenly thought I had gotten up earlier. Like her, I prided myself on punctuality, but today was an exception. She hadn't come upstairs to see what was keeping me until 7:15. I always set my alarm for 5:30 but slept right through it. With her assistance, I finally managed to drag myself out of bed and into the shower while she went downstairs to make me coffee. This was one more sign of how my life was spinning out of control, thanks to the person determined to end it.

My mother refused to let me drive myself to the farm, even with her following. I quickly dried my hair with a blow-dryer while she sat outside in her car and honked the horn. This didn't do much to improve my nerves. In her defense, mom worried that our one lone customer of the morning might already be outside waiting for a latte to fuel themselves for the coming day.

Once we arrived at the farm, she made me sit in the car while she unlocked the door, and then ran back to the vehicle to quickly usher me inside.

"This is ridiculous," I grumbled when we were safely inside. "I hate that this is happening to me and that it's affecting everyone else in my life. It's like being smothered."

Mom patted my arm absently as she went behind the counter of the café to get coffee brewing. "We have to do everything we can to keep you safe, dear, until Margaret's killer is behind bars." She tied on her dark-blue Sappy

Endings apron with a golden maple leaf in the middle. "Would you like coffee or tea before you go into the office?"

"Coffee, please. I need another cup really bad." I sat down at one of the tables and rubbed my eyes. Somehow, I had to get through this day.

Five minutes later, my mother brought me a steaming mug of coffee and a breakfast sandwich as I tried to decide if I should give in to my exhaustion. "This looks great. Thanks." I was hungrier than I'd thought and wasted no time devouring the food.

My mother said nothing. She was staring down at her phone with an unreadable expression on her delicate face. "Is something wrong?"

She looked up at me and frowned. "It's Jenna. She's not feeling well and won't be in today."

"Seriously?" I couldn't believe my ears. "She's been working here for less than a week and is already calling in?" Maybe I should be more relieved instead of upset. This might be the excuse I was looking for to get rid of her.

Mom tucked the phone back into her apron pocket. "It isn't a big deal, dear. People do get sick, remember."

"Well, I happen to think that she isn't sick." The words fell out of my mouth before I could stop them. Jenna must have been afraid that Noah would tell me what happened in the sugar house last night.

My mother's jaw locked in place. "You're making too much out of this. We probably won't have much business today anyway."

"That isn't the point. And why is she calling you? I'm the one who hired her." It sounded petty to my own ears, but I didn't care. Was I being unreasonable? Perhaps, but I'd been on edge about several things these days. Stick a fork in me, I was done. I didn't need Jenna and her antics adding to the stress.

Mom sat down next to me. "Leila, what's really going on here? Are you having second thoughts about hiring Jenna?"

I wiped my mouth with a napkin. "Mom, I don't want to get into this right now."

She eyed me suspiciously. "Tell me the truth. If you don't like her, why on earth did you hire her?"

"I didn't say I didn't like her. But if you must know the truth, we're going to have to let her go if business doesn't improve soon."

My mother looked horrified. "You can't do that. She needs the job."

It bothered me that my mother was defending her. "I'm sure Max would take her back. How can we continue to pay her if we're not doing any business?"

Mom pinned her sharp gaze on me. "I realize that, but still, I feel like you're not telling me everything. I've sensed for the last few days that Jenna has been annoying you. What has she done?"

I didn't want to say anything about the bond she had formed with my mother, because truthfully, I wasn't sure that was the problem. Instead, I went with the most obvious reason. "She asked Noah out last night."

"On a *date*?" She sounded like Heather.

"Yes."

My mother blinked, as if she still hadn't heard me right. "Are you sure?"

"Yes. Heather heard the entire conversation."

"I don't believe it," Mom murmured. "She knows that the two of you are dating. I even told her you were planning to move in with him and Emma soon."

"What did she say?" I asked.

My mother rose from her chair and went behind the counter. "Oh, something about how you two made a cute couple."

Oh, brother.

"Are you going to call and fire her?" My mother looked up while she stirred maple muffin batter and gave a brief nod.

"Not yet." My father's voice boomed loud and clear in my head. *You cannot control other people's feelings, habibi.* I knew that there was nothing for me to worry about, especially from Noah, but the thought of Jenna asking him out irritated me to no end. "Let's see how the next week goes."

"See how what goes?" Strong hands rubbed my shoulders, startling me out of my thoughts. I shrieked and turned around to find Noah standing there.

I placed a hand over my heart. "You scared me."

Noah's handsome face grew stern. "God, Leila, I'm sorry. When Selma saw me, I figured you knew I was there too. I realize you're jumpy because of—" He didn't finish his sentence. "That was a stupid thing for me to do."

"It's all right." I rose from the chair to kiss him, despite the fact that my mother was watching.

After our lips parted, Noah glanced over at my mother, and gave her a sheepish grin. "Good morning, Selma."

"Noah." She greeted him with a pleasant smile. "Would you like some coffee?"

"Thanks, that would be great." He accepted a cup from her as the farm's landline began to ring. Noah picked up the portable extension from the counter and spoke into it, his voice sounding sexy with a bit of Southern twang mixed in. "Good mornin', Sappy Endings." He paused, and a smile flickered through his eyes as they connected with mine. "Hey, Joel. Fine, thanks. Are you calling in your monthly order?"

There was another pause as I watched Noah's grin fade. "Uh, hold on for one second."

The nervousness in my stomach fluttered around like butterflies. "Uh oh. What's wrong?"

He placed his hand over the receiver. "It's Joel from Winnie's Waffle House. He wanted to tell us personally that they're cancelling their syrup order for this month."

A stricken look came over my mother's face, and she turned away. I sucked in a deep breath. Things were getting worse instead of better. "Is there anything we can do to change his mind?"

Noah shrugged. "Doubt it, but I'll try. Let me take this out back while I open up the sugar house." He gave me an encouraging smile and whistled cheerfully under his breath as he continued down the walkway.

My mother came around the counter and put an arm around me. "This isn't your fault."

My eyes started to fill. "Excuse me. I'll be in the office."

"Do you still want to stay open until five today, dear?"

What was the point? "You can leave early if you want to, Mom. I'll stay."

"But you're so tired," she began.

I shook my head. "It's fine. I'm riding home with Noah tonight anyway. We'll be stopping over at the house first. We're going to pick up Toast and bring him to see Emma." Noah's idea was far better than any I'd had. Even Toast gave his purr of approval last night when I'd mentioned it to him.

"That's a good idea, dear. Maybe it will help," Mom said gently.

"It's kind of sad when you think about it," I admitted. "I'm using a cat to bribe a little girl. Emma doesn't want to see me, but maybe she'll let us in when she finds out Toast is with me."

My mother laughed. "There's nothing wrong with it. Sometimes parents have to do those type of things with their children. The gesture might be enough for Emma to open her heart back up to you again."

"I hope you're right."

"Think positive, dear," she said.

I went into my office and tried to busy myself with rearranging the file cabinet and paying bills. In an attempt to be brave, I checked on the sales figures for the past week. It was something I had been putting off. As anticipated, they were worse than I'd thought. Not only was the pie contest deadly, so to speak, but it had turned into a huge financial disaster for us when we had no choice but to refund everyone's entrance fees.

I picked up my cell. Since I'd promised not to go anywhere by myself, the phone was my only real communication with the outside world. There must be *something* I could do to find this person. There was no way I would continue to sit around and wait for Margaret's killer to take another shot at me. Sure, the police were doing their best, but they couldn't protect me twenty-four hours a day. No one could, not even Noah. My mother had taken to locking the front door of Sappy Endings until she saw a customer approaching from the parking lot. This was no way for us to conduct business.

I went out to the café, where my mother was mopping a floor that didn't even need it. The woman couldn't stay idle for two minutes. "Mom, can I borrow your phone?"

She reached into her apron pocket and handed me her cell. "Did you forget to charge yours?"

"Yes," I lied. "I'll bring it right back."

My mother started to say something, then shook her head and continued on with her mopping. I took the opportunity to hurry back to the office before she realized what I was up to. I needed to have another talk with Abigail. She would be more likely to accept a call from my mother than me, although there was no guarantee that she'd pick up at all.

The phone rang four times. As soon as I convinced myself it would go to voicemail, the other end was picked up.

"Hello, Selma." Abigail sounded devoid of emotion.

There was no turning back now. "Abigail, don't hang up. This is Leila, not Selma."

"What do you want?" Her tone became suspicious.

I swallowed hard. "I wanted to know how you were doing."

"A lot you care," she said. "I shouldn't even be talking to you. If Eric finds out, he's going to freak."

"Abigail, I know that we've never been close friends, but I feel terrible about what's happened to your mother. My entire family does. If there's anything we can do—"

"Oh, please, spare me the lame excuses," she said angrily. "I know why you're doing this. You're afraid Eric's going to sue your precious farm."

"Is he?" My breath caught in my throat.

"He's drawing up papers as we speak," Abigail announced.

My chest restricted as if someone had placed a heavy boulder on it. "Abigail, please don't do this. Your mother wouldn't have wanted it."

"My mother's not here any longer." The bitterness in her voice spewed out like venom.

I couldn't believe my ears. Abigail had done a hundred and eighty degree turn since the wake, and I suspected that was because of Eric. "You know what happened at the farm was an accident. Don't you? We never wanted anyone to get hurt."

Abigail started to sob. "My mother's dead, and you killed her. Eric said that we're going to sue you for everything you've got."

My temper began to flare, and I fought to keep it in check. It would solve nothing to get angry. "Abigail, I hate to point out the obvious, but your mother was not a judge at the contest. What's more, my mother specifically asked her not to touch any of the pies until one of the judges had sampled them."

Abigail gasped. "So, you're saying it's my mother's fault that she's dead?"

"No, of course not. But you can't go around blaming us. It doesn't solve anything and won't bring your mother back. Your mother is dead because someone came to the farm and didn't care who they hurt that day." I almost told her that I'd been the intended victim, but that wouldn't help the lawsuit go away.

"Eric said that it's too bad you didn't get to taste it first," she sniffled. "Because then, you would be dead instead of my mother."

Her words, so similar to Taylor's, were enough to make my skin crawl. "It almost sounds like he wants *me* dead."

Abigail paused for a beat, as if to consider. "No, but Eric doesn't want me to have any contact with you."

"Because of the lawsuit?"

Abigail had always been meek, but it had become apparent to me that whatever Eric said went in their family. Still, it wasn't as if he was her father.

"Eric's not your boss, Abigail. Didn't you tell me you called him to come to town after your mother died?"

She was quick to answer. "Yes, he flew in that same night. What are you getting at?"

"I happen to know that Eric was already in town."

A stunned silence met my ears. "That's a lie."

"No, it's true. Plane records showed Eric flew into Bennington earlier that day. He was in town before the pie contest even started."

A sob burst from the other end of the phone. "Are you trying to say my brother killed our mother? He would never hurt her!"

"If he did, it may not have been on purpose."

Abigail's breathing became labored. "I don't understand."

"Your mother was not the intended target," I explained. "Someone was trying to get to me instead. And your brother isn't exactly fond of me these days. He asked me out several times in the past, and I turned him down."

To my surprise, Abigail started to sob. "You should have gone out with him. He gets very upset when he doesn't get his way."

"Upset? How?" I asked in confusion.

"Eric's not a murderer," Abigail announced. "He flew into town the day of your contest to see a friend."

"Who's the friend?" I asked.

"Stop it!" she yelled. "Just because he was in Sugar Ridge that day doesn't mean he killed anyone. And he never meant to hurt that other woman, either. She tripped and fell. It was her own fault!"

Cold, stark fear washed over me. "What are you talking about? What woman?"

Abigail let out a long, ragged breath. "Oh God. I thought you knew."

My heart began to pound rapidly against the wall of my chest. "Abigail, did Eric kill someone?"

"It was an accident. He didn't have anything to do with her death." Abigail sobbed, and the line went dead.

# CHAPTER TWENTY-ONE

**I WAS LEFT LISTENING TO** dead air as my stomach filled with a sickening dread. Breathing heavily, I punched Detective Barnes's number into the phone. He answered on the first ring. "Yeah, Barnes."

"Detective, it's Leila Khoury."

"Hello, Leila. Is everything okay? You're staying safe, I hope?"

*For the moment.* "Yes, but that's not why I'm calling. I just had an interesting conversation with Abigail Middleton about her brother."

"Oh?" His voice rose an octave. "What's Eric done?"

"Abigail made mention of an incident from the past, something I never heard about before." I paused to catch my breath. "It sounds like Eric might have killed a woman. Abigail's exact words to me were, 'It was an accident. He didn't have anything to do with her death.'"

There was an interminable pause on the other end. "Is that all she told you?"

"Yes. Do you know what she meant? Abigail said she thought that I already knew, so you must have an idea what's going on. When it became obvious that I didn't know what she was talking about, she ended the phone call."

"I've done some checking around into Eric's past," Detective Barnes explained. "He may be a criminal defense attorney, but he's got some serious skeletons in his own closet."

I had an idea of what was coming. "Like stalking women?"

"Yes, he's done it on a few occasions," Detective Barnes admitted. "I know he's done it to you, but there was a far worse situation before you entered the picture."

I braced myself for what was coming next.

Detective Barnes continued. "About nine years ago, when Eric was in college, he became infatuated with a woman in his dorm. Her name was Yvette Miller."

"*Was?*" My heart stuttered in my throat. "Did he—did he kill her?"

As soon as I uttered the words, I regretted them. That was a silly presumption on my part. If Eric had killed her, he'd be in jail—or maybe not.

Detective Barnes sidestepped my question. "He asked Yvette out repeatedly, and she told him not to bother her again or she'd get a restraining order. It got so bad that the poor woman was afraid to leave her room for fear of running into him."

"Did she report him to the administration or get the police involved?"

"She did both," Detective Barnes said. "Eric was not deterred. The woman was terrified for her life."

I could relate to her feelings even though, to my knowledge, Eric had never followed me around. One awful week after my breakup with Mark, he had called me about ten times. Thankfully, shortly afterward, Eric's interest started to decline. Once I moved to Florida, the calls and texts had stopped for good. "You didn't answer my question. Did he kill Yvette?"

"It doesn't appear to have been intentional," Detective Barnes admitted. "Eric approached her one night when she came back from another dorm. According to his story, he apologized for his past behavior and told her that he'd never meant to frighten her. Yvette tried to run from him and in the dark, she stumbled and fell against one of the iron bars of the dorm's gate. She hit her head and was knocked unconscious. Eric, to his credit, called 9-1-1. Yvette went into a coma from the head injury and never regained consciousness. Her family made the difficult decision a few weeks later to take her off life support. They tried to argue that Eric caused the accident on purpose, but it was never proven."

My entire body went numb. "I can't believe my family never knew anything about this. Margaret must have kept the secret hidden well." If my own mother had any idea, she never would have tried to persuade me to go out with the man.

"Eric went to school at Northwestern University,"

Detective Barnes continued. "The story made it into a couple of papers in the Chicago area, but from what I can tell, nothing was reported in Vermont. At least, I haven't been able to locate anything. He was never charged with murder."

"That doesn't make me feel any better," I remarked.

"Yes, I know, and I'm sorry," Detective Barnes said. "I can imagine what you're thinking, especially since Eric was in Vermont the same day his mother died."

My temper flared. "He should have been arrested for stalking the poor woman. Yvette never would have died if it hadn't been for him. Maybe he didn't push her, but he's still at fault!"

"I don't disagree with you," Detective Barnes said calmly. "Eric was studying law at the time of his arrest. He retained a lawyer when this all went down—one of the best in the country. Sometimes the justice system fails people, as it did in Yvette's situation." He paused. "But I will do everything I can to see that it doesn't fail you."

"Thank you, Detective. That means a lot to me."

―――――――――

At noon, I stood and stretched from rearranging the file cabinet. My back was killing me, and I needed a break. After some thought, I decided to finish the job on Monday. I was exhausted, and besides, there was no hurry. I figured there would be plenty of empty hours to fill on Monday.

Next week was Thanksgiving, my favorite holiday of the

year, which was followed by one of the farm's busiest days. Last year on Black Friday, the orders had poured in, especially with the fifteen-percent discount we'd offered. Even though I had sent out a newsletter the other day, we'd only received a couple of orders. The news about Sappy Endings' deadly pie contest had gotten out, and it looked like no one wanted to be associated with us anymore.

My mother had an appointment to pick up new eyeglasses, so I told her I would take over the café while she was gone. She told me to keep the main door locked while she was gone. I decided to spend the time updating our website and sat in the café while doing so.

I rubbed my eyes wearily and decided to take out my contact lenses. I searched through my purse for my eyeglass case, but it was nowhere to be found. Shoot. I tried to remember the last time I'd seen the case—yesterday afternoon before I left work. As Noah drove me home, he'd been forced to slam on the brakes when we'd almost hit a deer. My purse had fallen onto the floor. Perhaps the glass case fell out then.

Since I had extra keys to Noah's truck and house on my key ring, I decided not to bother him. I unlocked the front door and hurried over to his truck, all the while looking over my shoulder. There was nothing fun about living in fear.

As I unlocked the door of the truck, I was fully aware of the deafening silence around me. The only sound that could be heard was the rustling of the maple trees in the chilly November wind as they shed the last of their leaves in preparation. Noah would not be happy if he knew I had gone outside without telling him, so I didn't waste any time.

In seconds, I located the case on the floor of the back seat, locked the door, and hurried back inside the building. *Phew.* I was growing more and more paranoid with every waking minute.

I headed back to the office to grab my laptop. As I pulled it off the desk, I noticed that there was new email in the farm's account. Three messages had come through since the last time I checked the account at 10:00 am. *Wow, a landslide.*

One of the emails was an actual order for maple syrup. Hooray. It was only a couple of gallon jugs being sent to a resident's house in New Hampshire, but still better than nothing. I tried to see this as a positive sign.

I took a deep breath and closed my eyes. Whenever I was in the sugar house or my father's office, I felt his presence around me. Some days it was stronger than others, and today was no exception.

"We're not going down without a fight, Dad," I assured him. "I won't let anyone take our farm."

Full of renewed hope and vigor, I read the other two emails. One was from a reporter at the Bennington Journal, asking if I would consent to an interview about Margaret's murder. I promptly hit the *Delete* button.

The last unopened email had *Sender unknown* for its return address. My nerves began to tingle as I opened it. As I feared, the email was from my secret admirer.

*Are you afraid yet? You should be.*

*The end is coming very soon for you.*

Anger and fear ran through me. Enough was enough.

This cat and mouse game that Margaret's killer was playing with me had to end.

I hurried out of the office and dumped my laptop and cell onto a table in the café. With alarm, I realized that I'd forgotten to lock the front door when I came back in the building. As I turned the lock, I stole a glance out into the parking lot. Nothing had changed. The only vehicle outside was Noah's truck. I heaved a long sigh of relief.

When I headed back to the café, someone grabbed my arm from behind. I let out a shriek and struggled to free myself. I turned my head and stared into Cameron's angry face.

# CHAPTER TWENTY-TWO

**PANIC STARTED TO SET IN,** but I fought against it and struggled under Cameron's grip. "Let go of me!"

To my surprise, he let go. I started to run, but the expression of pain and despair in his eyes kept me rooted in place. "What—do you want?"

"Why were you at my house asking questions about me?" Cameron asked.

*Because I wondered if you were trying to kill me.* Sweat began to pool in the small of my back as I tried to think of a less offensive answer.

Cameron didn't give me a chance to think any further. His jaw hardened while he examined my face closely. "I had to go down to the police station. They asked me if I was at the pie-baking contest Saturday. You told them to question me, didn't you?"

I swallowed hard. "I thought it was kind of strange that you came to my farm."

He narrowed his eyes. "Sorry. I didn't realize it was a private event."

"It wasn't, but I never expected you to—" I stopped. The contest had been open to the public. Cameron didn't do anything wrong—at least nothing that I knew of. Maybe he had simply stopped for a latte or to buy some syrup.

"What?" A vein bulged in his forehead. "You act like you never expected to see me again. Do you think I'm still holding a grudge?"

His gazed was pinned on mine, and I didn't dare look away. The last thing I wanted was for him to think that I was afraid of him.

"Something like that." I rubbed my arm where he'd grabbed it. "You can't be very fond of me."

Cameron studied me for several seconds without speaking, then lowered his head towards the ground. "I know. Who could blame me, right? I read about the contest in the paper, and I—I was curious to get a look at you."

"I see." So far, he wasn't making me feel any better.

"No, you don't." Cameron's body stiffened. "You never knew this, but you were my favorite teacher—before the whole exam thing happened. You talked to me like I was a friend, not as a teacher."

My face heated and I was at a loss for words. "You were a good student, Cameron. I only wish that things could have been different."

"What do you mean?" He looked confused.

"I wish that you had come to me first, and let me try to help."

Cameron bit into his lower lip. "I didn't set out to cheat that day. Honest. Anyway, what good would it have done if I'd come to see you? You couldn't change things. My parents have always put so much pressure on my brother and me. Bs and Cs were never good enough. They wanted us to be the best. Anything less than straight As was not acceptable. Mom and Dad always made me feel like such a loser. They said I'd never amount to anything."

He swiped at his eyes quickly, as if ashamed of the tears. My heart went out to him. "So, that's the only reason you were here last week? Because you wanted to see me?"

"No," Cameron admitted. "There was another reason."

That's what I'd been afraid of. I braced myself for his answer.

Cameron paused for a moment. "I wanted to apologize," he said gruffly.

"*You* wanted to apologize to *me*?"

His mouth ticked up at the corners. "Right? Maybe that sounds like a lie, but I swear, it's true. I realize now what you did that day took a lot of guts. I should have trusted myself more, but I couldn't face my parents with a C. I'm sorry I put you in that position."

"Thank you for saying so."

"I did think about talking to you on Saturday," Cameron admitted. "When I was right in the middle of trying to work up my courage, you went over to the cafe. I thought about leaving, but then you came back. I couldn't get near you because so much was going on. When I started over, you began to slice up a pie—" His face turned as white as a bedsheet, and he didn't finish.

There was no need to say anymore. "Then you saw the woman collapse."

"She was lying on the ground, and her body was shaking like crazy." Cameron's eyes grew twice their normal size. "That was when I decided to get the heck out of there."

I had never expected Cameron to tell me all of this. Was it true? Yes, I believed him.

"What now? Will you continue to live with your parents?" I really hoped that he would find some way to move on without them, but it sounded inappropriate to say so.

"I'm transferring to Lafayette College when the semester ends. My parents don't know it yet." Cameron was silent for a few seconds, as if letting his words sink in. "I've already got a partial scholarship, plus a job on campus. And I even have a friend to share a dorm room with."

"That's great. I'm so glad everything's falling into place for you."

He paused. "My parents aren't going to like it, but I need to get away from them."

"I know how you feel." The words tumbled out of my mouth before I could stop them.

Cameron looked surprised. "You do?"

"Yes, except in my case, I left home to teach school in Florida. It was for a totally different reason than yours, but I needed to get away from here, and my parents—I mean, my mother. For most of my life, we never had a good relationship—not until recently that is. I'm living proof how things can change."

"Thanks, I needed to hear that." Relief flooded Cameron's face. "There's another reason, though."

I waited for Cameron to go on.

He shifted from one foot to another. "I figured it was about time that I took control of my life and faced things head on."

I smiled at him. "I think that's good advice for the both of us."

---

"You should have called me." Noah narrowed his eyes as he picked up Toast's carrier and placed it in the back seat of his truck. "That guy could have tried to kill you. We still don't know for sure he isn't the one."

It had been hours since my meeting with Cameron, but Noah was upset to learn that he'd been there and how it had put me in possible danger.

"Cameron's not trying to hurt me."

Noah opened the passenger door for me. "He could have killed you, and I wouldn't have even known about it until I found your—"

He let out a ragged breath as he shut the truck door. I leaned back in the seat, exhausted from the day and everything that had happened in the past week. Thank goodness tomorrow was Sunday.

As Noah got behind the wheel, I stifled a sob. "I hate this. It feels like my life doesn't even belong to me anymore."

Noah reached over to take my hand in his. "I know, babe. But this can't go on forever. The police will catch this psycho soon."

He was right about one thing—this couldn't go on forever. Either the police would catch the killer or I would join Margaret.

Noah started the truck and backed out of my driveway. "You're not having second thoughts, are you?"

"Of course not." I turned around to see how Toast was doing. He detested the carrier but wasn't yowling like he usually did when we went to the vet. Somehow, he seemed to realize that there was a much more important mission in store for him today. "Emma has no idea that I'm coming?"

"None." Noah turned left onto the main road. "I just called and spoke to Amelia. She said that after dance class, she and Em went out to lunch, and then baked cookies. She's in her room playing while Amelia's making dinner, which you will be staying for."

"That would be great, but if things don't go well, tell Amelia I might need a ride home."

Noah reached out and brought my hand to his lips. "None of that. You're staying no matter what. Em has got to learn that you're going to be a permanent part of her life. I won't lose you, Leila."

We both lapsed into silence. Sensing my unease, Noah decided to change the subject. "Amelia's been a lifesaver. I don't know what I'd do if she wasn't there to get Em off the bus every day and stay with her on Saturdays."

"Emma could always come to the farm after school and on Saturdays," I reminded him. "She's done it before when Amelia wasn't available."

"She does love the farm," Noah agreed. "Remember how

Amelia caught the flu last month? Em liked having the bus drop her off every afternoon. Personally, I think the main attraction is the maple candy. Every night she was so high on sugar it took forever for me to get her settled down and to sleep."

The comment made me smile. "I was the same way at her age. I lived for the nights when Dad brought home candy for Simon and me."

"I heard that he was only allowed to bring it home once a week." Noah stopped for a traffic light. "Your mother was strict about how much sugar you guys consumed."

"Did she tell you this?" I asked.

The color rose in Noah's cheeks. "No. I overheard her telling Jenna the other day when I went into the café for some coffee."

An awkward silence stretched between us. I had not mentioned to him what Heather had told me, but there was no time like the present. "I didn't want to get into this earlier, but there's something I need to tell you."

He shot me a puzzled look. "Whatever it is doesn't sound promising."

"I know that Jenna asked you out."

A muscle ticked in his jaw. "How did you find out?"

"Heather overheard you two talking in the sugar house."

Noah mumbled something indistinguishable under his breath and pinned his gorgeous gaze on me. "I should have said something last night but knew it would upset you. Honestly, I figured you didn't need any more grief in your life right now."

"I still wish you'd told me."

"I'm sorry," he said. "But it's not a big deal. You're the only woman that I love, Leila, and that's never going to change."

His words warmed my heart. "Has this kind of thing happened to you before?"

"Women asking me out?" Noah hesitated. "A couple of times."

A couple of times my foot. More likely it was a couple of times a week. Noah was being kind and didn't want to hurt my feelings. *Wake up, Leila.* Women always flirted openly with him at the farm, either while he waited on them in the gift shop or conducted a tour. It was nothing new. Last month, ten women under the age of thirty had come in for a tour, but I suspected it was not to find out how maple syrup was made. Noah was handsome, warm, and intelligent. He was also a hard worker and great father. What single woman *wouldn't* want him?

"What are you going to do?" he asked.

"There's nothing I can do." I stared out the window into the darkness. "I can't fire her because she has a thing for my boyfriend."

Noah stopped for another traffic light. "If it makes you feel any better, I told her we were engaged."

"I wish you had told me," I teased.

He laughed and leaned over to kiss me. The light changed to green, and a horn blew behind us. "It's nothing to worry about. Jenna's a nice kid, and to be honest, I felt sorry for her. That's why I told her about the job. She always asked me tons of questions about you and the farm, so I knew she was really interested in coming to work here."

Jenna was more interested in Noah than the farm or me, but I refrained from saying so.

"I don't think Jenna has many friends," he went on.

"Jenna told my mother and me that she has a boyfriend."

Noah shrugged. "Maybe she does, I don't know."

"That's even more disgusting," I spat out. "Jenna has a boyfriend, and she knows you have a girlfriend, but she still asked you out?"

Noah pulled the truck into his driveway and unhooked his seat belt. A wide grin spread across his face. "Are you jealous?"

"Maybe a little," I confessed.

"There's no reason to be." Noah pressed his lips against mine. When we broke apart, I'd almost forgotten what we were talking about.

Noah smoothed my hair back from my face. "Did that convince you?"

"For the record, I've never had any doubts about your loyalty," I said. "Besides, it really doesn't matter. It looks like I'll have to let her go."

He nodded. "I figured that might happen. If you can, keep her through Black Friday. Business might pick up by then."

"I'm starting to wonder."

Noah massaged my arms gently. "Think positive. The glass is always half full, remember."

He was so good at keeping me grounded. Despite the

terrible loss Noah had suffered, he always maintained such a positive outlook on life. It was hard not to admire him.

"I don't know what exactly bothers me about her," I confessed. "Ever since Jenna started at the farm, she's managed to rub me the wrong way. I guess I need to be more tolerant, but it's always been tough for me to have patience. That's one of the reasons I became a teacher. I love kids and figured I would learn patience by being with them. It looks like I still need to work on that."

"Don't be so hard on yourself." Noah leaned in and nuzzled my cheek. "You're a good person, Leila. The only thing you're guilty of is trying to please everyone. You've grown a lot as a person in the past year." He kissed me again. "We both have."

I placed my arms around his neck. "Remember the first day we met? I was so rotten to you!"

A mischievous look flickered through his eyes. "There was something about you that attracted me right away. You were so fiercely independent, and not about to take any flak from me or anyone else." Noah paused. "But you were also grieving for your father at the time. And I understood because I was grieving too."

In the past year, we had learned to heal together, and I felt closer to him than anyone else in my life, even Heather. The reference to his deceased wife made me think of Emma again. "I need to convince Emma that I will never try to replace her mother."

"I think Em's already coming around," Noah said. "She asked me about visiting the farm when she's off from school. I took it as a good sign."

He came around to my side of the truck and opened the door for me, then handed me Toast's carrier. Noah held the front door open, and Toast and I went inside.

Amelia was in the kitchen, stirring something on the stove. She set the spoon down and turned the burner off. "It's only macaroni and cheese," she said to Noah, then smiled warmly at me. "But there's plenty for three."

Amelia Royce was twenty and a student at the local community college. Her classes were always finished by 3:00 p.m., which allowed her enough time to drive over and get Emma off the school bus. Noah always said that Amelia was a dream come true. He hoped she would continue to watch Emma after she completed her degree but knew that good things didn't last forever.

Noah reached into his wallet and stuffed a few bills into Amelia's hand. "I appreciate everything you did today. Why don't you stay and eat with us?"

Amelia picked up her bookbag from the couch. "Thanks, but my boyfriend's taking me to the movies tonight. I'm going to pop in and say good night to Em."

Noah's cell buzzed. "My mom's calling," he said. "I'll take it out on the porch."

I set Toast's carrier down next to the sofa as Amelia came out of Emma's room, leaving the door ajar. She waved to me on her way out. "Take care, Leila."

"You too, Amelia. Have fun at the movies."

As soon as Amelia had left, Emma wandered into the living room. It was only 5:30, but she was already wearing a pair of American Girl pajamas. She stopped when she saw me, and I couldn't help but notice how her little body stiffened.

"Hi, Emma."

She glanced around the room. "Where's my daddy?"

I swallowed hard. "He's outside, talking on the phone. It's nice to see you."

The child regarded me with suspicious eyes but said nothing further. She turned on her heel and went back to her bedroom, shutting the door quietly behind her.

# CHAPTER TWENTY-THREE

**IT WAS NOW OR NEVER.** I picked up the carrier, which Emma hadn't seen, and tapped on her bedroom door. No response. I opened it a crack. Emma was sitting on her bed, holding the doll. She looked up as the door opened.

I lifted the carrier in the air. "Look, Em! I brought a friend with me."

Emma let out a loud squeal. She jumped off the bed and started towards me, then suddenly stopped. She stared at Toast, then back at me, and bit into her lower lip.

"It's okay," I said gently. "You can go ahead and play with Toast. If you want me to leave, I'll wait in the other room." I reached down to open the carrier door and Toast trotted out. He was familiar with the house, having been here before. Toast wasted no time and immediately jumped on Emma's bedspread. She giggled and followed him, hugging the cat close to her body. Toast loved to be hugged and didn't even attempt to move away. He was a lap kitty through and through. His purrs grew louder until they resembled a V-8 engine.

"He sure does love you."

Emma kissed Toast on the head and didn't reply.

My heart sank into the pit of my stomach. I had harbored a secret hope these last few days that Emma would come around, but it looked as if nothing had changed. I decided not to stay and upset her any further.

As I turned towards the door, something underneath Emma's bed caught my attention. I stooped down for a better look. It was the Cinderella book I'd bought for her birthday a few months ago. She had begged me to read it to her whenever I was at the house.

The book lay open on the floor, with the spine face up. I picked it up and turned it over, noticing that a page had been ripped out. That seemed odd. "Did you have an accident with the book?"

Emma lowered her eyes and didn't respond. I'd read the book to her a few times, and so had Noah. I tried to remember what page was missing when it suddenly dawned on me. It was the page where Cinderella was scrubbing the floor. Her stepmother had been standing over her, laughing. I thought I finally understood what was wrong. I walked over to Emma and gently laid a hand on her shoulder. Fortunately, she didn't move away.

"Emma." I took a deep breath, trying to decide where to begin. "Are you afraid that if your daddy and I get married, I would be like Cinderella's stepmother?"

She buried her face deep into Toast's soft fur. "Stepmothers are bad. Cinderella's stepmom was mean and made her do all the work around the house, like dishes and stuff. She didn't like Cinderella."

"But it's not a true story, Em. Cinderella is only pretend. It never really happened."

Emma stared up at me with Toast in her lap. He glanced from me to her and opened his mouth in a wide yawn, closing his eyes again. At least he didn't seem to share her opinion of stepmothers.

"You mean there isn't a real Cinderella?" Emma asked.

I sat down on the edge of the bed and ran my hand over her blond curls. "That's right. It's a fairy tale. There's lots of stories that aren't true, like *Goldilocks and the Three Bears*. Everyone knows that bears can't talk."

She pressed her hand against her mouth to smother a giggle. "Oh yeah. I forgot about that."

"And I want you to know something else," I continued. "When your daddy and I get married, I would never try and replace your mommy. There's no way I could do that. But I can promise you I will always love you like my own little girl."

Emma sniffled and reached out her arms to me. I wrapped mine around her and Toast in a tight hug and let out a huge sigh of relief. Why hadn't I seen the writing on the wall sooner? For crying out loud, I'd been a teacher. I should have realized what the problem was, but that didn't matter anymore. Maybe some people would think it was silly, but her reaction seemed perfectly normal to me, especially considering what she had gone through. Even grownups had a difficult time detecting between reality and fiction at times.

"If you were my step mommy, could we still read stories and judge another pie contest together?"

"Of course we can."

She considered my response for a minute. "I guess it would be okay then."

I kissed the top of her head. "I'm so glad you feel that way, because there's nothing I want more."

Emma was silent for several seconds. I waited until she felt like talking again, hoping that she had grown more comfortable with me. "Mommy would have liked you," she finally said.

Her statement brought a lump to my throat. "Thank you, Em. I'm sure I would have liked her too."

She sat up and stared up at me with a curious expression. "If you and my daddy have a baby, will it be my sister or brother?"

I'd known that this question would pop up sooner or later. My choice would have been for much later because I was still unprepared. Emma deserved an answer, and I knew Noah wouldn't mind if I told her. We'd discussed the topic once before, and Noah agreed that I should be the one to tell her.

"Yes, they would be your brother or sister." I hesitated for a minute. "But your daddy and I won't be having a baby."

"Why not?" Emma looked shocked.

"Because I can't have any babies, Emma." I tried to keep my voice steady. "But you know what? It's okay and will make you all the more special to me. Maybe someday your daddy and I will decide to adopt a brother or sister for you."

"You mean somebody else's baby?" she asked.

"That's right. It might be someone who lost their mommy—and their daddy." I winced inwardly, not wanting to bring back painful memories of her mother's accident. Emma seemed okay with the topic, so I continued. "Someone who needs a new mommy and daddy to love them, and a big sister like you."

She lifted her chin in the air. "I'd like to be a big sister."

"That would be lots of fun, huh?"

"Hmm." Emma stroked Toast's fur as he purred in contentment. "Can I come and visit Toast at your mommy's house sometime?"

"You don't have to go and visit him, sweetie. Toast will live here too."

"He will?" Emma's eyes shone with anticipation.

I had to laugh. She was more excited about Toast moving in than me, but that was okay. "Yes. My mother is going to adopt a kitty from the shelter. This way, we'll be helping another cat like Toast find a home. Then you, your daddy, Toast, and I will all live in the same house together."

Emma hugged Toast tighter. He lifted his pink nose proudly in the air and sniffed. Toast was used to being held in such high regard.

"Yay!" she squealed. "I'm so glad."

"I'm glad too. I didn't want to leave Toast behind."

Emma bounced on the bed. "So, I get to adopt Toast, right? He'll be like my brother."

I hadn't expected this but started to laugh. "Well, kind of, I guess." I leaned in and whispered conspiratorially. "But I have to ask you a very important question first."

She regarded me with a slight frown. "What is it?"

"Would you still let me live here if Toast wasn't coming?"

Her eyes twinkled like her father's. "You're teasing me."

"A little."

Emma giggled happily and laid her head in my lap. "I guess that would be okay. Will you be here for Christmas?"

"How about at the beginning of the new year?" I suggested. "There's a lot for me to do before Christmas comes."

"You mean like shop for presents?" She looked at me hopefully.

I tweaked her nose. "Yes, but also other things like take care of the farm and figure out what I'll be bringing with me."

Emma snuggled closer to me. "I'm sorry that I was bad."

"Oh, you weren't bad, sweetheart. You could never be bad. You were worried, that's all. And guess what? We don't ever have to read Cinderella again if you don't want to."

Emma took a moment to consider this as Noah opened the door and stuck his head in. "Leila, can I talk to you for a second?"

"Sure. I'll be right back, Emma."

Emma was rubbing Toast's head like it was Aladdin's lamp. She chattered happily with him, as if he was a friend, and I wasn't even sure she'd heard me.

I followed Noah out to the kitchen. "Is something wrong?"

Noah's face was pinched with worry. "My mother called. She fell down the stairs and is in the Emergency Room."

"Oh my God. Is she okay?"

He pursed his lips together. "I think so. But she broke her leg and is in a lot of pain. I'm going to try to convince her to come and stay with me."

"Of course. She can't be on her own right now."

"Exactly." Noah rubbed the back of his neck. "My mother is really independent. She always told me that she never wanted to be a burden to anyone. My brother is in South Carolina, so I'm the closest and most convenient one to help."

"Say no more. Go to her."

Noah hesitated. "I hate to ask this, but would you mind staying here with Emma? I might not be back until really late or even tomorrow, if you don't—"

"Of course, I'll stay. You take as long as you need. Emma and I will be fine."

"Thank you." Noah cocked his head in the direction of Emma's room. "I take it that things are going better in there?"

"They are." I wrapped my arms around his waist. "I think Emma and I are going to be okay. Correction—we're *all* going to be okay."

Noah exhaled in relief. "That's great to hear. I knew Em would come around. What was the problem?"

"She had a case of Cinderella-itis," I quipped.

Tiny frown lines appeared on his forehead. "What does that mean?"

"Emma was afraid that I would turn out like the wicked stepmother in the story."

Noah blinked. "You're kidding. I never even thought of that. But I'm glad it's all over. Are you sure you're okay staying here? I hate to ask, but it's either that or bring Em with me."

"It's better this way," I said. "There's no sense in keeping Emma up all night. Now go to your mother and give her my love."

Noah's face lit up. "What would I do without you?"

"The feeling is mutual, Mr. Rivers."

He kissed me. "Thanks so much. I'll say goodbye to Em and then be on my way." Noah went into her bedroom while I stood in the doorway. "Em, I've got to go see Nana. She hurt her leg."

Emma's smile faded and she jumped off the bed. "I want to go too!"

"No, sweetheart." He chucked her under the chin. "I might not get home until real late. Leila will stay with you until I get back, and then Nana will come home with me."

Emma didn't argue any further. She threw her little arms around his neck and kissed his cheek, then laid back down on the bed with Toast. "Bye, Daddy."

I walked with him to the front door. "You don't know how much I appreciate this."

"Will you stop thanking me?" I swatted him playfully on the arm. "That's what a family does for each other, right?"

"Absolutely." His face brightened like the sun. "Okay, I'll call you soon."

"Drive carefully," I called.

He waved over his shoulder and jumped into the truck.

I waited in the doorway and watched as he zoomed out of the gravel driveway, his tires causing a flurry of dust to fly in the air.

I shut and locked the door, then returned to Emma's room. She was still on her bed, playing dress-up with Toast. He had a straw doll's hat on his head with pink flowers all around the brim. We both laughed.

"He's going to a wedding," Emma explained.

Toast let out a lion sized yawn and closed his eyes. He had other things on his mind besides a wedding.

"Well, he looks very pretty." I chuckled at how silly Toast looked. "Amelia made us mac and cheese for dinner. Do you want to go have some?"

Emma shook her head. "No, I want to stay here and play with you and Toast."

"Sounds good to me." I stretched out on the bed next to her.

"When you and my daddy get married, can I be the flower girl?" Emma asked suddenly. "My friend Hannah got to be a flower girl in her aunt's wedding."

"Of course you can be the flower girl. I would love that."

"And Toast can be in our wedding too."

I loved the fact that she referred to it as *our* wedding. Toast opened one eye, and I swore that he winked at me. "Maybe he should be the ring bearer."

Emma nodded and fell silent. "What's wrong, honey?" I asked.

She took the hat off Toast's head. "I wouldn't really mind if we read Cinderella again. Would that be okay?"

"Of course. We can read it whenever you like." I leaned back against the pillows, my arm snugly around her.

Emma was still talking. "Are there any real princesses?"

"Oh, yes." I yawned. "There's a lot of them. Not around here, though. Mostly in other countries."

"What about princes?"

The room was warm, and sleep beckoned me. I had to force myself to sit up and read the book to Emma, but maybe she wouldn't mind if I took a little nap first. "Well, I for one happen to think that your daddy is a prince."

She giggled. "I bet the lady at the bagel place thinks my Daddy is a prince too. She said that he's really cute."

A flicker of annoyance shot through me. Not again. I opened my eyes to address the little girl. "Do you mean Jenna? I didn't realize you knew her. She doesn't work at the bagel shop anymore. She works at my farm."

"I know." Emma gently stroked Toast's head while he stared up at her in adoration. "My daddy told me so the other day. He stopped for bagels on the way to school, and I asked him why that lady wasn't there. He said that you gave her a job working with your mommy."

Which might have been a mistake. "When did she tell you that he was cute? At the pie contest?"

Emma shook her head impatiently. "No. I didn't see her that day."

"Oh, that's right."

"The lady—I mean, Jenna—asked me if I was going to the pie contest," Emma went on. "And she said that her favorite kind of pie was chocolate."

With a sigh, I leaned back again and closed my eyes, trying to force the image of Jenna from my brain. I wished that Emma would stop talking about her, but didn't want to hurt the little girl's feelings. "That's a good choice."

"After that, Daddy went into the back room with Max," Emma explained. "He asked Daddy if he would look at his oven. It got broken. Max said the oven wasn't getting hot. And my daddy can fix anything."

"I know. He's very smart." My sleepless nights had finally caught up with me. I snuggled up against the child, grateful for our time together. The comforter was soft and warm, making me feel like a butterfly safe in its cocoon.

"The lady came over to the table where I was sitting and talked to me," Emma said. "She asked me what my favorite kind of pie was. She said she makes really good pie."

"Mmm hmm. That's nice." I reached out a hand to stroke Toast's fur, and he rewarded me with a deep purr. Far off in my mind, I thought I heard the sound of a car backfire, but I must have imagined it. "Why don't we take a little nap until your daddy gets back?"

Emma prattled on, as if she hadn't heard me. "I told her that I liked chocolate pie too. And apple pie. My mommy made really good apple pie. That lady asked me what kind of pie you liked best. I told her it was pumpkin, and not just because Thanksgiving was coming up."

It took a few seconds for what Emma said to register with me. My eyelids flickered open, and I shot up in bed. I stared down at the innocent little girl cozying up to me. She had no idea of the impact her words had made.

Jenna knew what my favorite kind of pie was. She was a baker. Her boss at the bagel shop had bought a maple leaf mold. Jenna wanted me out of the way and Noah for herself. Was that enough of a reason to want to kill someone?

Without a doubt.

Emma was still talking. "I started to tell Daddy all about my talk with her on the way home that day, but he got a flat tire. Then I forgot all about it." She paused. "Until now."

Bile rose in the back of my throat. Like an intricate puzzle, pieces had started to fit together. Everything was falling into place. Jenna had been at the farm for an interview. How convenient that she'd come in the same day as the pie contest. She could have easily dropped the pie off before I'd talked to her.

My phone must have fallen out of my pants pocket. I rose from the bed and scanned Emma's bedspread, but it wasn't there. Had it fallen underneath the bed? I got down on my hands and knees to check, but didn't see it anywhere, and I needed to call Detective Barnes right away.

A tap sounded at the front door, and a shiver ran down my spine. "Who can that be?"

Emma bounced on her bed. "Amelia always forgets her phone. Sometimes her keys too. Daddy said she ought to tie them to her wrist."

"Why don't we play hide-and-go-seek?" I suggested. "You go ahead and hide in here while I give Amelia her phone." It would be a good way to distract the little girl while I tried to figure out what to do next.

"Okay!" Emma clapped her hands. "You'll never find me

in here. I'm the best hider in the whole world. I know a great place."

"I'll bet you do. Okay, once I shut the door, you hurry up and get into your hiding spot. Ready, set, go!"

I closed the door to Emma's bedroom and crossed the living room. I needed to get rid of Amelia quickly so that I could call Detective Barnes with my suspicions. There was a chance I might be wrong, but I didn't think so.

Before going to the front door, I took a quick look around the living room, but Amelia's phone wasn't in sight. Not a big deal. I'd let her in to search for it while I called the detective—once I found *my* phone, that is.

I glanced out the peephole, but no one was there. My blood ran cold. Was someone setting a trap for me? I moved away from the door and flattened myself against the wall. At that moment, I noticed that the front door was unlocked. What the—*No.* This was impossible, because I distinctly remembered locking it. As I turned the lock back into position, a clicking noise sounded behind me. I whirled around and gave a gasp.

Jenna stood there, wearing a tight, sparkling purple mini-dress, as if dressed for a night out on the town. Her dark hair was loose around her shoulders and curled at the ends—exactly the same way I wore mine. She wore little or no makeup—another similar trait that we shared—except for some pink lip gloss, a personal favorite of mine.

"Hello, Leila." Jenna pointed a pistol at my face. "I heard that you've been looking for me."

# CHAPTER TWENTY-FOUR

**"WHAT ARE YOU DOING HERE?** How did you get in?" I trembled with fear. All I could think about was the little girl in the next room and her safety. *Please, please, don't come out here, Emma.*

Jenna held up a key. "You stole the key to my boyfriend's front door. So, I took it back."

My mouth went dry. "Did you get that from my office? How dare you go through my personal things!" Since I'd never even noticed it missing, Jenna must have made a copy on her lunch hour and then quickly returned it.

She pointed at her chest. "*Me?* You need to stop following my boyfriend around. It's really getting annoying."

Sweat pooled on my forehead, and my heart began to pound at a frightening pace. I needed to stay calm, and at the same, stall her. Stall her from what, though? Noah was on his way to New York. There was no reason for anyone else to come out here tonight. Somehow, some way, I had to protect Emma. Maybe Jenna would think she had gone with Noah.

Jenna grinned, but the smile didn't quite reach her eyes. "Why so unfriendly? Is it because you know that you're going to die tonight? You shouldn't be in my boyfriend's house."

She had clearly gone off the deep end. This was worse than I'd anticipated. I decided to tell her what she wanted to hear. "Uh, Noah made some candles for the farm and asked me to come over and pick them up. He had to leave, and I was on my way out."

"Where did he go?" Jenna glanced around the room.

"Noah will be back soon," I lied. "He knew that you were coming over, so he asked me to stay and tell you that his mother broke her leg. He and Emma went to see her."

Suspicion was etched into Jenna's face. "I don't believe you."

"It's true," I insisted. "He—"

Jenna raised a hand in the air. "Please. I don't want to hear any more excuses. You shouldn't even be here. This will be our house soon." Jenna tipped her head back and laughed. "Noah's going to marry me."

"Congratulations." My voice sounded hollow to my own ears.

"Thank you." Jenna's voice was as sweet as maple syrup. "We've been dating for about a year, ever since I came back to Sugar Ridge. You see, there was a death in my family. Because of it, I had to take over responsibility of the maple syrup farm."

"You're doing a great job."

Jenna sighed. "Noah was so kind and welcoming on my first day. He was attracted to me from the very start."

Disbelief swept through my body. Jenna had deluded herself into thinking that she was me. But there was no way I would try to correct her thinking, especially when she held a gun in her hand.

Jenna didn't only want Noah. Jenna wanted my entire life.

"You killed an innocent woman," I said. "Margaret Middleton never did anything to you."

Jenna waved the gun in my face and backed me up against the living room wall. "Yes, I knew there was a chance that someone else would sample the pie before you did. But she was old and probably would have died soon anyway."

I couldn't believe my ears. Jenna had no real emotions or feelings. She couldn't care less who her actions had hurt.

"Why do you want to kill me?" I sputtered. "I've never done anything to you."

"Don't play stupid," Jenna warned. "You know why I have to do this. I've seen how you've been trying to take Noah away from me. You're always following him around like a puppy, hoping that he'll notice you. It's pathetic."

"You're right. I'm sorry."

A dreamy look came over her face. "I've been in love with him since the first time I saw him. That was way over a year ago." Jenna's eyes darkened. "Before you came back to town and tried to take him away from me."

Jenna clearly wasn't playing with a full deck. All I could do was continue to play along and hope she might become distracted for a second. "If you hurt me, you'll go to jail. Why would you want that to happen? You have a wonderful life. Noah loves you, not me."

My mouth was as dry as sandpaper, and the last few words were difficult to say. Perhaps I hadn't always been as grateful as I should have, but it was true. My life was wonderful, and I didn't want to lose it.

"Yes," Jenna agreed and lifted her nose into the air. "I also have a successful business and a great family. My mother is simply the best."

"Yes, she is." My stomach twisted into a giant knot. If only Jenna would look away for a second, I'd take my chances and try to get the gun away from her. I had to protect Emma at all costs. "Tell me all about your mother."

"Mom is a terrific cook." Jenna beamed. "She crotchets and gardens and helps me make clothes. I let her run the café at my farm. You should taste her baklava. It's to die for."

What would happen if Jenna shot me? Emma might run out of her room with Toast. Part of me wanted to believe that Jenna wouldn't hurt a child or animal, but the truth of the matter was, I didn't believe Jenna cared who she hurt. She'd already proven that with Margaret's death.

My eyes shifted towards Emma's door, which remained closed. "Please believe me, I would never interfere in your relationship with Noah. I promise not to bother him again."

Jenna shook her head. "That's not good enough. The pie seemed like the easiest way to kill you, but when it backfired, I had to think of something else. Shoving a towel in the furnace pipe couldn't fail, right? But once again, you managed to stay alive."

"That's when you decided to take a shot at me in Bagel Palace's parking lot."

She tapped her finger on the side of her head. "Yes, but you still wouldn't go away and kept causing all kinds of trouble. Well, that's three strikes, so guess what? You're out."

"Please don't do this," I said.

The gun began to shake between her hands. "But I have to get rid of you. It's the only way."

Words stuck in my throat. Time was up, and I had to think of a plan quick.

A loud, clattering noise from Emma's room startled both of us. It sounded like the lid of her toy box had fallen on the floor. My heart sank into the pit of my stomach.

Jenna swiveled her head towards Emma's room. "What was that? Who's in there?"

I took that split second to charge at Jenna. Before she could react, I pushed her down onto the floor. The gun fell from her hands, and we both made a grab for it. Jenna reached it first, but I quickly dug my nails into her hand. Jenna screamed in pain but managed to hold onto the gun. We both continued wrestling for it as sirens wailed in the distance.

Jenna jerked her head up. She made an inaudible noise in her throat and let go of the gun, but not before backhanding me across the face. I staggered to my feet, still holding the gun, as she bolted through the back door of the house in an attempt to escape. I ran out into the night after her. Jenna was headed in the direction of the woods when a squad car appeared from out of nowhere, blocking her path. Panicked,

Jenna turned and ran back in the other direction, where she was met by a policeman on foot. He wasted no time in pushing Jenna to the ground, then pulled her arms backwards to position the handcuffs on them.

I hurried into the house, where I was met by Detective Barnes. "Are you okay?" he asked.

I nodded, too breathless to say anything for a moment. "How—how did you know she was here?"

The door to Emma's room opened. She peeked around it and out into the living room. When she saw me, she rushed over. I lifted her up in my arms as she began started to cry.

"Don't cry, sweetie. Everything's okay."

"I was so scared the bad lady was going to hurt you," Emma sobbed. "So, I called 9-1-1, like my daddy taught me."

"You're a very brave girl," Detective Barnes said.

I hugged her tightly against me. "Thank you so much, Emma." A tear rolled down my cheek and disappeared in her curls. "Wait a second. How did you get a phone?"

She stared up at me and smiled. "I used yours."

"Where was it?" I asked. "I looked for it before I left your room."

Emma wiped her eyes with the back of her hand. "Toast was hiding it. I found it when I picked him up so we could play hide-and-seek."

I went to the doorway of her bedroom and stared in. Toast had not moved from his original position. He was fast asleep on Emma's bed. The excitement had clearly been too much for him.

A slow grin spread across Emma's face, causing dimples

to appear on both sides of her mouth. "That's when I found your phone. Toast was sitting on it the whole time. He knows how to hide things too."

———————————

"I still can't believe it." Noah shook his head as he poured the wax mixture into glass jars.

It was Monday morning, and the official week of Thanksgiving. Noah and I had started the holiday season in full swing. He was busy working on candles in the sugar house while I sat in the opposite corner, making maple candy. The building smelled wonderful, with the scents of maple and evergreen floating through the air. Noah had decided to create a new gingerbread scent for the gift shop this year. With Jenna behind bars, there was some hope that the farm would quickly get back to normal.

"It was hard for me to believe it too." I turned the pan upside down and tapped the bottom with a spoon, then flipped it back over. The pieces of maple candy were perfectly formed. I dipped them in syrup to coat them and moved the pans back to the shelf. Afterwards, I covered the trays with white cloths. They would remain there through tomorrow, at which time we would box them up for Black Friday.

Noah's deft fingers skillfully arranged red and green ribbons around a glass jar. "It goes to show you that anyone is capable of murder."

As uncomfortable as the words were, I knew he spoke the truth. It had all started for me a year ago in this very room, when I came face-to-face with my father's killer. Sugar Ridge was not a town known for a high murder rate, but the statistics had increased once I arrived back in town.

"Did you have any idea that—" I struggled to find the right words. "That Jenna was in love with you?"

Noah's cheeks flushed crimson, and he didn't answer right away. "I guess there were a couple of signs, but I didn't think really think much about them. She asked me to dinner once before when I went into Bagel Palace, and I told her that I had a girlfriend. Jenna asked me lots of questions about you all the time, but I figured she was just curious. She never did anything else to show that she was interested in me until the other night." He paused. "You know, when she came out to the sugar house. I hope she gets some help."

"She will," a deep voice boomed from behind me.

We turned around to see Detective Barnes standing there. He was dressed in a pair of jeans and a hooded Harvard sweatshirt. "This casual attire is getting to be a habit with you, Detective," I teased.

He laughed. "The sweatshirt was a gift from my nephew. He's a sophomore at Harvard."

"That's funny," I mused. "You seem like a Harvard guy to me."

"I'll consider that a compliment since I never made it to an Ivy League school," Detective Barnes said. "I had to settle for Stanford."

"I wouldn't call that settling."

Detective Barnes grinned. "I hope I'm not interrupting anything, Leila. Your mother told me you were down here."

"Hello, Detective." Noah cut off a few more lengths of ribbon and wrapped them around another glass jar.

"Good to see you, Noah." Detective Barnes leaned against the desk where Noah was working. "I'm headed out of town today for the holiday but wanted to stop by here first."

"The police department is actually giving you a few days off?" I teased.

"Can you believe it?" Detective Barnes asked. "But don't worry, they still have me on call, in case something goes wrong in Sugar Ridge during the holiday week. Maybe I should have told them to get in touch with you, Leila. You can take care of any issues while I'm gone, right?"

I couldn't resist a snort. "No offense, Detective, but I think they'll be fine without me."

"We owe you a debt of gratitude," Detective Barnes said. "Jenna wasn't even on our radar. You did a great job finding Margaret's killer."

My face warmed. I always disliked being the center of attention but appreciated the kind words. "There's someone else who deserves praise." I exchanged a look with Noah. "If it wasn't for Emma, I might not be standing here right now."

"That little girl is amazing," Detective Barnes agreed. "Most six-year-olds wouldn't have handled the situation so well. She's very mature for her age. Emma knew you were in trouble and didn't waste any time getting help. There are grown-ups who could take a lesson from her."

I nudged Noah in the side. "She gets those self-sufficient skills from her father."

Noah gave a mock bow, and we all laughed.

Detective Barnes cleared his throat. "I wanted to let you know that Jenna is being held in the county jail until after her trial. Once she's convicted, it looks like she'll be transferred to a psychiatric hospital."

"Has she confessed to Margaret's murder?" I asked.

Detective Barnes nodded. "Jenna denied making the pie at first, but after we found a canister of cyanide hidden in her jewelry box, she broke down. As you probably suspected, she borrowed the maple leaf mold from the Bagel Palace."

"And put it back before Max knew it was missing," I added.

"The house she lives in belonged to her parents," Detective Barnes went on. "Jenna's an only child. Her father killed himself when she was a baby, and her mother died from a drowning accident shortly after Jenna graduated from high school. She lied about going to college—and many other things as well. From what we can tell, she has no friends or living relatives."

"So, she's been living on her own all these years without anyone?" I asked in amazement.

"It looks that way." Detective Barnes folded his arms across his chest. "She told Max that she lived with her mother, who was sickly and didn't get out much. From what I've been told, her father suffered from the same type of mental illness as his daughter, which led him to take his own life. I spoke with a couple of his former coworkers. They confirmed he had a couple of breakdowns before he was admitted to a mental ward for observation."

"Jeez, it's almost makes me feel sorry for her," I remarked.

The detective's expression was grim. "I can understand that, but, remember, Jenna took another person's life. I'm guessing that her attorney will tell her to plead insanity, but don't worry. Either way, she won't be bothering you or your family again."

He hesitated, and I sensed there was something else. "What is it, Detective?"

Detective Barnes nodded and his gaze wandered over to Noah. "There's one more thing I need to tell you."

Noah narrowed his eyes. "Do we want to hear this?"

"Probably not," Detective Barnes admitted. "Jenna has pictures of you all over her bedroom walls."

Noah's face turned scarlet. "Pictures?"

Detective Barnes nodded. "We found a folder of them on her computer. There were at least a couple of hundred photos, and all of you. She must have taken them with her phone, and you probably weren't even aware of it. There's some of you getting out of your truck at Bagel Palace's parking lot, and several others of you here at the farm, giving tours, or working in the sugar house. She also snapped a few of you working outside your house, mowing the lawn."

"Oh, my God. She's obsessed with you," I said.

"Did she give you any idea that she was interested in you?" Detective Barnes asked.

"Not really." Noah exchanged a look with me. "She knew I had a girlfriend, so it's not like I ever tried to lead her on. She asked about Leila—what her favorite color was and things like that. It sounded liked she wanted to get to know her better. She even suggested that we all go out together sometimes. It didn't seem like she was jealous."

"It sounds like Jenna was obsessed with both of you, because she clearly wanted to be Leila and have you for her boyfriend," Detective Barnes pointed out. "She went into Walmart a few weeks ago to print out some pictures. The photo clerk remembered seeing her because Jenna needed help with the machine. When the woman asked her who the good-looking guy was in the pictures, Jenna said it was her boyfriend."

Noah's jaw went slack. "I never imagined that she was living in some kind of fantasy world."

"There's more," Detective Barnes went on. "We found an envelope with pictures Jenna had printed yesterday. They were of your mother."

My mouth went dry. "What sort of pictures?"

"See for yourself." Detective Barnes held the envelope out to me. There were two pictures inside. My mother was standing in front of the gas stove in the kitchen area of the café, holding up a tray of baklava with a pleased expression on her face. The other photo was a selfie Jenna had taken of them both. She had her arm around my mother's shoulders as they smiled for the picture. I turned the picture over and read the words Jenna had printed on the back. *Me and Mom.*

A shiver ran through me. It all fit now—why Jenna had bonded with my mother, worn the same clothes as me, and even had the same hairstyle. "This is beyond creepy."

"It's all my fault." Noah came over and put an arm around

my shoulders. "If I hadn't told her about the job, this might never have happened."

I leaned into him. "Don't blame yourself. Even if we hadn't hired her, she still would have found a way to show up at the farm, hoping I would eat the pie she made."

Detective Barnes scratched his head. "Here's a bit of good news you might not know about. Eric Middleton has gone back to New York, and Abigail told me he's dropping the lawsuit against the farm."

I almost fell over with relief. Thankfully, Noah was there to support me. "That's the best news ever."

"What made him change his mind?" Noah asked.

"I can't be positive," Detective Barnes admitted, "but during our questioning, the incident with Yvette came up. I think Eric was afraid more of the sordid details would leak out if it became known that he was suing a local farm."

A buzzing from the intercom interrupted us. I picked up the receiver. "Yes, Mom."

"Leila!" My mother's voice sounded excited. "Please come up to the café as soon as you can, and bring Noah with you."

My heart nearly stopped. "Is everything okay?"

"Everything is perfect." she said. "About twenty people have come in for coffee during the last ten minutes. I can't keep up. And there are people in the gift shop, waiting to buy candles and maple syrup. Please *hurry*."

"We'll be right there." I put the receiver back down. "Detective, can you please excuse us? We're needed up at the main building right away."

Noah slipped his hand into mine. "This is fantastic. It looks like things are finally back to normal around here."

"It must be due to the article Simon printed in the Maple Messenger this morning," I said.

"That was a great write-up," Detective Barnes agreed. "And he gave credit where credit was due—to his sister."

My face warmed at his compliment. "Emma deserves the credit. And so do you, Detective."

He brushed my compliment aside. "While I'm thinking of it, I need to get a couple of bottles of syrup for my parents. I'll follow you both up."

"By all means," I said. "And it just so happens that my mother made fresh baklava this morning. Can we offer you a piece with some coffee? On the house, of course."

Detective Barnes rocked back on his heels and grinned. "I'm not a big fan of sweets, although I've heard that your mother's baklava is wonderful. Maybe we can work out a deal for a breakfast sandwich instead?"

I looped my other arm through Detective Barnes, and the three of us started towards the main building. "I think that can be arranged."

# CHAPTER TWENTY-FIVE

**EMMA CLOSED HER EYES AND** breathed in deeply. "That smells so good, doesn't it, Daddy?"

Noah leaned down next to his daughter and sniffed. "It sure does."

My mother laughed at Emma as she set the turkey on top of the stove to cool. "It will not be long now, *habibi*."

She glanced over at me, and I smiled at her use of the nickname my father had reserved for me while growing up. It had been a long time since I'd heard anyone else use it and seemed appropriate for my favorite holiday.

"I wish Nana had come with us," Emma said wistfully as my mother handed her spoons and forks to set the table. "She's gonna miss me so much while she's in New York."

"Nana is fine," Noah told her. "She wanted to have dinner in her own house, and her friend Jay is going to cook. Besides, we're going to see her this weekend, remember?"

"Is Nana going to marry Jay?" Emma asked.

Noah looked amused by her question. "I don't know. That's Nana's business."

Emma nodded wisely. "Don't worry. I'll ask her this weekend."

Noah and I both held back a laugh at the serious expression on her face.

My mother was bustling around in the kitchen and busy giving us all orders. "Leila, mash the potatoes, please. No, not with the masher. It's easier and quicker to use the mixer. Emma, honey, would you like to put the silverware on the table? Remember, forks go on the left. The napkins are already set up. Noah, why don't you take the knives and help her, then grab two extra chairs from Victor's office for Heather and Tyler?"

Because my mother was boss of the kitchen—the entire house, actually—we didn't think twice about doing her bidding. Even when my father was alive, he had followed her orders to a tee. It didn't bother me as it used to. My mother was like a well-oiled machine. She believed in organization, and that would never change.

She picked up one of her blue willow china bowls and started to fill it with stuffing from the turkey. Emma, who had returned from the dining room, lifted an eyebrow in confusion as she watched. "Why is there rice in the turkey? That's not stuffing."

A huge grin spread across my mother's face. "This is the way the Lebanese eat their turkey, little one. You will like the taste. It is very good."

She spoke the truth. My mother had not used Stove Top once in her life and wasn't about to start now. Her stuffing was made from a mixture of rice, pine nuts, cinnamon, allspice, and nutmeg. There was also a plate of kibbi, traditional mashed potatoes, homemade cranberry sauce, tabbouleh, stuffed squash with meat and rice, and homemade rolls.

My mother inspected the potatoes with a critical eye as I spooned them into another china bowl. "They look good, dear. Simon," she called out to the living room. "Can you please come and carve the turkey? Leila, bring the potatoes to the table, and then you and Noah go ahead and sit down."

I placed the bowl of mashed potatoes on the table as Noah set up the extra chairs for our guests. "Your mother certainly goes all out," he remarked. "There's only the seven of us. This feast could feed at least twenty people."

"It won't go to waste," I assured him. "She packages up the leftovers into separate meals and gives them out at the café—free of charge to anyone who's hungry."

He looked impressed. "Your mother is amazing."

"She really is." My mother and I had come full circle since my father's death, and I felt closer to her than ever. I reached for a chair at the end of the table, but Noah stopped me.

"I—uh, thought I'd sit there. Why don't you take this chair."

"Okay." I waited as he pulled out the chair for me, not sure why it mattered where I sat. I thanked him and reached for my cloth napkin. My mother had shaped them all into crowns on the dinner plates. The napkin fell away as I picked it up and revealed a small red velvet box inside. My heart leapt into my throat as I picked up the box with trembling fingers. "What's this?"

Noah's eyes were shining into mine. "Open it."

Emma was standing at the end of the table, wiggling with excitement. "Open it and see, Leila!"

I lifted the lid and gasped. Inside the box was a beautiful one carat marquise diamond with a smaller setting of diamonds all around it. Speechless, I continued to stare at it in shock.

Noah lifted my hand to his mouth. "Last spring, I told you that I needed more time until I could make a full commitment. But I realize now that I can't live without you. When you come and share my—I mean *our* home—I want things to be settled. Leila, I guess what I'm trying to say is, will you marry me?"

My eyes misted over. "Yes. Yes, of course I will."

Noah put the ring on the third finger of my left hand, then placed his arms around me and kissed me.

"No, Daddy." Emma frowned. "You did it wrong."

We broke apart and waited for her to go on.

"What did I do wrong, sweetheart?" Noah wanted to know.

"Leila is marrying both of us," she said. "That's what you told me the other night."

He smiled and reached over to tousle her curls. "You're right, baby. We're a package deal, aren't we?"

"And I wouldn't have it any other way." I lifted Emma onto my lap and hugged her.

My mother appeared, followed by Simon, who was carrying the turkey. Her face lit up, and I realized what happened. She and Simon had deliberately stayed in the kitchen to give us some privacy. "Emma, dear, would you like to grab the basket of rolls off the kitchen counter?"

"Sure." Emma jumped off my lap and ran into the kitchen. She returned in a few moments, balancing the basket between her tiny hands. "Where should I put it, Selma?"

"Here, baby." Noah reached out and grabbed the basket from his daughter and placed it in the center of the table.

My mother leaned over my shoulder to admire the ring, then kissed me and Noah. "*Narju 'an takun seydan dayman.*"

Noah's eyes searched mine for an answer, but I didn't have one. My mother laughed out loud. "It means may you be happy always."

My mother didn't speak much Arabic these days. She had decided when her children were born that they should only use English, as she didn't want them to have trouble making friends. For that reason, she had never taught us her native language. Over the years, Simon and I had managed to pick up a few Arabic words and phrases here and there.

"Welcome to the family, my son." Mom dabbed her eyes with a napkin.

A tap sounded on the front door, followed by Heather's

voice. "Hello! We're here!" A few seconds later, she and Tyler entered the dining room. Heather was wearing a maroon-colored dress and had her blond hair piled high on her head in dramatic fashion.

Heather gave my mother a kiss and handed her a bottle of wine as Tyler came over to shake Noah's hand.

"I thought we were early, but it looks like we're right on time," Heather said. "Thanks for inviting us, Mrs. Khoury. This is a great excuse not to eat my mother's cooking tonight. She doesn't come close to you in the kitchen."

"There was a reason why we wanted you to come a little later." Noah grinned and lifted my left hand in the air.

Heather clamped a hand over her mouth when she spotted the ring. "Oh my God!" She squealed so loud that Emma put her hands over her ears. Heather ran over and hugged both of us. There were tears in her eyes. "It's absolutely gorgeous."

Tyler pulled out a chair for Heather across from me. She unfolded her napkin and dabbed at her eyes with it. "Do you guys have a date yet?"

Noah reached for the basket of rolls and put one on his and Emma's plate. "That's up to Leila."

"A Christmas wedding would be nice," I admitted, while Heather's fork clattered against the plate. "Relax. Not this Christmas."

She breathed a sigh of relief. "Thank goodness. Even I can't help you plan a wedding that fast."

Tyler squeezed her hand. "And here I thought you could do anything, babe."

"There won't be a ton of planning to do, not like with your wedding. We're not having two hundred people." I glanced sideways at Noah, who nodded in approval.

"Again, it's Leila's decision, but I think something more intimate is the way to go," Noah agreed. "I don't have a lot of family anyway."

I took the platter with the turkey from my mother and caught her eye. I tensed, waiting for her to drop the bomb. She had always dreamed of me having a large wedding, and I knew this would not sit well with her.

To my surprise, she nodded in approval and added a meat pie to her plate. "I think that is a very good idea."

Shock must have registered on my face. My mother didn't care if I had a big wedding or not. Had the world ended and someone forgot to tell me? "Mom, I never thought I'd hear you say those words."

She smiled. "I guess you're never too old to learn new things. And I've learned a lot this year." She passed the plate of meat pies to Heather. "I only want you to be happy."

It took a few seconds before I could speak. "Thanks, Mom. I appreciate that."

Noah's hand closed over mine. "We both do, Selma."

"Have it at the farm." Simon winked. "Then, I can write an article for the paper about your special day. 'Extra, extra, read all about it. First of its kind wedding held at Sappy Endings Farm. More to follow as this is now the hottest new venue in town.'"

"Sounds like you're on to something there," I agreed.

Noah squeezed my hand. "Do you want to get married at the farm?"

"I'm not sure." My mother, of course, would want me to get married in the Maronite Catholic Church, but she didn't seem bothered by the question. "It would be a great way to generate more revenue in the future."

"Yes!" Heather squealed. "Outdoor weddings in the summer and early fall could be absolutely lovely at Sappy Endings. There's a perfect spot in the sugar bush that overlooks the mountains. You'd be booked up for months in a heartbeat."

"Okay, that will be my next project then," I said. "After the holidays are over, I'm going to start looking into it. Are you up for some catering, Mom?"

She grinned. "As all you young people say, bring it on."

Noah turned my hand toward the light to admire the ring. "Okay, I admit, I've had the ring for a couple of months. I was going to wait, but after what happened with Jenna—" He didn't finish the sentence. "Anyway, I decided to show it to Em. She's the one who suggested that I propose to you today."

"My goodness," my mother exclaimed. "You are such a smart girl."

Emma shot us a huge grin, which showed off an adorable gap in the front of her mouth, where her two front teeth had gone missing the other day. "I told daddy that this would be the best day to ask you to marry us, since it's Thanksgiving. Cause it's a day when we give thanks. That's what my teacher told me. And I'm thankful you're going to be my new mommy."

I glanced sideways at Noah, who was smiling proudly at his daughter. I reached over and wrapped my arms around her. "That's beautiful, sweetheart. I'm thankful to have you as my little girl. It's the biggest honor I'll ever have in my whole life."

THE END

# RECIPES

# MAPLE CREAM PIE

## Ingredients

- 9-inch pre-baked graham cracker crust, cooled
- ¼ cup and 1 tablespoon cornstarch
- ½ teaspoon salt
- 1 ¾ cups whole milk, divided.
- ¾ cup pure maple syrup
- 2 large egg yolks
- 2 tablespoons unsalted butter
- 1 ¼ cups heavy whipping cream, divided
- 3 tablespoons confectioners' sugar, divided

Combine the cornstarch and salt in a heavy saucepan. Whisk in ½ cup cold milk until the mixture is smooth. Gradually whisk in the remaining milk and ¾ cup maple syrup. Cook over medium heat until thickened and bubbly. Stir frequently starting out, but as the mixture heats, stir constantly to keep from scorching. Reduce the heat to low once it begins bubbling and cook an additional 2 minutes, stirring constantly. Remove from heat.

In a separate small bowl, whisk the egg yolks. Whisking constantly, add a ¼ cup of the hot milk mixture to the egg yolks. Slowly and whisking constantly, add the egg yolk mixture into the saucepan containing the milk mixture. Over medium-low heat, cook the mixture until it begins to bubble, then cook an additional 2 minutes, stirring constantly. Remove from heat and whisk in the butter until melted. Cool to room temperature without stirring.

Once filling has cooled, add 1 cup heavy cream to a chilled medium-size bowl. Whip on high until soft peaks form. Reduce speed to low and slowly add 2 tablespoons confectioners' sugar. Increase speed and beat until stiff peaks form. Fold 1 cup of the whipped cream into the fully cooled filling. Pour filling into the cooled pie crust. Spread the remaining whipped cream over the pie filling. Refrigerate overnight. Just before serving, whip the remaining ¼ cup heavy cream on high speed until soft peaks form. Reduce speed and add 1 tablespoon confectioners' sugar, then increase speed and beat until stiff peaks form. Using a piping bag and large star tip, pipe the whipped cream around the edges of the pie to decorate.

# S'MORE PIE

## Ingredients

### For the crust:
- 2 cups of finely ground graham crackers (about 15–16 graham crackers)
- 6 tablespoons melted butter
- ⅛ teaspoon salt

### For the filling:
- ¾ cup of semi-sweet chocolate chips
- ¾ cup of milk chocolate chips
- ¼ cup of butter
- 2 whole eggs
- 1 egg yolk
- 1 cup heavy cream
- 1 teaspoon vanilla

### For the topping:
- 2 egg whites
- 1 cup of corn syrup

- pinch of salt
- ½ teaspoon vanilla
- ¼ teaspoon cream of tartar
- 2 tablespoons sugar

Preheat oven to 350° F. Grind graham crackers in a food processor or place them in a Ziploc bag and whack them with a rolling pin until they are crushed into a fine crumb. Place graham cracker crumbs into a bowl, then add the salt and the melted butter. Combine with a fork until the crumbs stick together. Place the crumbs in a 9 ½ pie plate, working the crumbs up the side of the pan with the palm of your hand. Set aside.

Place both chocolate chips and butter in a heat-safe bowl. Heat the heavy cream in a saucepan until it simmers, pour it over the chocolate chips, and whisk until melted and combined. Add whole eggs and yolks, and mix until combined. Add vanilla. Pour chocolate mixture into pie crust and bake 15–20 mins until pie is set and a toothpick comes out clean. Meanwhile, place 2 egg whites, corn syrup, salt, vanilla, and cream of tartar in a bowl, and whip on high until stiff peaks form and mixture is glossy. Slowly add sugar. Allow pie to cool, and then add marshmallow topping on top, creating decorative swirls as you go with a spatula. At this point, if you are not serving right away, the pie can be refrigerated until ready to serve. Then proceed with last step of broiling. Place pie under the broiler for 1–2 minutes until marshmallow topping turns golden brown. Marshmallow burns quickly so keep an eye on it while broiling; do not walk away! Note: Do not use marshmallow fluff as it does not have the same texture.

# MAPLE APPLE PIE

## Ingredients

**For the crust:**
- 1 ¾ cups white whole-wheat flour
- 1 cup all-purpose flour, plus more for dusting
- 2 tablespoons maple sugar
- ½ teaspoon salt
- ½ cup cold unsalted butter, cut into chunks
- ¼ cup avocado oil or vegetable oil
- ½–¾ cup ice water
- 1 egg yolk
- 2 teaspoons turbinado sugar

**For the filling:**
- apples, peeled, cored, and sliced*
- ¾ cup pure maple syrup, dark or amber flavor
- ¼ cup all-purpose flour
- 1 tablespoon fresh lemon juice
- 2 teaspoons cornstarch

- 1 teaspoon cinnamon
- ¼ teaspoon nutmeg
- A pinch of salt

## To make the crust:

Pulse whole-wheat pastry flour, all-purpose flour, maple sugar, and salt in food processor. Add butter and process until the butter is cut in and the mixture resembles coarse meal. Open lid, drizzle on oil, and pulse to combine. Open lid and drizzle on ½ cup ice water. Process until the mixture just comes together. If the mixture seems dry or does not come together as a ball, try squeezing a handful of the crumbs together. If it still won't come together, add up to ¼ cup more ice water. Divide dough in half and form into two disks, wrap in plastic, and refrigerate until firm and chilled, at least 1 hour.

Lightly dust work surface with flour. Roll one dough disk out to a circle, about 14-inches across. Transfer to a 9-inch-deep dish pie plate. Press dough gently into corners of the pie plate. Roll the second dough disk out to a circle, about 12 inches across, and set aside.

Arrange oven rack in the center of the oven. Preheat oven to 350º F. Line a baking sheet with foil or parchment.

## To make the filling:

Toss Macintosh apples, firm apples, maple syrup, all-purpose flour, lemon juice, cornstarch, cinnamon, nutmeg, and salt in a large bowl.

Add apple filling to the pie shell, arranging so they are as compact as possible. Lay second dough disk over the apple filling. Roll edges under, and crimp edges to make fluted edge. Brush egg yolk over the crust. Sprinkle with turbinado. Cut five 1-inch-long steam vents in the top of the pie.

Place pie on the prepared baking sheet. Bake pie until the crust is golden brown and the filling is bubbling out the vents a bit, 60–80 minutes. Let cool on a wire rack until room temperature before cutting.

*Note: It is recommended that you use 4 large Macintosh apples and 4 firm apples, such as Honey Crisp, Mutsu, or Ginger Gold at about 1.75 pounds each. The macs will break down and become very juicy and the firm apples will hold their shape and give great texture.

# PUMPKIN SPICE PIE WITH MAPLE SYRUP

## Ingredients

- 1 9-inch pie crust prepared but not pre-baked
- 4 medium eggs
- 1 cup heavy whipping cream
- 1 ¼ cups pumpkin puree, homemade if possible
- ⅔ cup pure maple syrup
- 1 seed of 1 vanilla bean scraped or 2
  teaspoons pure vanilla extract
- 1 teaspoon sea salt
- 1 tablespoon pumpkin spice blend
- ½ cup sweetened whipped cream for garnish

Preheat the oven to 350º F. Keep the pie crust chilled in the refrigerator while you mix up the pie filling. In a large bowl, whisk the eggs and cream together until blended. Add the pumpkin puree and the maple syrup and again whisk well.

Finally, add the vanilla, salt, and spice blend to the pie filling and combine.

Remove pie shell from the fridge and place on the middle rack of the oven. Slide the rack out carefully a couple of inches and pour the filling into the pie shell. Slowly, slide the oven rack back in place, taking care not to spill the contents of the pie shell onto the bottom of the oven. Check pie after about 30 minutes and rotate, if necessary, to ensure even browning of the pie crust. When the center of the pie has puffed up and jiggles only slightly when the pan is moved, the pie is ready. This will take about one hour. Remove pie from oven and cool on a wire rack. When the pie is room temperature, cover with plastic wrap and refrigerate until ready to serve.

Pie will keep, covered in the fridge, for up to three days, or well-wrapped and frozen for up to 8 weeks. Serves eight people.

# STRAWBERRY RHUBARB PIE

## Ingredients

### For the crust:
- Single crust pie dough

### For the filling:
- 2 ¾–3 cups (340–455 g) sliced rhubarb about ¼-inch thick, about 5–6 medium stalks
- 2 cups (about 455 g) sliced strawberries
- ⅔ cup (141 g) granulated sugar
- 3 tablespoons (28 g) cornstarch
- For the topping:
- 1 cup of all-purpose flour
- ½ cup of brown sugar
- ½ cup of cold butter, cut into tablespoon-size pieces

In a large bowl, combine the rhubarb, strawberries, sugar, and cornstarch. Mix well. The mixture will start to turn thick and syrupy as it is stirred. Roll out the pie crust and place in a 9-inch pie plate, trimming and fluting the edges. Pour the strawberry/rhubarb mixture evenly in the crust.

To make the streusel topping, combine the flour and brown sugar in a small bowl. Add the butter, and using a pastry cutter or two knives, cut in the butter to the flour/sugar mixture until it has the consistency of coarse crumbs. Sprinkle the streusel topping evenly over the top of the pie (but not covering the edges of the pie crust).

Place the pie on a rimmed baking sheet (in case any of the filling bubbles out), and bake at 375° F for 50–55 minutes. Cover the pie crust edges halfway with foil or a pie crust shield to prevent over-browning, if needed. Note: over the years, I've started baking this pie for 75–90 minutes so it's fully set up and not runny.

When the streusel is golden and the filling is bubbling and hot, remove pie from oven. Let the pie cool completely before cutting. (The filling will thicken as it cools.) Makes eight servings.

# BROWN SUGAR MAPLE COOKIE PIE

## Ingredients

- 1 pie crust round (homemade recipe below)
- 1 egg, beaten, for brushing
- vanilla sugar or coarse sugar, for sprinkling (optional)
- 4 tablespoons salted butter
- 1 cup light or dark brown sugar
- 2 large eggs
- 1 egg yolk
- ⅓ cup maple syrup
- ⅓ cup heavy cream
- 2 teaspoons vanilla extract
- 1–1 ½ cups semi-sweet chocolate chips or chunks
- flaky sea salt

### For the Vanilla Cream:
- 1 cup heavy cream

- 1 tablespoon real maple syrup
- 2 teaspoons vanilla extract

Position a rack in the lower third of the oven. Preheat the oven to 350° F. Fit the pie crust into an 8-inch pie plate. Brush the edges of the crust with beaten egg, and then sprinkle with vanilla sugar or coarse sugar. Lightly prick the bottom of the dough with a fork. Freeze for 10 minutes. While it is freezing, add the butter to a small saucepan set over medium heat. Cook until the butter begins to brown, about 3–4 minutes. Remove from the heat and transfer to a heatproof bowl. Let cool. Whisk together the brown sugar and two eggs and one egg yolk until well combined. Add the maple syrup and heavy cream. Whisk in the brown butter and vanilla until smooth. Fold in the chocolate chips and pour the mixture into the crust. Bake for 55–60 minutes, until the pie is puffed on top but still wiggly in the center. The longer you bake, the more set your pie will be. While the pie is baking, prepare the vanilla cream by whipping 1 cup heavy cream using an electric mixer until soft peaks form. Add the maple syrup and vanilla. Whip until combined and fluffy. Remove pie from the oven and let cool between 20–30 minutes, then serve warm, sprinkled with sea salt (if desired), and dolloped with the vanilla cream. Or serve at room temperature.

# Acknowledgments

Special thank you to Jenna and Jacob at Baird Farm in Vermont, which serves as the inspiration for "Sappy Endings." During Covid, I made the three-hour trip to North Chittenden to learn more about the maple syrup process, and they were generous in sharing their knowledge. I've been a big fan of theirs ever since. Jenna, I said you'd eventually wind up in one of the books, so here you go!

Thank you to my editor, Margaret Johnston, and the rest of the Sourcebooks/Poisoned Pen Press team for making the series come alive, and to my agent, Nikki Terpilowski, for her belief in me and the storyline.

I also need to thank Kathy Kennedy and Constance Atwater for always being faithful beta readers and for their honesty, no matter how difficult it is to hear at times! A huge shout-out to Kim David for the use of her delicious maple cream pie recipe.

Lastly, thank you to my family, especially my husband Frank and sons Phillip, Jacob, and Jared for their support. I'm extremely lucky to have them in my corner.

# About the Author

*USA Today* bestselling author Catherine Bruns lives in upstate New York with an all-male household that consists of her very patient husband, three sons, and several spoiled pets. Catherine has a BA in both English and performing arts, and is a former newspaper reporter and press release writer. In her spare time, she loves to bake, read, and attend live theater performances. She's published more than twenty-five mystery novels and has many more stories waiting to be told. Readers are invited to visit her website at www.catherinebruns.net.

# PENNE DREADFUL

**First in the Italian Chef Mystery series—
tomato sauce isn't the only thing that runs red!**

Local Italian chef Tessa Esposito is struggling to get back on her feet following her husband's fatal accident. And when the police knock on Tessa's door, things just get worse. They've discovered Dylan's death wasn't an accident after all, and they need Tessa to start filling in the blanks. Who would want her beloved husband dead, and why?

With the investigation running cold, Tessa decides it's time to save her sanity by reconnecting with her first love—cooking. And maybe the best way back into the kitchen is to infiltrate Dylan's favorite local pizza parlor, which also happens to be the last place he was seen before he died. Tessa has never been a fan of detective novels, but even she can see that the anchovies aren't the only thing that stink inside the small family business. And with suspects around every corner, Tessa finds that her husband's many secrets might land her in hot water.

# *IT CANNOLI BE MURDER*

Teresa's biscotti have always been killer,
but not like this

Six months after her husband's death, Tessa Esposito is hoping to
drum up reservations for her restaurant's grand opening. And since
a signing with bestselling author Preston Rigotta is sure to draw a
crowd, Tessa agrees to cater her cousin's bookstore event, whipping
up some of her famous Italian desserts. But the event soon takes a
sour turn when Preston's publicist, an old high school rival, arrives
and begins to whisk up their old grudges.

That night, a fight breaks out in front of the crowd, and it
becomes clear there's bad blood in Harvest Park. And when the
publicist is found dead on the bookstore floor the next morning,
a stray cannolo at her side, Tessa knows who will be framed as the
prime suspect.

To clear both her cousin's and her own name, Tessa must investigate the murder. But Preston's publicist has many secrets to hide,
and in the end, the truth is bittersweet…

# THE ENEMY YOU GNOCCHI

It's the deadliest thyme of year
for the Italian chef

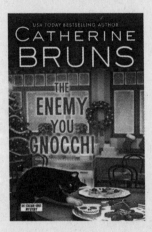

With snow dusting the ground and sauce sizzling on the stove, local chef Tessa Esposito is ready to serve up some holiday cheer. And with the annual Festival of Lights underway, it seems nothing can dim her spirits. Not even Mario Russo, the newest scrooge in town whose espresso bar has been quickly disrupting businesses and stealing customers from Harvest Park's favorite coffeehouse.

But when Mario is discovered at the festival's opening, face-down in a Santa suit, Tessa realizes the bah humbug runs deeper than she could have imagined. And when one of her dearest friends is implicated in the crime, she must make a list of Mario's enemies, check them twice, and discover the cold-blooded killer. Especially before they can sleigh again.

For more info about Sourcebooks's books and authors, visit:
**sourcebooks.com**